More by the Author

Poetry, Essay & Short Story Collections

Across the Deserts of My Ghosts
Collecting Shadows
Deukollectrum
Hyperborea
Small Events

Novels

The Nightingale's Stone

Anthologies

Unnerving (Volumes 1—3)
The Mighty Pen

Collecting Shadows

by David Mecklenburg

BLUE FORGE PRESS
Port Orchard, Washington

Collecting Shadows
Copyright 2020, 2022
by David Mecklenburg

First eBook Edition August 2020
First Print Edition August 2020
Second Print Edition July 2022

ISBN 978-1-59092-942-1

"The Slubburge Man" appeared in Issue 2 of *The Dark Fiction Spotlight*.

"The Ladies of Keldmere" appeared in the December 2010 issue of *Darker*, the online magazine of Dark Speculative Fiction.

"Church of the Hidden Children" appeared in Issue 1 of *Lisette's Tales of the Imagination*.

"Let Me Fly Away" was published in the August 2014 issue of *Silver Blade Magazine*.

Blue Forge Press is the print division of the volunteer-run, federal 501(c)3 nonprofit company, Blue Forge Group, founded in 1989 and dedicated to bringing light to the shadows and voice to the silence. We strive to empower storytellers across all walks of life with our four divisions: Blue Forge Press, Blue Forge Films, Blue Forge Gaming, and Blue Forge Records. Find out more at www.BlueForgeGroup.org

Blue Forge Press
7419 Ebbert Drive Southeast
Port Orchard, Washington 98367
blueforgepress@gmail.com
360-550-2071 ph.txt

*For Tree Swenson,
in gratitude and respect
for your wisdom, insights,
and most of all, friendship.*

Table of Contents

Collecting Shadows

by David Mecklenburg

Preface

I study him for a time and wish for something to remember him by. I never had anything of the sort from Modran. Downstairs, amongst the old tools in the boot room, I find a mason's hammer.

I climb upon his hideous form. The stone of him is smooth and pleasant, though, like a freshly carved statue. It almost pains me. I take the hammer and break off his ear: once flippery and supple as the cool skin of a salamander but now turgid stone. Inside the ear, I can hear his invasions, observations, inventions, tales, whispers, trespasses, and stolen memories.

Smiling, I walk away from him. I shall write all of this down.

I wrote the above words—the closing of my memoir *The Nightingale's Stone*—upon my return to the Free and Hanseatic City of my birth: Hagen. If you have not read it, know that I outwitted a hungry being of the night who wished to eat me. We talked over my life and, it being summer and a short night, the Sun came up and saved me.

The following collection of stories contains both narratives I heard through the troll's ear, along with some experiences I have had myself. Some of the stories have been published elsewhere and some have waited for this anthology.

In putting this collection together, I was constantly reminded of how misleading the sunlight can be; we are easily blinded by its brilliant distortions. However, in the shadows—the places where the light does not quite reach—we can find more of ourselves. If we take a moment to collect those shadows and consider them carefully, the full artistry of ourselves reveals itself.

—Ada Ludenow

The Strand

The wind blew in from the open window, indeed, the very reason Julian had gone into that room, and it stirred the grey hair, lanky in hanks and crawling with wolf spiders moving in their independent locomotions. And then as neatly as a courtesan, it swung its legs out to the floor and with the crunchy pops of heel bones upon the wood, it moved swiftly toward him. The moon, just turning to last quarter filled the room with soft light and shadows.

Julian Harbasch was a quotidian sort of man, in that most of you see his like every day, and every day was the same for him in the measured hours, the predictable tides of people, water and money. There was nothing remarkable about his appearance, no striking narratives of childhood or doomed love affairs with heiresses. The steadfastness of his mind and its ability to receive abstract information in careful, distinct strands and craft it into careful, sober tallies made him one of the best accountants at Green and Margaux, so they chose him specifically for this task of auditing some books in the coastal town of Storling. His inn was unremarkable and he would not have stayed there had it appeared remarkable. The concierge was aloof and rude: just the sort Julian liked. The most he got out of the man was a gruff recommendation on Wednesday's chicken pie. The patronage appeared to be old, listless and blessedly unconcerned about anyone else's business. The rooms were clean and well-furnished and the beds were very comfortable, so it was quite easy for him to hide in one.

It had been only a few hours since he saw the thing on the bare linen sheets. He knew this because dawn was turning the Eastern sky the color of lilacs and he could now clearly see his traveling case, a pewter wash basin and ewer, the firm solidity of the mirror and floor. He traced the lines of planking, old fir planking worn smooth by hundreds of feet; the seams ran out under his locked door to the hallway, where he could see shadows moving upon deeper shadows. Julian could not say with certainty when the morning had returned, but he was a not the sort given over to the philosophical minutia concerning the seamless slip of time. His eyes now having captured the scene of his room, his body felt the warm coverlet of down and denim, but his mind was still in #16: the room at the end of the hall. He became aware of his hands clutching at sheets, fidgeting, clutching in cycle with the repeated memories of his mind's wheel.

Rats, thinking about the rats of his childhood with their little nails scratching on the walls, and their little feet treading the ceiling, their undulational black bodies, soft furry black bodies and naked snaky tails shooting below his father's boot, or scattering in the barn with the clap of opened doors. Reason lamely asserted that it was rats on the bed, mating, eating, or just rustling around in their impenetrable ratness. Or a joke of the mind, or a joke of his landlord, but by now, the greater part of Julian knew that the thin leathery legs, stretched tight over brown bones, the grasping claws that had been hands, and the long grey hair, had been on the bed under the rats who squirmed and moved over it.

After the sunshine had chased most of the fearsome shadows from his room and mind, he finally got out of the bed and looked at the ledgers, the ink, pencils and other extensions of himself that lay neatly stacked upon his desk. He washed his face and changed his clothes, eager to hear the topics of conversation over the eggs and porridge below. Owing to its remarkable restorative powers, greater than perhaps any visitation from the other side, Julian could just now smell the breakfast coffee's aroma and laughed off the apparition. The slow steady method of his conscious mind began to rationalize and construct an explanation based primarily on the whimsical and perfidious nature of the human dream-mind. With a clean shirt and collar and combed hair, he descended down to breakfast with the other guests, in a rather quiet and cheerless parlor. It seemed at first as though the only spots of color in the room were the yellow egg yolks and raspberry jam pots, but then things are not always what they seemed, he reminded himself. But the porridge was hot, the eggs were cooked to his liking, and best of all the coffee was strong and black. Outside, figures in the gray mist on a pier were indiscernible. The sun shone brightly enough, but through an almost dry fog so that the canvas of the world was a bright grey like a beautiful old woman's hair in the summer. A wind stirred clouds of this mist during the turning point: where the tide hissed upon itself and fled, and the sun burned away the fog. Julian enjoyed his momentary respite from the rigors of the world while breakfasting. In fact, only once did he think of the head with its unclosing jaw, dangling there like a broken branch in the wind. Resolving to mention something about the vermin problem in Room 16--it was understandable, the seasonal change, the proximity of ships and fish offal--he did no such thing and went about his business at the herring exchange. Later, satisfied at the state of things in on the pier, he went next door to the office of the Vasily Cooperative where he spent much of his time in quiet contemplation, getting the feel of the books which were in terrible disarray and did not match up at all with the sales figures purported in Hagen.

"Incompetence before malice," Julian said to himself, and he sharpened up his pencils and got to work. He felt that men and women were by and large incompetent beings, lovingly so perhaps, but usually not attuned to the details of the universe enough to really plumb its complexities and utilize that knowledge to further humanity. Of course, he *was* the sort of man who could plumb complexities, and yet no matter how many pound-reports of herring he counted, nor gross salt expenditures, his mind would often return to that room and the queer silver diffusion of moonlight. It made the squirming hair seem like the welling up of deep water in current-pools. That was Monday.

He returned in the darkness of the evening, had a fairly good dinner of roast beef and potatoes and went past 16 on his way to his own room. The door was shut, of course. Julian paused and came close to putting his ear to the wooden panel itself but dismissed such an action as hopelessly childish; picture himself a grown man, a fully accredited accountant to act in such a way. But standing close by the door, with an expression as though he was caught in such a transporting memory that he was compelled to stop his movement and consider the recollection until its power over him had dissipated. Well, that would be perfectly acceptable. To make this appearance complete, he tried to think of his sister and he rowing a boat as children. She sat upright on the thwart laughing with her long hair in the wind. There was a sharp snap beyond the door, as if a knot of wood was popping in the heave of boards or a socket cracking after much unmoving rest. Julian knew in the spontaneity of memory, that the rats could not have raised up the torso so quickly, nor turned its neck, not in the semblance of human conversational posture, but in the actual motion of one who has been sharply awoken from sleep. The door remained shut, and he hurried away from it.

Julian lay under his bedclothes, accounting these sights and the eerie half-quietness of it all, as if he had been struck deaf in one ear in that room, his good ear pointed to the hallway and sanity as he fell asleep.

Tuesday and Wednesday followed on much the same way as Monday. He breakfasted, and took a long mind-clearing walk upon the strand. Then he would be at the Cooperative, scratching with his pencil, amending, recording, revising, tabulating and any of the other activities that make up the constellation of accounting labor. His lunch was provided by the Cooperative and unfortunately consisted of their stock in trade, grilled and served with mustard and dark bread. However, Julian Harbasch steeled himself up, as a mathematical soldier must, to serve under diverse conditions and get his mission done. Aside from the smell of herring, which he grew used to, the general uncleanliness of the Cooperative irritated him. There was always sand, and fish scales, and hair, most monstrously single long hairs in his butter, or perhaps floating down with the unseen motes to rest upon his books.

The sun would set earlier and earlier upon the North Sea, and the wind would pick up and bend the beach fires flames leeward. The tide would leave forests of laver upon the sand, tangled inky weeds, crawling with sandfleas, crustaceans, growing more indistinct as the sun disappeared. Julian would walk along the strand for his evening exercise and dread his supper and the sleep that would come. The most common dream was one of his father. His father had worms in his eyes and his hands had grown long and thin, like wood shaped by the sea, and they were slick-black giving off a misty shadow of blackness, as if they were evanescing into the air. And he waved those long hands wildly above his head as though Julian was very far away and his father wished for Julian to see him. Yet there they were, in the empty dining room in the moonlight together. And Julian was only perhaps ten feet from him. And he waved his hands still.

It was Wednesday, and the concierge was out, perhaps rudely sharing dinner with the other rude inhabitants of his family. A different couple managed the affairs of the inn that night, and perhaps this explained the reputation of the chicken pie. The old man was garrulous, friendly and inquisitive.

"Upstairs in 14? I hope everything has been to your liking. The sun doesn't bother you in the morning, that being the Eastern wall and all?"

"No, not at all. I welcome the sun every morning."

"That's good. Haven't been sleeping well as of late?" The old man looked at him under ridiculously bushy eyebrows that only seemed to ease Julian's mind. Although this man could not be Julian's grandfather in reality, he might as well have been spiritually, or so he felt. Julian felt comfortable enough to have a glass of beer with the man in the dining room and learned some of the old stories of the village.

"Hauling out the old books of the Herringmen and rubbing it down with holy stone and sand? Well it doesn't surprise me at all. Not since they began overfishing here did anyone ever bother to notice that their accounts weren't square. But when you're flush who cares to count, eh? I'm sure you've seen it all before."

"Oh yes. It's sad but that is precisely true, Mr. Schmidt. The flush times are precisely when accounting needs to be done the most for it can help prevent the sour times from harming the company, its shareholders, or wage-men.

"But people don't usually take stock of themselves or their assets in good times, no matter what."

"No, my experience has taught me otherwise, so that rather than steering a great ship into uncharted waters, but with a strong keel for profit, a seasoned crew, and a pilot who knows how the sea works, I find myself doing what you describe: scraping barnacles and patching holes in the hope the ship won't founder any further.

Feeling rather good of himself for his nautical turn of metaphor, he listened to Mr. Schmidt's tale of Mud Mularkey being dragged through the town on a chain to his own boat for stealing salmon, and how the locals used to have a great Spring parade with the most beautiful girls dressed in silks and gold stitched lacework, but then the next day they were simply plain young women again. And there were darker stories as well.

Schmidt stopped and walked about the dining room, lighting lamps and telling Julian the tales of dead sailors, mad women, and other unhappy souls that had lived in the village, until Julian felt so at ease that he began his own careful questions. Perhaps the beer and better company and a good dinner would finally give him the sleep he was craving, indeed needed for a proper day's rest since the office would be closed the next day. He had thought about hiring a rowboat, or perhaps exploring the beach far up into the North end, where the picturesque Mystic Hills ran down to the Ocean.

"Room 16, Mr. Schmidt. I have been here a week and yet I have not seen anyone come or go from that room."

Schmidt looked up from lighting a lamp, briefly letting the naked flame reflect in his eyes, as he looked straight into Julian's gaze. It was momentary, brief, and in spite of the adamantine obdurance of Julian's emotional understanding, he felt the flicker of shared fear between them. His mathy mind was quick to shovel the earth of preposterousness upon that realization, but Schmidt was not so easily buried.

"There's a very good reason you don't see anyone come out of that room." He paused for a moment. "No one stays in that room anymore."

Julian drank more of his beer and licked the froth from his mustache. The silence that followed was mysterious, not confrontational, but laden with the serious stillness of broken decorum, although Julian was at a loss as to how he had broken it until—of course, what was he doing in that room in the first place? He then picked up Schmidt's thread.

"I'm afraid the door was ajar the other day, and so I endeavored to close it and wondered why I had not seen any occupants."

"Did you now? A careless cleaner, I suppose. Ellie, most likely, for we use that room for storage only now. Thank you for your attention, Mr. Harbasch." And although the explanation was surely a rational one and indeed explained why rats would make their home there, Julian felt that the conversation had been firmly closed by Mr. Schmidt. Yet, the conviviality of this new host did not diminish in the least, and indeed, once the guests were arranged at their tables, he and his daughter brought forth the famous pie, with sautéed red cabbage that was fresh and crunchy, unlike the soggy mop Julian was used to. The smell of chicken and hot pastry, another pint of good beer, there was even some laughter from other tables, and Julian felt for the first time, alone, but cheered all the same. There was a good fire in the grate for once; Schmidt did not stint on the wood, and Julian had quite forgotten about the rats, the bony feet and the terrible dreams of the last nights. He watched Schmidt's pretty daughter tie up the loose strands of her long black hair with a grey ribbon, and he smiled, drifting into the silly perambulations of a bachelor's mind, and then another minute he was listening to an old woman talk about her father's hounds. Julian was so happy that when he pulled a long gray hair from between his teeth, he attributed such inconveniences to be amusingly common to the town. Mrs. Schmidt, who appeared to be a larger, more mature version of her daughter emerged from the kitchen and began to play upon an old harp. She played old songs mostly, and sang in languages he did not understand, but the Pie was excellent until a large clump of hair stuck in his throat, and he choked. Schmidt was quick to hurry over and clap him on the back. At that moment, Julian looked down and saw that his slice of pie was nothing but gouts of gravy-clotted hair, long grey lanky hair, with spiders dead and streaked through it. There were bits of leaf and earth. Some sand.

The hair was between all of his teeth now, and he had no idea how much he had eaten, but he could feel it coil in his stomach like a squirrel turning in on itself.

Around him, everyone else's face was beaming, cherry happy in the fire and song. They all ate the hairy pie, an old man sucked the long strand up into his mouth like Italian pasta, and then they all looked at him. A silence fell upon the dining room. Not an uncanny silence of immediate deafness, but the silence of suspended breath, interrupted gesture, halted song. The crackling of the fire made one of the only two noises, for above there was also the click pop of heels—someone walked upon the bare floorboards above, going toward the hallway door. And you can imagine how loud the thick oak table thunked upon the floor, upended and the secondary and louder crash of china and flatware in such a quiet room. Whether the guests were used to men tripping and falling over their tables in a rush to get out of the dining hall, or rather, they were taciturn, reserved folk who withheld demonstrative reaction, it did not matter. There was no shouting to follow Julian out of the dining room, but only blank and silent stares.

The wind had cleared the sky of clouds, but it was dark, profoundly dark since the moon was nearly new. The stars shone more brightly on the strand, the town, the waves, and there in the dim light, the figure's hair blew in the wind, upon stiffly moving legs, its patchy clothes all fluttering. It walked in jerking steps down the street becoming more fluid, until it almost seemed to glide towards the pier and then it disappeared in the shadows of the buildings.

Forsaken by the safety of numbers, numbers clear and untouched by light or by darkness, Julian was found cowering and working in the only other place he knew in Storling—the counting tank of the Vasily Cooperative.

The Cooperative were understandably vexed to incur the costs of an accredited accountant such as Julian and his lodging, arguing that while they were very pleased with his rectification of the previous three years' books, there was no prescriptive advice, a promise that Green and Margaux had made. The Cooperative felt that there was little they could do with a ledger full of childish drawings that recollected rats or drifts of seaweed. Perhaps it was poorly drawn hair. And then there were his figures. Stick-figures outstretched and walking, as if drawn on a cave, or perhaps at waist level on the nursery walls: these were not the figures the Cooperative paid for. However, Julian's bills were paid for, and he was sent back on a boat to Hagen. His companion passengers remarked on his distant, cold expression and his rude compulsion of having his fingers in his mouth, digging for food perhaps. His father, a well-to-do farmer of the neighborhood received him and took him back to the family farm claiming the work had wrecked his son's nerves. Or perhaps it was the rats.

The Slubburge Man

The music of the world is sad, and I hear it in the water, in the weeds and reeds and the suck-thuck of the mud and in the lonely wind that gives the evening its lyric. The twilight helps me in my way upon this water. Twilight is the time of my work. The fish and I are unbound from the night and unfettered by the day, but I am no fisherman. The fish are my silent companions. In the twilight of morning and evening, they feed on sleepy tired things like flies and worms. I pull things, people that once were, out of the water. I find the work of monsters in the water. I am the Slubburge Man.

This slough and its water have been here for many years. Since the beginning? Before my beginning, and before writing, and before the songs of the Old Peoples' voices sang the memories of it in dream language. The water does not move through it much. I know this. My father taught it to me. Unhallowed, the water smiles in its iniquity, its jealousy, and its distance from the river that carries desires into the North Sea. It layers like old tea and keeps secrets by revealing. So close to the City, the world of men: it mocks them. It asks for the drag of the hook, the thocking knock of the boat-club that shakes the bubbles. I watch for them to breach, pop, speak of what is there. I know that there is nothing in the world like looking if you want to find something. But the slough does not always give you what you are looking for.

I know the river. It is all rivers, for it is never the same river; whenever I row out upon it, it is a different river lying under the illusion of its flow and I have heard of this fact from books about many different rivers. The flow is what makes all the rivers one and yet always different. The river tricks and hides things in its currents, ever moving beneath the deception of its immovable surface. And yet, if I look into the river, it reveals like the slough, only more quickly. The stories rise in silence, in the eddies of the river's own time like grass blades, the undulating fish, branches and limbs. If I watched and listened too closely, I would lose my mind upon the river.

The marsh stinks. Neither earth nor water, it is full of creatures and spirits. I know where to look in its bog pools and tidal orphans.

The North Sea is unpredictable. Deep and cold, and it keeps its bodies, for there are many creatures with great eyes and teeth, wriggling into you from ass to mouth, and you disappear with the whales, the ships and the sundered lovers. It can carry a story far in its own currents, just as it does the flotsam and the jellyfish. Sometimes the story will go unnoticed by the salt-water creatures and washes upon distant sands.

The moon shines and my path across the water is so long.

I have been outside for a long time. My work demands it and my work demanded me, chose me, for I never could pull a living thing from the waters. The other boys landed fat salmon, or even great halibuts out in the sea, but I found boots, dead fish, all but their heads eaten off, or the white cottony bag of the bloating octopus. Its egg-spent life was over, and the once-intelligent tentacles rotted, crab-nibbled and delicate in decomposition.

I was ten or twelve when I went outside although I didn't know it then. I do not remember the years on purpose.

He was a cold, whitened child on the fishing line: his body, naked, thin veined: his sockets open and filled with water: to see the terror and darkness of the water. He could not sleep for he had become dream. I remember his hands were blanched and bony. He was small. Perhaps only five. I knew him, remembered him in the instant recognition of a face I had seen but never marked. He had a dirty face then, but now the waters and the tongues of fish had cleaned him.

"Your boy will be a Slubburge Man," they had said to my father.

"I know that. Never getting a live fish, and now this," he said.

I was given a shilling for finding the boy. The women

knew him better, and knew the mother and father in the nearby hovel-town. They knew who had drowned him when the food was gone, who had thrust him under the ice of the slough. Desperation drives bodies into Winter's water, but the Spring always reveals, gives you things you were not looking for.

When I was fourteen or fifteen, I found Georg: in two pieces. I found his head first, for I was dragging a hook through the river to find a missing woman. The dogs had trailed her to the waters, but I knew she was gone; the river had taken her to the sea, for I saw her at night. Her gown was white, and the stones in her pockets were now as light as the cottonwood seeds that blow through the Summer air. It was twilight. She walked upon and followed the flow of the river. She paused and gracefully gestured to an eyot on the far side, looked at me and then continued the flow of her body into the sea that consumed and remembered her when no one else did.

But I remember her.

I found Georg in the eddy by that eyot. Part of him. I remember the blood-drained head. His body came up upon my hook not long after. In those days I cared about what had brought them to the water. Cared enough to listen at the inquest and go to see the trial and sometimes watch the murderer hang from a tree. They buried Georg's killer in the ground.

As I grew older, and went further outside, I no longer cared to go to the trials, and I did not need to go to the inquests anymore. My skill, they said, was enough as was my word, not even set to paper. I have enough to read in the bubbles, the currents, and the flies in the marsh. And so I lived until I was alone.

"Why should he care? His father and mother are both in the earth where his hooks will not find them. His family…"

"What family?"

"The family, his kin. Dispersed, like memories, upon the wind. Forgotten."

"I never knew he had kin. He has always been the Slubburge Man."

The moon shines and my path across the water is so long.

I watch the stars upon the water, for they seem clearer there: the Great Hunter and the Wain: the Dragon curling and pointing. The water then clears of their images. The wind that had faintly sung all night stopped and the surface matted into smooth black. A summons. Always in the flat waters. I row into the flatness. It surrounds me like dull ink and I see the hand. It is a woman's hand, tattered, still stretching out to stop the knife that made the wide wound, cleaving the palm in two. Her slender white arm is there behind it. An arm that held someone. An arm that rose to draw the curtains apart in the daylight. An arm that cast shadows in the flame light of the Fall. Is it the water that moves it so?

I returned to my cabin by the water, and placed her arm in the resting box. I gently covered it with the preserving salt and went to sleep upon my bed. But she returned. In the darkness the hand alone beckoned to me. Just her hand and arm in the darkness beyond the firelight of some old house of memory.

"Come, be with me, it is dark, and I am afraid," she said.

I reached out and her hand vanished in the light of dawn and wakefulness. I rose, still in my cabin; still alone and remembered that dreams speak many tongues I do not understand. I had forgotten something. Not that the memory had just disappeared then, but rather a memory recovered, only partly, like the arm in the water. I searched in the sloughs and salt marshes of my morning mind until I grew hungry.

"But you would come, and I knew it, for I had not been looking for you," I said.

My family is all gone now, and I had forgotten them in the daylight world. I thought that was the best way to lose them. I have no wife. Why would any woman marry the Slubburge Man? What prospects, what riches come with the payment of finding that which was discarded, shamed and mourned? The whores thought me unlucky, save for Mary Delight. She was older; the bloom of her youth spent upon her work long ago. My closest neighbor, I knew her sometimes, knew her body, heard the nostalgia in her names of other men and women, but most often we talked over warmed whisky and tea by the fire, trading stories of our work. We made up stories of our youths, of what happened in the other dreaming that never quite met the grey one we both lived in. Until she died. She left me then, although I found her where I did not expect. Not on her pallet but seized up and still:

hard and cold along the path from the city.

I go out in the boat with Minke the Dog, for her old nose is still quick and seldom wrong. She finds what she wants, but often not what someone else desires. I found her in the hovel-town one night. I had to pass through from the farmland in the North. I had been retrieving someone, turned them over to the family's grief, when I walked through the hovel-town. There was an empty hut and something was mewling in it. Awash in only the filth that men and women can make upon the earth, there was a dead bitch-dam, and hanging from her was the tail end of a puppy, trying to find its way deeper into her mother or out. I could not tell. Its feet flopped on the earth and squirmed in the air. No one was there except an old woman who was either dead or drunk unto death. The dead bitch-dam's eyes were open, white turned. Its tongue upon a rag of poison. And so I pulled the puppy out of her. She has been with me ever since. Although she will die before me, for such is the way with dogs, she is precious to me as the only living thing I ever found.

The moon shines and my path across the water is so long.

I can see the lights of the City at night, because it is very dark out here. There is a seething life there, erupting in its lust and glory. There are moments of tenderness, of remorse and fierce anger and sometimes the ends of these passions find their way onto my hooks. I look at the moon and think of the poet who leaned over too far to kiss the moon and so a Slubburge Man in China had to find him.

I have had much time to think upon desire. I looked for it once, but I quit looking for that because I found too much aside. Too much is in the water. Too many desires of the others, for death, or for others' deaths, which is the perverse mirror of love.

I pole the boat; Minke sniffs at the water and whines, for she can smell the death rise up from it, knows the smell of woman or man in the deep mud, held there by bonds, by rocks, or by desire. The dog paws toward the new patch of flat water that is swallowing the stars and the moon.

The water is a mirror and on the other side of its surface is the endless night and day. That is why the woman is there now, where none but the water can have her. No one else. Her freedom taken and given unto the water, for there are her legs, which could have carried her away. And with them, still joined, her naked hips and the vessel of her womanhood, her motherhood perhaps, just beneath the water, waiting wraiths, white now in the moonlight that returns and floods the slough.

I return to the cabin and resting box. I return to the resting bed and wait.

Where did she go?

I know this place but I cannot remember it.

The rain had come in the night and came among the green, new leaves. It left with the night and she stepped out upon the damp earth. There was mud between our toes and we played in the happy, young light. The timeless adventure of the waking garden had unfolded into the wild woods, that drew closed with a run to grandmother's washtub. Full of clear water, we studied it for an age, a moment, and then obscured its clarity with our clean muddy feet. Berries cooked and called with perfume framed in pastry so golden I can still feel it give way to honeyed red.

The moon went unto the West. Of course the West, calling my skin, bones and this stupid heart. Courses of blood, the rivers, the sloughs of it in my cold legs for I stand and knock-knock and push the great pole into the thirsty mud and pull the hooks behind my boat. Her legs ran upon the damp earth. Where is her blood? I have heard that the earth drinks man's blood, no matter how hard the feet have beaten it, no matter how hard the press of years have pressed it into stone. That is the idea of the thing, the old things gone: the daisies embroidered on the hem of her summer dress.

The moon shines and my path across the water is so long.

I go out upon this third night without Minke, who sleeps by the stove and its embers. I hear you then, upon the wind. Ever have I found what others wished I would not find, for my discovery is the end of hope. I close the false doors blazing with airy light and the green persistence of ivy-promises, until the darkness of the house reveals them to be impenetrable sepulcher-stones. I do not want to see those doors, and so I am afraid. In my boat there is a puddle that waits to join the wide water it is sundered from. The transient planks are momentary, as am I, rowing at rusty oarlocks that keep the unrelenting beat of the world's twilight.

"No. Do not go. The pain is too fresh, too much, my friend.

A lifetime of pain is still a life and not the death of the white unknown," you say.

"I will look for you, I once said, and I forgot that promise. We make many promises we never mean to break. The promises do not break, but simply disappear like the ice upon the slough. The memory remains."

It is now as clear as the Moon upon the water. It is as clear as the water upon your face. Veilings of years and your long hair swim in the night, and your lips part, to breathe the water. The water on the boat's chine is like a kiss.

In the darkness, I remember kisses inside. It was warm. In grandmother's house, we lay together watching the fire tell stories in shadows, and we kissed. I remember your kisses and your blue eyes. We smiled and kissed children's cousin-kisses because for one moment it felt good and so that is a kind of love.

Your father was so angry without words. He rose like a mountain for mountains do not know words or deign to learn them. I have waited for you although I did not know it. I have seen his anger on those they dragged to the hanging tree in fury. It is jealousy. It often drives the bodies into the water and drives them upon my hooks. Its eyes are fierce and red, bloodshot through, and thirsty. He took you away that night, called shame upon us. In the short family days of my youth, I saw you less and less until finally in his madness and your mother's madness you were all driven out of the town. You disappeared, unspoken. Unlived, then and my memories of the Yule night faded until this night came upon me.

You must forgive me. I fell in love with the outside and yet you were always in it. Like so many things that fell away into this water. This is where the frail flowers fail. Those that do not run away. Some will not. Some cannot. I know this now.

What rage can crush a flower? What wrath can take a knife and cut you, stab you. What mutilations upon your body? I have seen them all in the corpses I have found and found them all in you. It is as clear as the water upon your face.

I did not know you were married to a man much like your father and that you lived in the hovel-town just over there, for I have been outside. You hold your hand to your lips, to beg me to stop the agony. I ask the only Why I have ever begged from this old slough with its water that never moves. Your hand is tattered, comes up from the water, stretched out to say stop. To your father? Your husband? You are there among the cattails. Your body and form bend and shift in the light, not one, but shredded like the clouds, like flesh.

Your bones and flesh, white from the cold water speak and are whole again: the girl with long brown hair and blue eyes and the memory I never knew outside in the light. You sit beside me, and the mute years go by. I do not know what we will find in the slough, the river, the marsh and the sea. You whisper with the wind:

"The moon shines and our path across the water is so long."

The Ladies of Keldmere

She comes at twilight, with kindly hands that soothe.

It is summer. The towel lies upon his forehead, the linen is cool and kept in a stoneware jar of clear water, kept in the cellar darkness. Pure water, not the salt sweat on his body. It is her gift.

"The cellar door is ajar," she jokes to him in his delirium. "The stoneware is a jar." She says this to him in the darkness that belongs to his fever. There is a bat in there, it watches them with little ticks, ratchet-ritchetting tongue clicks. What does he see in the deep gloom with his large ears? The bat waits for the dark outside, when it is cooler. There are many stagnant pools in old broken fountains, hollow stumps, forgotten buckets, and they breed thick feasts of mosquitoes.

"I do not like them, they prick and bleed, they flutter in hair and terror," he says and tries to sleep again. She stays with him there in the cellar darkness, the cellar coolness, and he is less miserable to feel Ingrid touch him and hear her regular breath, like a slow drum. Her thigh presses against his shoulder and he feels the softness of her flesh, the nakedness of her flesh.

"Don't leave me today."

"We won't," she answers. "It is not day but eternal night down here. Cool and nice, like a night in April when you first came to Keldmere House."

"I have forgotten April."

"Shall I tell you how we met? Again?"

"Yes."

"This is the beginning, yet ending of this story," she says.

Once, when you were younger, stronger, but no less handsome for your ruin becomes you, you were a cook—a young man, strong man, in that flush of youth hardened into wise muscle and fool's hope, brash, cock-sure of yourself but in need of accommodation. We are all in need of accommodation, even those of us without houses, since we have no houses for our souls if they are naked and unclothed in the world, as blind souls, each one in the bright light of the Sun. The Sun makes this world real, delineates the form and shape of things, gives life in her blood and hides the rest of the world in her shining. We hide from her in workhouses, our kitchens, our offices in foster homes of brick, stone and wood. We hide beneath the trees, who cover us with their wide, splayed hands.

It is April. Remember April. Outside. I do. It is a beautiful month, like the first moments of kicking when my baby would begin to test his little arms and legs against my stomach, my kidneys, my spleen and liver and my blood flowed through him like sap. That was long ago. But April always reminds me of that.

Go on.

You need a place to stay. Remember the cherry trees on Kirsa Ride are blooming, leading up the hill and they are remembering Japan, wishing the Sun into Spring.

You walk away from the thick rush of the Central City and the Commerce Circus with its great press of merchants, customers, lawyers, government and hanseatic clerks and other loiterers, to a new situation within the deep Marckstan Dale, where the woods are slowly taking back the old hollow. At the crest of the hill, two enormous oak trees lay their strong, long boughs in arches over the pavement like a great green gate. Beyond them, the street plunges down into the cedars, beeches, chestnuts and maples, while a multitude of butterflies flutters over their tops. A few red brick chimneys can be seen, perhaps the ghost outlines of a roof or two—these belong only to the grandest houses, each sitting in its own park.

You walk down into the woods and see many old proud facades, carriage houses, and mazes of overgrown hawthorn hedges. You become lost in turning from this street, onto that one and down that lane, following the vague directions to one of the oldest houses: Keldmere. To here.

It is an old house in an old neighborhood with old people, their necks hang until they jut from the body rather than riding atop it. Things tend to lean. The mortise-and-tenon timbers sag out of plumb. Guy wires are not taut and the dogs' tails do not hook sharply but droop. These roads are old, untouched by the rationalist engineer's desire for order, geometrical straightness and perpendicular intersection. These roads under the trees hug the curving arms of the Marckstan Dale. The old creeks, once tamed into smart stonework watercourses and ceramic culverts, splash through and over broken masonry; the trees have crushed and broken the old waterways; amphibians and water rats lurk in the moist darkness.

And there is the old stone bridge spoken of in your directions, decrepit but still strong enough for a carriage, although only the grocer's cart or handymen's tinkerwaggons cross it. The lane, little more than a pony track now, runs beneath old massive grey boles of beeches, through an ancient iron gate. It is rusty, delicate and held up more by the riot of ivy that infiltrates its once intricate arabesques.

Remember the ad you tore from the *Hagen Weekly Stem,* that dubious newspaper favored by the literate underclass of hansamen, musicians, clerks, courtesans and idlers?

Mancook wanted. Hallward's Hansa only, please. Keldmere House. Gardener, carpenter and general steward duties. Pay is scale with lodging & board.

Your referral note adds little more detail; it is stamped with the embossed seal of the Hansa and possesses an elegant signature in the traditional, bold purple ink.

"They will not open it for you," the dispatcher said, "so

you had better wish for luck and tap the postern three times and then go through."

"Knock, you mean?"

The dispatcher barely seemed to pay attention, focused more on completing the referral paperwork on her desk. "No, just let the old ghosts there know you are friendly and wish to live with them in peace."

"What else can you tell me?"

"Flowers don't bloom there. You will never see any children. It rains more there. Dead people walk there."

Yes. I remember. I did not believe the first and third comments; I did not particularly care about the second.

The fourth troubled you slightly.

But I did not care.

Nothing had need of you and it pulled you in slowly. Nothing pulled you in day by day, that is step by step, as the music of the world played on in the notes and bars of love and loss until your feet had little need of direction but turned in the gyre of the dance

Hilda had left you when the first cold rains last October began to fall, coming across the wide ocean to wash the last love she had for you away. The old flat was dirty for it was seldom cleaned, and all of the dreams you had evaporated one by one in the doldrum days until that atmosphere of indolence replaced each of her breaths with a struggle not to cry out: "this is all?" And then she did say that, and it broke the spell some magician must have laid upon that narrow pallet you shared. She was young and beautiful with long brown hair upon a head precocious with wisdom and knowledge beyond her years. You made her laugh, once, when you were younger and lay together on the grass of the Seapark. The shafts of light bore through the clouds and illuminated your love—that brief flower—like the narcissus and lilies all around you, a single day of sunlight and warmth in May, a fleeting eternity lost in the mist of the endless clouds. Those cloudy days were spent inside, drifting apart as the tedium wrecked your love.

The Koorsala Hall then let you go for absences. You lay on the straw bed and grasped for the memories of ambitious dreams: the desire for a red chef's coat, for adulation and the brick house on University Hill. The stolen wine helped you until the rent was gone and the dispatcher gave you this last chance.

The last chance waits at the end of the pathway. Three knocks and the gate creaks open slowly. Inside is a wilderness of old oaks and maples. You pass green burial mounds, yews and the standing stones that last a little longer than you and speak like trees in solitary forests. You hope that mowing this down is not part of your job, that a hired man will perhaps come and take care of this nightmare. And yet you wish the verge to stay, for the noise of the city is far behind you and the green opens itself like the memory of a dream clearly and unexpectedly recollected in an unconnected moment of time. Perhaps this is happening in the future? You cannot tell, can you?

Keldmere House: ancient, eclectic and melancholy. It is

cobbled together from all of the desires of the architects and builders, the contrasting whims and angers of owners now all dead, gone to the West so their bones can rest beneath the barrows beneath the midnight green and reds of the yews. Heavy timber-framed in the front like the old long halls of your ancestors, the Old House is made of oak trunks hewn by broadhead axes and they make a face of shadow beneath the high shake roofed porch. The southern wing rises up in hard blocks with long windows, their frames rotting and the glass held in by long acquaintance and sentimental attachment. They do not open. The north wing, a listing pile of bricks, waits under a thick coverlet of ivy—windows occluded in green. Robins sing to one another and flit about, gathering their nests. What magic holds this box of old tree and earth bones together? Then the Sun breaks through the April clouds and illuminates the entirety of Keldmere.

"This house is old and full of memory," you say. And the woman answers.

"Yes. It is. Can you stand to listen? Like many old people you think she is perhaps senile and not all of the memories are true. Some are forgotten and some are long remembered and they possess both senseless lust and crushing sadness."

"Are you Mistress O'Niall?" you ask.

"I am one of them. You must be the man the Hansa sent. What is your name?

"Erik Holzhaus, ma'am. I have my letter of referral if you would like to see."

And she did and she took the letter in hands that seemed

as old as the house, parti-colored from age, spots, wrinkles, twisting calcifying lumps, but perfect nails. You realize they must have once been beautiful hands. She speaks to you in a voice you place slowly; it is plucked strings, silver strings upon a Celtic harp, yes, and the notes run in rills up the octaves in questions. Her hair was once blonde, and the long tails of it that sweep the wooden boards around her chair give evidence of that memory. What hands ran through it once, was it brushed while idle fantasies crossed her mind? There is a sense of young winter about her: red apples drying in this cellar perhaps, and straw, and the husks of lily stems, beautiful in grey gracile peace while the water begins to freeze in thin panes and the nights grow long.

"This appears to be all in order and you are young and strong looking. Can you garden?"

"Yes."

"You lie," she says this with an ironic smile that you cannot parse. "I think you learned in the hall from a book, I'm sure, but you have never really touched a spade to the ground nor swung a scythe. That is not an issue. You only need to tend the market garden. I rather like the turn this place has taken; like the rest of this quarter, it is now wild and forgotten by everyone except the birds and polecats. But you must keep the path clear. Do you understand?"

"Yes, ma'am."

"You do cook? Good. My sister and I are somewhat particular in our diet, but that comes from overindulgence in youth. Of different appetites." She does not explain this, but looks out on her estate for a long while, and the blood in your legs pools. "My sister's needs are simple now: porridge, custards, milk-bread puddings, perhaps consommé. You can leave it outside of her door."

"And your sister…"

"…Is an invalid, although she is slightly ambulatory and wishes to listen to the birds singing in the daytime. She fancies that she changes into a cat at night and steals milk from the neighbors. The less contact with her the better for you."

You nod.

"Are you really a carpenter or just a banger of nails into places with hopes that they hold until your situation changes?"

"My father was a carpenter, and I would have apprenticed under him had he not been killed."

"I am sorry for my comment then."

"Thank you, but I assure you that whatever fixing you need I can accomplish, or at least hire the right builder to rectify more… imposing tasks."

"And I know what you mean by that. This house was well made, Master Holzhaus, it will not collapse on you tonight, but you are right. Perhaps you can start by re-framing those windows you keep looking at. I don't care much for them, but my sister likes to sleep in the open air at night and cannot. My brother's son is somewhat useless in that regard, and he begrudges us your salary. But he is incompetent in everything but the law, and for that he is passable. You shall seldom see him so do not knit your brow. The only enemies one finds here are ones that come through the gate and it is unusually adept at keeping the wrong sort of person out."

And she talks and talks, as she is wont, about her brother's death, which she had missed owing to her many travels. She holds forth your night and day off, and where the larders are, and the shed full of tools—most rusty and in need of sharpening—to stay out of the old wine, and how the Mighty O'Niall family has fallen on the last of their times, how the entire world is a degenerate mess of avarice and lies. As your knees were locked to stay attentive, they forsake you, inevitably, but you heard enough at the end.

"We lock the doors here at night and do not venture into the park. You will think I am an insane old woman, which is not up to me, but I am your employer and I therefore make the rules here. So do not open the doors and if you are coming back from some tipple in the Vale, simply stay at some whore's house and do not pass through the gate at midnight…"

She thinks I am afraid. I was afraid. But my mind left me, and I awoke, and you were there in the parlor. No one had said anything about a beautiful woman with long red hair living there. Your eyes were wide and bright in the darkness; they shone, as if you were going to cry. But you smiled at me and touched my heart with your hand. Then my mouth. Then my eyes. You gave me brandy and held your finger to your lips to silence me.

And I wore the Cheongsam I had from when I was younger, for it always fit me best. Such a handsome young man on the sofa, so asleep and silly. Do you remember how green the silk was?

Your arms were bare, white. I could almost see the sun through them, and I knew it was day outside. It was not midnight. The silk did not rustle, and you were gone.

Robert, the dead brother's son, is in his study, which is his office and his cell. Over four thousand spines present themselves in failing gold letters and dust, which is terribly thick in places for he does not consult on the wide expanse of the law, but only commercial torts which touch the very ground, the real property of his clients who acknowledge his mastery. He still thinks he may touch the other realms of the law and so the books remain. He prefers the darkness of the north wing, for it is away from the singing at night. A tray of roasted chicken, sliced cabbage with vinaigrette, berries from the thicket in the garden. You bring him new lamp oil, pens, papers and correspondence, and twice a week he leaves in the early morning to visit his chambers at the old firm, which tolerates his eccentricity for the lucidity of his counsel.

"You know I disagree with having any outsiders here," he says.

"But I am professional help."

"That is an outsider, as far as I am concerned and as far as this house is concerned."

"I am a professional, sir. I intend to respect this house's policies and rules. I am very grateful for the situation."

"Do not take my hostility personally. I do not like people very much, and I like them less in my own house. But my aunt still owns this place. You may be sure your situation will end when she finally does." He waves his hand at you in the old dismissive gesture and you know the interview is over and so you can return to your chores, your errands.

At first the house is a kindly place. You patch, you trim, you bring lumber on the small pony cart down the lane you keep clear, but you do not cross the line into the wilds of the park even though you know it to be only few acres. There is something foreboding in the sunlight. There are millions of shadows for each leaf on each tree, and each forms its own secret memory, shielded from the full light of the sun. And you are tired in the early summer nights and retire to your garret room with a bottle or two of wine and do not remember anything of them for they are short and warm. You feed the five old, fat Koi in the pond, shielded by a wrought iron cover from the hungry hands of polecats. The fish are caged but do not know it and thrust out their gentle mouths for food. But someone sings in the house at night and through the thickness of your sleep, you hear it. Although upon waking, it is a nameless memory from the night, never coming quite close to your consciousness so that the song, when you whistle it, simply seems to come from somewhere else. You know it comes from the door on the hallway below you.

"Anthony, you must go to my chambers and release the pogonip from inside the cupboard. It is cold. When will you fix my window?"

You are in the Invalid's room and she stands before you in

a long yellow gown. It was white linen once, with small flowers embroidered into the hem and blue ribbons tied in bows at her neckline. Her breasts hang nearly to her stomach, which is also paunchy, decrepit. The expanse of her once beautiful skin hangs behind the threadbare gown, revealing, alluring and antique. Her eyes are wide and set within a hundred wrinkles and her hair is a long shock of uncombed white, clogged with cobwebs, visible dust in their gossamer threads. Her feet, with brown horny nails, protrude and rest like claws upon the fir floor. She has three teeth in her head for this is the one who eats the custard and gruels, the thin food that marks the last transition from humanity to dust, just as it welcomes the baby into the world of people. They are bookends, these bland concoctions of grain and dairy.

"I am sorry, ma'am. Yes, I can fix your window." And so you do. You stand with square, saw, the brace and other tools of the carpenter's trade. You are skillful and quick but must still endure her talk.

"Have you seen my baby today? He wandered away from me last night and I have not seen him all this day. It is always the same. At night he sucks my teats dry, leaves them as these dangly things." She is showing you, lifting up her gown, but you focus on setting the new pane into putty, but the corners of your gaze are drawn still, as if she is some accident of horses sprawling broken-legged on the pavement in the City.

"I know what you are, Anthony. You have come to take me away and put me in that hospital. My sister is smart, but I am not stupid."

"No ma'am. I am simply here to tend the house."

"The house was old when I was born here, when you came to me at night sneaking over the walls of hawthorn and stone. Do you remember?"

"My name is Erik, ma'am. You can call me that or Holzhaus, or whatever you please, but Anthony is not my name," you say.

"Anthony, you are lying to me again. Just like you lied when you said you would marry me. It was out there. I remember the night. We had been dancing all night under the stars. All of the people were in their fine clothes and the China lanterns hung in the trees like planets and moons of moths wrapped around them. The moon was a crescent. Do you remember the wine? It was red and juicy like a raspberry and we were drunk. You took me out there, away from everyone. I bent over a rock and you stuck your big thing in me and stirred it around like a wooden spoon. I want you to put whiskey in my milk next time and quit forgetting about it!"

"No, ma'am. I am finished here, good day." And you were not finished but you hurried by her as she climbed into bed, naked now. You leapt over the gown, remember? And you were caught then, even though you felt as if the episode were over. You drink two glasses of brandy below in the cellar to steady your nerves.

You see Leena, your employer, every day at luncheon, and seldom see Robert. You have not seen me and wonder if I was simply a dream. But I have grown impatient. The sculptures of the women in the garden are covered with ivy, and they yearn for you to set them free. The bats fly out at night, and one night you wait to watch, something, you do not know, but you watch.

This night, the garlands of ivy unravel from breast, from waist and thigh and slowly the singing begins in an old language from across the Sea. And the statues commence the slow liberation of living stone, Three Graces, Greek, fair visages and flowing hips, legs and arms that weave together over the old pond. The fish rise in the night and breach the still surface; their voices, liquid and ancient, join the song. You do not know the words, but you understand the woman's child is dead and cold in her arms, and the rain and shame of the world descend upon her and its little corpse until the darkness touches each tiny fingertip, the barely formed nose, the thin eyelashes. But the night is kindly and does not reject them. The rain and night take them and cloak them. You know the song from many nights and you softly hum with the melody.

And you were singing. I heard you in the maples, joining the fish, and like them, as if scale and fin had become flesh, you stepped blue marble skinned in the night. You were clothed in fern, in ivy, in streaming moonlight that fell as mist upon the ground. The fire of your hair was bright and undimmed by the twilight and I loved you. A single touch and the wrought iron cage upon the pond disappeared and you bathed in tears beneath the moon and the arms of the Graces.

You do not remember how long you watched and gazed upon me. You find yourself in the small bed across from the window, and then you feel it growing in the midst of the room. It is very young and yet old and is shapeless in hunger.

It is like a blue light, the gas jet flame glowing without heat in the room. It is horrible, Ingrid. Please. No.

It has no teeth, but it bites angrily upon you, Erik. Do you feel your bones melt into its mouth? Do you feel your milk drawn out from your breasts? It is always thirsty, it drains you and you cannot breathe. The pressure mounts upon your lungs and they shrivel in its hunger. Why is your hair so long? Why are your breasts so full and painful in their slow drain into the child's mouth, and why will you die here in the bed with your last gasp forgotten by Hilda, by your friends, by your mother, even your father as he rests in the grave and waits with open eyes and crushed limbs?

This next morning you are tight chested. You are gasping still and cannot believe that you are whole and not in the grave with your father. The light of the Sun is now driving away the last of your shadows, Erik, as you stumble to the chamber pot and pass cloudy urine and your head throbs, your thick tongue stuck, choking you into coughing. There is not enough air in all the world. You remember the dream and it shrivels you.

"You've been drinking again," the Invalid Sister later says. She ferally sniffs the air and trains her eyes upon you. "I told you father will not tolerate that. He knows we are meeting outside. He has forbidden me to leave the house. Why did you come back here, Anthony? I loved you and you left me."

"I did not leave you, ma'am."

But it is useless. She chatters at you until it is easier to follow the dappled courses of her ruined thoughts and you are Anthony. She pounds upon your memory, upon your back while the last dribbling milk spills from the porridge bowl you carry away. And so this day you scuffle from her, down to the cellar, to the one place of peace and solace. The brandy is fire. It eases the throb of your head and dilates the veins.

Later, for the sun has climbed now and cast the garden and park into that peaceful green of maple-shade—when its power to transform the world is at its height—you feed the Koi and listen to June whisper in the breezes through wide leaves. All pavement is gone from your mind, the earth is young again and so are you. Road left, not taken, but should be now. It courses away from the drear world of keys, desks, chopping blocks, paper, words. There are trees, and they welcome you.

I am young and want to climb in them. There is no cooking to attend to, no studies, for it is deep summer. I watch the butterflies and run after them.

Yes, I loved them when I was a girl as well. The world is forever, and laughter is the only language we have to speak.

You are laughing in the woods. I hear you and catch the flash of white. I walk forward while the Koi nibble and converse and soon forget me. Deep in the park, beneath the oldest maple tree, you are swinging. The ropes are old but strong and covered with ivy. Your legs are so slender, your toes pointing forward with the swinging flex of your calves. The green of the maples ignites your red hair. White dress, bare shoulders and shadows deep in the curves of your bones.

"I want to swing higher, push me," I say.

"Yes, ma'am. As you wish. If you will pardon my asking, are you in the O'Niall family as well? I have not met you, I think."

"Oh yes, you have. You had fainted while Leena was interviewing you, don't you remember? We carried you to a sofa and you slept. A touch of brandy on your lips awoke you. You are very handsome, you know."

"Thank you ma'am." You say this and put your hands upon my shoulders. They are cool to your touch. You push gently and I rise in the air.

The sun shines through your dress, you are naked to my mind, and I am happy again. The flutter of the ivy and your white linen, sun-pierced so that your body is revealed, arching in arching, and I cannot count the times I put my hands upon your shoulders under the maple, and push out to breathe the perfume of gardenias upon your skin.

We do not need to count, my love. If life is an endless day beneath the maples swinging, then enumeration is an absurdity, nor need we have language to cut the world in thirds. It is one day beneath the maples, with soft stone fruits, apricot and peach, waldmeister wine, a bed of sword fern and we are one.

"Dereliction of duty is something I find both inconceivable and unacceptable, Mr. Holzhaus. I am not much of a mind how you disport yourself with my relatives, only that it does not interfere with your charge in maintaining this house for which we pay you handsomely. This is precisely why I was against hiring your sort into this household, and I find it both irksome and tedious that I find myself in the position of castigating help for shirking work.

Insofar as the stolen wine and brandy, I must admit that on a personal level I do not really care, for as you know, I do not drink liquor, but some of the more expensive wines are missing, and those are investments I plan to liquidate upon my aunts' demise." Robert says this with his usual appropriation of outrage, but he is cold and distant nonetheless.

She is in the room, Leena O'Niall, but she does not seem to take offense at this slight, as if she were not in the room or her son was not in the room. There is an entire subjunctive mood about the place, as if many things were not what they seemed and if only you could get away from this tiring interview.

"I suppose that you will say Ingrid lured you into this and it is all her fault. That may very well be the truth, but even if the most beautiful woman in the world brings you a silver cup those are your hands that accept it and your lips that taste it. You must make the choice and you have done as I expected. Am I making myself clear?"

As water. As running water. You think of the summer rains outside and resolve to check your behavior, to see me less, or perhaps talk about this with me. You have a job to do here after all, and our love can accept the inconvenience of employment. You will make it so. And so you nod sagely through the meeting, putting on your best show of dignity and remorse at your ways. "It is summer, and it gets the better of me, sir. It shall not happen again." Robert does not believe you, and I know it is not true.

"I know what you are up to, Anthony. Don't think father and Brian have not noticed at all. Nor have I. It won't be long before they notice the swell in my belly and then what are we to do? Come, have some wine with me and we will make our plans. It shall be a beautiful wedding in the Park. We must hurry before I show too much. We will travel far away from here, perhaps to Ireland where I will bear our son, and when we return we can simply lie about when he was born. There will be no finger counting or suspicions, and you can then put another child in me and another, and we will have a house of love and children running through this place."

She has been drinking the Port again. The expensive Port from down below, and for someone so dappled, you cannot fathom how she is able to sneak past you, as if she had some sort of magic ring or a Master Key, as they tell in stories, that can open any lock on earth. You will find out, you will show Robert who the real thief is around here.

The cellar is cool in the end of July. It seems to be the one place of retreat from the heat that pools in the Marckstan Dale. There are the heaps of old potatoes, the cheeses, the confit, the hams and the preserves of summer that you bottled away. The oddments of a household's life are strewn here: frames of old paintings, a child's crib in the corner is broken and smashed with rage, not time's gentle decomposition. There are the racks of wine, like an old honeycomb forgotten, filled with dusty necks and more empty holes. But you are tired and it is cool and you lay down to sleep.

The light is colored like grey new steel. It makes the shadows indistinct memories of what their cast was above the ground. A cat steals in on black liquid limbs, quick, silent and rough tongued for the rats and mice. Quick snip, quick bite at the neck, and she serves you as do we all. The fever makes you king of the ghosts, it tremulates the chords of life like fine horsehair upon the catgut. And we speak to you in old languages that the dead speak from across the Sea: of immutability, of the singularity of a window frame, Hilda's profile there and the brown hair, water, the rains of autumn. The oak desk where she wrote you love letters. These are good things and all within you. And you can forget the world above and the crying at night.

It is so cool down here and I am so hot. My body has become clear I think, like water on the floor of this cellar. I do not go out into the night to you, but I retreat to here. Above, in my room, night after night it comes. The singing brings it.

And you do not see her at first, so silently she steals in through the door without a single click of lock. And she moves in her yellow shift without walking it seems to the great racks of purple wine brought all the way from the Douro, rife with lateen sails. Is it the same sun that shines so brightly on them in the wide expanse of that river? But here it is late blue evening. She uncorks the bottle and lifts it to your lips.

"No, he won't be coming in here. He does not come here, Anthony, so you do not need to fear your son. Yes, he comes in the deep night, just as he did in the first great pain that opened me up to the world. The brandy was so fiery on my lips and in my throat if I could drink enough of it. The doctor came with his red coat and long thick needle of opium. He came secretly, under the promise of much gold, and with it the threat of disbarment, banishment to rude lumber fields to finish the jobs on hands and feet that axes and wayward saws had started, if my condition were made known to the world. And the child was a misery to me. I was put up in the garret with him, for my father would not have a wet nurse witness to his shame: his own daughter ruined, abandoned in this house that accepts so many abandoned lives. And at night I prayed and became an owl and flew over the world on wings flocked with whispers. I had eyes like the moon and I watched you sail across the sea. I watched the whole world move without me, armies in Italy, the fishermen on Tangyanika, the temple engineers in Gujarat, the mothers bearing millions in far China under limestone spires."

She rises and walks away, to the door she did not open, to the stairs that lead to the world. "Even though you did not come for me, I will return for you. Stay here, my love."

Ingrid?

Yes? We are here, Erik. You are dreadfully ruined. Your body is like clear water upon this floor. I will tend to you. I will bring you the cool water that you are. And we are here. See? She sits across the cellar on the old stool and plays upon a moldy cello without strings, and it tells the story over again, speaking the old language from across the sea. Listen, for the tongue has all the words of wonder and misery, of green maple light and the mother who hates and loves the child at her breast, and the deep places of the world where this secret sea feeds all the rivers of the earth. The cat waits, licks her paw and cleans her ears; her eyes are bright jewels in this darkness.

"Ingrid?"

"She is not here, not now. It is afternoon. She is in the garden, perhaps, or in her room. Or both." Leena's tone is distant, sad. She sits in a chair, looking upon you.

"No, I mean Ingrid, the girl who was here... who I met in the garden,"

"My sister is Ingrid, you fool. How can you not say that you do not know that? You have lain with her every day. You fixed her window and shared all my bottles of Port with her. Yes, she is like that in the daylight and night. She is horribly ugly and beautiful and young. I cry for her when no one can see me. In the garden she is most beautiful and sad, when the evening is in twilight like the color of her child when we found them. The night of my betrothal, she was paralytic drunk, dancing naked in the fountain for the guests, and father struck her down and took her upstairs to her room and the child. Alone, save for the child, the blacking drunk came on her, for she hid bottles of brandy, and had smothered the poor little boy in the early morning. He was hungry, I think, for Ingrid's breasts were bare and full upon the child when we rolled her over. It still comes at night for milk, if you let it in an open window. And Ingrid is still here."

"But I have seen them, both here with me. Forgive me, Ms. O'Niall, I did not mean to..." and your body fails as the last gasp of servitude is spent.

"You have seen her together? I understand now." And you both sit in the dark cellar for a while. Leena speaks again:

"It is true that the older you get the less you know. Sometimes the memories are false; sometimes it is because the universe breaks every rule you were taught. One is only left with hope, like the Greeks thought, but whether that is a cruel joke or a great pity, or both, I do not know."

And she lays her hand upon your head. And looks at you with kindly eyes for my sister has seen much in her time, before she returned to this place.

"I sense that your place will be here. Now. And that is the crucial word. To recollect memory without a future in a timeless house."

The Child is the Wasting Fever, my love. The Cat's eyes are our bright jewels. The bats are feeding and you are cold with memory, as am I. I will soothe you here, in the cellar, forever in this kindly summer twilight.

She comes at twilight, with kindly hands that soothe.

The Blue Children

Blue light carved out the snow all around Kip, for the sun was now tripping lightly, lowly in the southern misty sky and all the dark long shadows came out to stand around him. Bundling tightly, the scarf and hood tickled the boy's neck with searching scratchy wool-tendrils, coarse hairlets escaped from mother's spinning and carding. A ringlet of coyote fur kept his cheeks and brow warm as he made his ice castles and danced with the ice princesses that ran free above the sugar-crispy snow. No other children played with him in that snowfield so distant, on the outer edge of town, where the Forest began and the endless marshlands now dead beneath the sleep of Winter.

The daily chores and studies were over. Cold chores like milking: cows' teats the only welcome warmth; labors of writing, reciting basic maths and listening to the short tales of the long saga of the land and its people. And as they had, so too did Kip grow from the black rice in the marsh, the potatoes in the dark cold soil and the meat of the pigs nosing around with misty breaths.

The other children considered Kip lucky to be alone, to have no little brothers to tend, or older sisters who scolded, teased and bossed. Kip grew up somewhat spoiled, although he was not mean of spirit, but rather innocent of sibling law. Jealousy rarely entered his heart, and if it did it seemed a strange thing, like a bad walnut that you spat out and forgot about. And he seldom felt alone, being used to a solitude filled with many friends and adventures that left no tracks in the snow but his own.

It was getting late. Kip knew that when the sun set low in the South and the last cold moon of Autumn winked through the wracking clouds, whole families of the dead flew at night with the great ravens and the wendigos. As the sun began to settle down behind naked birches, the green, cold pines, the air grew noticeably colder, and Kip saw the child: a boy twisted by the cold. Naked and shivering, his pale skin was now as blue as the hollows of Kip's footsteps in the snow. His skin was blue-veined, blue-white like skimmed milk forgotten, frozen in the bucket. The boy's hair looked like black ice: solid, striated by the wind. His penis was a tiny nub beneath his sunken belly.

The boy was cold and dead, and he looked at Kip. He did not speak but clasped his hands beneath his arms. Kip then saw that the boy had no legs beneath the stumps of his knees, so he left no tracks when he turned and disappeared into the blue, snowy shadows of the Forest.

Slowly, a mewling, a howl, a dry throat wracked with cold moaned like wind upon a distant lake, but it came from deep within the Forest. The cry carried just the hint of humanity, like words started but stopped in the stammer of weeping. Low grunts, gurgles, bird caws of discomfort and memory moving closer. Kip looked down, and around him. There, just over at the old locust tree, or at the fence. There, over by the barn. Kip began to walk toward the barn and then stopped; someone was following him, and he turned around expecting to see the boy without legs gliding behind him, his mouth an open dark hole howling, tongue a frozen stick of meat. But the boy was not there. With each turn, Kip was sure the boy disappeared into the darkness and dying light, leaving a flicker of disappearance, like the shadow of a fish darting away into deeper waters. The refraction of mortality and evening occluded the boy in the corners of Kip's sight and the mewl continued its darting game of hide and seek.

"Kip, you get in here, *now*." The sure strong contralto voice of his mother clapped the air and broke the crying spell, leaving one last gasp: a short intake of breath Kip heard above the sound of his snow-crunching boots.

His mother stood in the doorway, and streaming, steaming past her was the smell of dinner: braised cabbage, bright beetroot red, white sour cream, roast pork with baked apples, rice cooked with flecks of mushroom and bacon. There would be cider and buttermilk whipped with last summer's blackberry honey, fresh baked loaves and butter. It was a kindly house near the Forest. The windows were bright and cheerful, and his mother made it a wonder of good smells throughout the year: lavender, sweet verbena, honey wax and always the baking smells of sugar and vanilla. Mother did not allow any tobacco smoking inside.

"Be quick tonight! I'll eat it all up before you get the chance!" Alda, his father's pregnant niece, gallumphed with him to table. Karl, her childhood best friend, and now her husband, joined them. Grandmother was there too. Her word-hoard was rich and deep, and her memory was long. She remembered things that her old friends had said more than fifty summers ago, and she knew much about the herbs, roots, and wind, where the aquifers ran close to the surface, and how to set a Percheron's leg so it was hardly lame at all. She loved Kip the best, since he was the closest grandchild. His cousins all lived many miles away, and he only saw them in summer time and at Yule. Kip's father was a lawyer and he worked in the township. He was a big inquisitive man with a big laughing belly. In addition to her cooking, his mother taught music at the local school in the mornings. Karl and Alda managed the farm. That was his family, as he knew them, and he loved them.

At dinner, he was quiet, although his father asked him for a story about an ice castle of the snow elves, or a talking pike down in the lake. But that was silly. He told his father that nothing interesting happened, for Kip worried that he had held onto the fancies of childhood too long, and that no one would believe him. But little dead boys could talk, or cry and they waited out there in the darkness.

Grandmother looked at Kip and knew something; her wits remained keen, even after a great dinner of pork shoulder, red cabbage, and a mug of cider.

"Father, was there another family who lived here before?" Kip asked.

"Here, in this house? No, you know that Karl and I built this place with Grandfather a long time ago, but not that long. But there have always been people here."

"Our family lived around here," Grandmother added "and many of our people died here, in the great plagues. And people lived here before when our families lived by the ocean and met the Nordiques. But they have all gone unto the West."

Dishes were cleared, and the family then moved to the front room with its great hearth full of logs, where they toasted cheese on rye, and watched the fire. While Mother sang, the fire showed stories from the past, the future, sometimes even the present, which was the briefest of flames, as it rapidly flowed from potentiality into regret and then distant nostalgia.

"How do we die, Grandmother?"

"Death comes for us in many ways. To the South, the far South, I mean, there are poison snakes and spiders and wasting diseases of diarrhea and the shakes. Here in the North, the cold, which can kill the serpent and the spider, will likely kill us all. The earth is not a kind place."

"Grandmother, do we all go to the West when we die?"

"Most do, but some do not."

"Why not?"

"There are many reasons. Some are bound here, they never go, but come back in different forms each year like the crocuses your mother likes. I think squirrels do that as well, for I have known the same one several times, and you know that their lives are short. Some never leave, like the spirits here, the deep elves, the manitou. They have always been here and it's a trick of our sight that we see them at all because we are flying, flying on the brief flight through the warm hall. They are the kings and the thrones and the pillars of the hall."

"But people?"

"Sometimes people don't either. Whom did you see today?"

"How do you know."

"I can tell by the look in your eye at dinner, and you acted different, of course."

"I saw a dead boy."

She looked at him and blinked slowly. Searching through her thoughts, the memories were coming and they would leap out of her eyes if she did not close them. And then she let the sun set upon the memories, and opened her old eyes, the crow's feet deepened in shadow line.

"Why don't you get that nice coat your mother made for you. I want to go outside and smoke," she said, and then leaned close in whisper, "come with me, we'll have more privacy."

The Outside seemed quiet to Kip after the noise of the warm house, the comfort of the fire, the music, the whispering plans of Karl and Alda. His grandmother carefully filled her pipe with tobacco and then struck a match. She puffed thoughtfully, her mind searching old places and so Kip turned and looked into the moon-silvered indigo of the night sky. In that wide darkness of Outside, the Forest's ice night conversation spoke in cracks and pops from refreezing branches, split stones. Wind caught on whistles of bough and limb, hollow bole-knots, and the hidden deep places of the woods. Slowly, a soft cry began to sound out from the trees, born along with the rest of the music and sounds. Kip looked at Grandmother, who simply stared out into the night.

"Unresting," she said. "I have heard them before." Clicking, tinkling then, old fingers knobbed with arthritis worried through the necklace of charms, worn against the blue breath of the Forest. Charms against the dead who walk in the brief foyer of winter twilight.

"Is that what you heard this afternoon?"

"Yes,"

"The Blue Children." She sighed little at saying it. "Ghosts should never be younger than you Kip. It makes you feel as old as the trees. What did they say?"

"They didn't say anything."

"People speak with more than words, you know, and the dead are no different."

"The cry wanted me to find it, to follow it. It was hungry."

"It is hungry. Don't follow it. Though I fear you will some day. Your father was right of course about people who lived here before. And he was a little misleading as well. Your mother's brother lived on this land before your mother and father took it over." Kip had heard of Old Uncle Bill who was a drunk trapper living in the Forest where it came close to town. A ghost himself, almost, he was seldom heard of. When rarely seen, he would assume human shape to visit the Iverson Tavern and the Trading Post to buy whiskey when he wasn't making his own from gleaned corn. Then he would disappear into the woods, to the traplines he set. His family warned Kip to stay away from him, but since their paths never met, the opportunity to actually avoid the old rednose never arose.

Kip was about to ask, but Grandmother anticipated all questions. It was an annoying gift. "He lived here with his wife and it was hard. They had to put out a child, in the old way, although no one spoke of it. But we knew. Some of us heard it crying in the night. It died the first night, surely, the fire of its body quenched quickly. The Frost does not tarry in his work, Kip. I do not blame them. It happened in those days when the animals were dying in the Forest, the traplines were empty and the larder was emptier. I have heard of people eating their children under such circumstances, but that didn't happen in this case. Things got better for Bill. The next year was better, and better still after that. More people meant more corn and rice. More help when you needed it and he and Julia had another child. That was when it came back the first time and its spirit was harder, and tougher than anyone could have guessed."

"The first time?"

"Yes, an utburd can smell a pregnant woman. That is why

this one is back now. Babies are angry, selfish little things. They think of only themselves and the breast. You have no brothers or sisters so you haven't heard the angry screaming and crying at having to come into this cold world. But when they die, and they aren't released to the West, they sometimes come back terribly strong. Across the water, they used to pin them down in the earth with a stake, and that should have been done here. But Bill hadn't wanted to do it and so it came back crying and pawing at the door and Julia cried to let it in, to have it to her breast once more but Bill wouldn't have it. He began to drink more then to keep the noise out of his mind. And so one night, when he was thoroughly gone in the whiskey at Iverson's, Julia opened the door."

"What happened?"

"We don't really know. While he was still drunk in a corner at Iversons, we found his wife on the floor with her neck twisted around like a wrung chicken. Her eyes were black and bulging. Her tongue stuck out and her fingers were bloody from scratching the floor. My teacher, Ingmar Willow, knew what had happened, and he laid that hammer up over the door to make sure it never came back inside, and it hasn't. But it waited outside, and so eventually lured the other child out into the arms of the Frost to keep it company. It was all over for poor Bill at that point. Julia would come to him in dreams and so he drank more and more to sleep through the winter like a bear and he left this place to live in that hut in the woods. I do not know how long this will happen. The utburd and his brother go away in the summer. It is now, at Midwinter, they are strongest."

They sat for a while longer, listening to the soft crying and Grandmother sang an old song, bidding the child to leave and sleep in the West.

"Here, take this." She handed Kip a bird's leg bone, long and dry and cunningly carved into a whistle, and a little hammer of steel hung from it. "When you feel them near you, feel them drawing you into the Forest, blow this."

"Will you come?"

"Someone will."

Kip made sure that he stayed inside during the darkness and watched the sun in its course through the sky, avoiding the late twilights that brought out the crying. Only once was he late and as he ran over the meadow, almost home, there near the coop, he heard the soft chattering of teeth. And crying, crying out in the twilight blue, and there it was. A face, a baby's face with no eyes; enormous angry mouth-hole howling in the dark army of the boles. He clutched for his whistle but suddenly looked up and Grandmother was looking out into the woods scowling. The crying stopped and he quickly crossed the chicken yard.

But the school recess of Midwinter ended and he had to go back to chores, to work and to school, and the Blue Children feigned retreat.

The old pond was wide and open and irresistible to boys and girls with glittering skates or rusty skates, or no skates at all, just sprawling shoes. The teachers let them all go early that day, indeed the whole town was there and the men skated with their wives. Kip even saw Karl twirling upon his blades while tottering

Alda watched. Five times three Kip and the boys cracked the whip, and there was a man selling hot cider from a cauldron, and corn was popping. The living moved over the old pond: deep ice over summer swimming. And Kip forgot to say goodbye to Karl and Alda who were going to a dance that night anyway and would not be home until late. He had his whistle after all.

The Sun had fooled him. She ran quickly now to the West, and the afternoon became the threshold of evening. Kip knew the long way to home and he would have to go along the road that touched the eaves of the Forest. They were there, watching him, invisible through the daylight hours. He fingered the whistle in his pocket, touched the steel hammer, felt the smooth bone and remembered everything his grandmother had told him. He should not run. Running led to panic and panic led to a quick death in the cold. He set his jaw, like an old hero and continued following the too-swift Sun.

Ravens followed him along the road. He was so quick and swift that he surprised rabbits; they darted quickly in panting surprise and he thought about how much he must scare them and how really silly that was. A crooked wood lay before him. The old locust trees stretched up their twisty wood, old persons' arms, along with pines stunted and full of deep green needles. They reached over him in silence, blocked the sky and waited. He knew their hungry roots would eat his bones. He took out the whistle but did not raise it to his lips. No, it seemed immediately more peaceful, a sleepy old copse of trees now that they knew he could summon help. Kip wondered what sort of help and Grandmother had not said another word about whom the whistle summoned. It was a beautiful thing, he thought, with cunning old runes carved deep into it, painted scarlet. He shivered and then he heard the first sniffle, like a sick person in a far off room. Kip knew it was one of them, unliving and waiting for the right time. He cleared the little wood and looked up at the sky and saw the purple twilight begin fading into grey, for snow clouds were coming from the East and the Great Lakes, and he quickened his pace again.

One, two, one hundred, he had closed his ears to the outside, focusing on the wash of blood through them and the sound of his lungs. He was tired from the skating, and his skates were heavy. He stopped and looked at them in his hands and heard it.

Low, gurgling, baby gurgle almost cooing. Waking up again at night, like it had when it was a living baby in the folds of a blanket, staring at a wide ceiling, perhaps. Hungry now, it began to softly cry. Kip began to sniffle snot through his own nose, breathing quickly now in the cold. His eyes smarted and lashes froze. Kip stopped his legs from running and looked around. No boy. No baby. Not yet. An old raven stood upon a branch and studied him.

Help me. But the raven did not move. It cocked its head and watched him struggle on into the deepening night. The snowflakes began to now fall upon his black feathers, upon the leafless limbs and upon Kip's hood. He turned once again and saw the raven was now gone and he was alone. And the crying began again. Nearer. Quick walk, quick walk he had to pee but dare not stop. The blue of the snow deepened, and then, just there vanishing behind the tree, a naked shoulder.

Kip said aloud, "I will not listen to you."

In answer, loud, like a dying rabbit, or cow, all the cold voices of everything that had died in the Forest below the hand of the Frost, rolled round every trunk and struck Kip to his heart, jumping, bumping against his chest. His coat was tight and hot because now he was running. He dropped his skates, father would be cross. Mother, more cross. Grandmother would explain, he thought and he loosened his coat and felt the snow, now falling, drifting fast against his face. Off there, in the woods, but not deep enough he saw it finally. A blue cloud, misty cloud with shaking fists, growing angry growing bigger than the world, its mouth was black, a single open hole, one tooth long and white, icicled. Black tipped hands, blue naked cloudflesh it moved to follow him.

Do not listen to it, do not look at it! Follow me! The boy stood in his way. Legless, naked, blue veined and frozen hair. It was the older one. The one who had learned to speak before coming out here to join the Forest. *I hate it, come help me,* the boy said this and turned into the darkness, for now it was night. And Kip felt the ice of the thing behind him grow colder and its lowing grew louder, angrier. Following, stumbling, Kip watched the boy move across the snow, into the Forest, away from the thing behind him and they continued on. Four hundred breaths? Quick panting, quick stopping. Where did he go and where is the road?! Kip stopped in a pine clearing and looked around him quickly. The stars were veiled and no use in their indifference far above him.

Stay here with me. It won't find us here.

"No."

You will be warm. The boy glided out again from the depths of a huge fallen oak and moved toward Kip, his hands were no longer clasped under his arms, for he held them out, black tipped, frozen dead and *you will be safe with me Kip. Here. Wait, sit down, we cannot play, yet. This is serious, you know.*

Kip ran the other way, away from the boy and then the crying sounded twice, the boy calling for him and the thing in the woods was hunting him. It knew where he was because Kip did not know where he was. He stumbled over broken dead boughs and a saw a frozen deer before him, its stomach ripped out from the wolves. It began to move as well, and looked up at him with its deep black eyes and the sound that came from it was the moaning, the lowing, the freezing cry of death and the deer began to uncrumble itself up, up upon its feet.

Kip, do not run. It only makes it harder. Falling through the Forest, dead flies swarmed around him with the snowflakes. They were close now. *Breath light and dying, you are cold, cold. We are cold we will be cold together forever.* The gurgling angry wail, the yelling of the cloud was upon him and Kip fell on his face.

Sleep with us, cousin, oh we shall never have to come inside again, oh cousin. You are warm and we are cold. Let us warm ourselves. In the summer we shall go swimming and sleep below the lake and there will be no more chores, cousin. The other was raw hunger, naked angry hunger and pain, fist-shaking terror-curses without poetry upon the world and the unclean forces of its wrath.

And there in the snow, where it had landed a few feet from him, the steel of the hammer caught some last blessing light and glinted. Squirming, swimming toward it, Kip reached the whistle and blew a sharp high note.

No. No damn you I'll kill you now.

But the crashing deer corpse had stopped, the ice thing had paused in its childwonder to consider the noise. Only the legless boy did not stop but moved in front of him. With the last of his strength Kip rose, blew again and fell backward, dim-confused and wrong-remembering the road before his snow-drifted mind. The boy moved quickly now toward him, through tree, branch, drift. It was over, now and I'm going to join them was the only thing Kip thought.

The dead boy stopped. The ice wraith moved up behind it, dead baby grown monstrous in the Forest, in every warp of windward movement, but then Kip felt something else looking at him. It looked at the dead boy. It looked at the ice-wraith, the dead baby, blue and somehow checked.

Huff. Huff. Hurff, harumff, growling lower than the deep roots of the sleeping trees and deeper than the hiding places of the ghosts. Growling. Angry. Awake. Kip felt a tremendous resentment, so huge and strong it stopped his breath, as though a thousand jumps from tall trees and hitting a thousand hillocks on his back. He rolled over coughing.

The great bear stood there, two jets of long thick living steam blew out, curling the snow in eddies. Kip lifted the whistle and blew again, faintly. This is death. Cold bone on his teeth and his lips had now frozen to it. A little dying bird. I am a little dying blue jay, he thought and then the warmth of the cold death began to climb his legs.

Old beard. Long red brown beard, a musty marten smell of skins and corn and crushed micelings. Hands, big paws big hands with fingers missing from old leg-hold traps snapping, or the frostbite blacksnapping fingers free and left for Old Wolverine. He smelled the Wolves of the Forest, heard them howling in the darkness then and their warm fur under his body. The breath smelled of meat; is arms were great bear arms bearing him away.

Over the trees and under them, the sweet smell of corn and deep pinch of man-stink, musk sweat and all around him Kip wached the Forest move swiftly past, distant. Was he in the clouds? The red-brown beard, old mossy wooly beard, tobacco smoke and corn whisky smelling richly now, Kip pressed against the big fur chest and the red-brown beard fell over him like a blanket and the ice of their breaths formed the frozen ice pavilion, like pergolas in summer sky, only snow-cave blue. The mewling disappeared and all Kip could hear was the heavy breaths of the great man. Or was it a bear? Am I already eaten and inside the bear? Are we going West?

The morning light barely came through the oilcloth window. Everything was stuffy, but Kip was warm beneath the heavy bearskin and blankets on top of him. Tobacco smoke, heavy, and boiled herbs and the sweet corn whisky smell lingered. A gamy rancid fat-smell was everywhere. Burning lamps. A low fire of alderwood glowed in the little fireplace. Kip rolled over beneath the heavy weight of skin and went back to sleep. He did not know how long he was asleep. The living wind awoke him. Up and looking around, he saw old traps, a gun against the door post and many dead animals, skinned neatly, but mess and disarray everywhere: old stone jars tipped over, a knife stuck in the wall. This was a hunter's cabin, dark and lonely without a mother to clean it. It was a small place, and he was afraid of the owner returning but he was afraid of the outside. and waited until the outside came to him. Later, he crawled out of the skins and found dried stick of old cured venison and ate it hungrily.

A head, well wrapped in fur, long grey hair streaming out, thrust itself quickly through the door and Kip started with a scream.

"Stop that, you little fool! I'll kill you myself, dig you up and kill you again," and Grandmother was on him in an instant, all hugs and tobacco kisses. "I told you, but you didn't listen, and I knew you wouldn't."

They walked out of the little cabin into the bright sunshine. The snow had fallen deeply over everything, everywhere.

"Where are we?"

"Your uncle's cabin. Come on, they're still looking for you in the woods. You followed them, didn't you" and Kip told her all about the night, and the blue baby ghost, the little boy, the dead deer and the Great Bear while they walked toward the men who were shouting deep in the Forest. The men abruptly stopped shouting, but Grandmother knew the way and kept on straight and true to the last clearing. "This is where I was, I was right..." but he stopped, for now, tightly holding her hand, he saw the dead man leaning against a tree. His long red-brown beard was frozen stiff and full of snow and ice. His eyes were frozen open and the tears were clear icicles on his cheeks.

"He is gone too," was all grandmother said. Kip got to sleep on the couch in the house that night, loaded with eggnogs and brandy but he could not sleep and listened to whispering talk between Grandmother and Mother, who cried throughout the night and sang for her brother in the Forest.

The old house was cold and empty and no living person entered it. Animals sheltered there in winter, but the chickens, the pigs, the people were all gone. Kip stood on the porch looking out into the moon-silvered indigo and saw them, for they were now very hungry. No one lived there to feed or remember them, although Kip did when he sat alone on the porch of his big house in town. Karl and Alda and their children owned a farm, now some miles distant. Grandmother and father had passed unto the West, and Mother was old but full of song and wonder. Kip had come back one last time, to that porch, to say goodbye to the old farm. There were the three of them, the legless boy, the stooped frozen bulk of their father, and the shapeless, hungry angry ice child beyond them convulsing in coursing clouds of wrath and death. No one could live there until the Forest was cut down and their lost bones lay as distant dust upon some other land.

Kip whistled softly to them, a song of the West. They

drifted slowly into the Forest and let him be for they had no power over him now, but they were family and so he loved them still.

The Church of the Hidden Children

I woke to the breaking wheel, spokes and shards and the agony of the snapping thoroughbrace. In the death of that year, the afternoon had come as quickly as a storm upon the sea and so the westering Sun's orange light disappeared into fields of raw earth.

"We are broken, Ms. Ludenow," the coachman called down and there amongst the Imperial mailbags, my dark nest of letters, words, admonitions and taxation notices, I considered the comprehensiveness of his observation. I opened the door and unfolded to the ground. The old mail coach lay in the dirt beneath the fog, a linen-colored smoke-mist, touched here and there with yellowed shrouds of phosphor. The damp air drew the heat from my body. I pulled my shawl over my head and huddled closer into the warmth of my cloak.

"How long until we are underway?"

"We? Or do you mean you? Perhaps tomorrow night. The coach and I will stay here until another can fetch a carter from the next station."

An old road led off from us stretching between fallow plough lines and marked only with a rough carved stone: *Moriah* it said.

"Is there not a town that way?"

"I shall not go there."

"But we are still within the Emperor's borders. They may have a carter."

"I shall not go there," he said again as he tended the horses. They stamped and chomped in their nosebags, resigned for the wait.

"Is there lodging, at least?" I asked.

"I do not know. Perhaps. They are a quiet folk, desiring to be left alone. Even a Scrivener of the Emperor would find no welcome there."

"Then I shall go."

"Good, then take these and make yourself useful." He threw a parcel of bonded letters on the ground, most bearing the Emperor's Seal. "I would be careful and keep your head covered there, Ms. Ludenow."

I walked away, carrying my bag, into the fog. Fruitwood orchards lined the road to Moriah. Crows hunted over the fields for worms and ignored me. In time, I saw a ploughman through the even luminescence of the fog. Old grey beardman, old black-cloth man, I waved and he moved away from me behind the plow. Parallel, we kept our silent courses to town: the ploughman, the crows, and me.

The houses were single-storied, plain with no paint or decorations: single plain stories. Covered women and dour men walked about as the evening set upon Moriah. There were no children, but there were eyes, old and so bereft of happiness that the memory of it had utterly faded. Gazes followed me and studied every inch of garment, though my dress was as plain and black as theirs. Yet it was a new black, with unseen yet discernable ornamentation: the flourish of a weaver's black lilies set against their straight and even warps and wefts. I looked at the blacksmith and he shuttered his shop. The carter's door closed with a bang, even louder in the curious silence. There was only an inn, perhaps only a gathering place: not an establishment.

"I am a traveler, is there lodging?" I asked to anyone.

No answers. I opened a dark door adorned with a cross. There was a meager fire and a palisade of aging faces and stares. Another cross was on the wall: plain, wooden, and waiting perhaps for a corpus of tortured light. Again, I repeated my plea, and asked with the Emperor's coins for something to eat, a place to sleep the night, and a carter. I spoke to a nation of mutes and there was no thaw in their resolve or distance. To shut my mouth, a woman slid a bowl of porridge across a plain oak table. There was no salt. Her husband whispered to her and left.

I ate the insipid food and forgot my warnings. The first sin: I laid my journal on the bench. They all wished to crowd but would not. I touched my pen to ink, and wrote the beginning of this story. A titter, whispers like trees outside and jealous in a sorrowful breeze. Grievous sin: when I grew warm and took away my shawl, and my long black and grey hair fell away there was a single sound, like the last intake of breath that bid the quiet hush of death.

Then a whisper: "Witch of Emperor." Quiet, yet loud in the dark timbre of smoke and fear, I replaced my shawl.

"I am a Scrivener of the Emperor. Have you never seen one?" I asked.

"Are you lost, Witch of Emperor" I barely heard this.

"I wander, but I seek. I am not lost."

They fell silent. How I wished to kill them with a word and give them their truth, but then a strong voice rolled across the room, like a deep river in the desert beneath the comfort and vastness of a star-filled night.

"You are strayed from the Lord you never knew, but that may yet be the path of righteous seekers." He wore the same black clothes and plain cross, but his old starched collar, frayed a little, was his mark of office and the crook for his sheep. "Why have you come to Moriah, child?"

The broken coach, the cold and dark, even the letters for the town found their way as explanation although I did feel lost.

"There is more than a call for taxes, which we shall pay. We give unto Kaiser what is his, but he is not the Lord. And yet the Lord shall not turn away the lost, nor those that follow his path in the wilderness of this lesser earth." He smiled then. "No, not even tax collectors, which you are not."

He was even older than his flock, this pastor-whitebeard, with his grooved and elegant hands and eyes that burned like blue stars. Kempt, stately, patriarchal, he came and sat with me. Then to test me, he leaned close and spoke the old language of the Septuagint.

"You misheard them. They call you the Witch of Endor, but you must forgive them. You are as strange as a creature of the moon. You must know we wish to be left alone and worship in our way. Why are you here?"

"It was an accident, Reverend," I answered in Greek.

"My name is Reverend Mordecai, and there are no accidents in the Providence of the Lord. You are here to deliver something. Or have you sought deliverance?"

And then a marvel for that dreary space: a child cried out and summoned a scampering to quiet it. The Reverend then spoke again: "I shall speak with Caleb, here, and you shall have a pallet to sleep upon. I am afraid we can offer no aid for tomorrow is our Sabbath and we do not labor on that Day. As you know. You may come and join our worship for the morning service, but had best return to your coach before Noon. Another of the Emperor's coaches comes at that time."

I drank pure water in the deepening evening and received some blankets, mistrust and a removed alcove for my bed. I asked their God for sleep and life the next day, and remained awake until dream and night became one.

The livid flowers once opened for the sun, and were crushed on the day of God. Pulp and perfume linger for a moment. It is the time for things to die and the promises of ignorant rebirth seem naïve optimism. There is only death and a few moments of joy. I stood outside the circle of shunning mothers, as though I was the mother of words and lies and those children bring neither wealth nor comfort to age.

I rose and left to enter the trackless Outside. Deserts do not need to be warm and dry. They must only be deserted. From that desert, I could hear a woman's keening. It was not the cry of a selfish girl, usurped, vengeful, but rather a long question, held in the ululation of How. It was the maqam of lamentation asking the wherefores of broken small things: eggs, children, roofs and hearths: *"I am alone in the desert and my child thirsts."* Our Lady heard the woman's cries, but She could only cry with her. The child continued to cry in the desert and the Sun descended.

I left the harsh light of dream and unveiled my eyes to the welcome black of the closed alcove. Yet the crying and a thin light pierced the doors. A stirring, a pacing, life was outside and I could feel it in my body. I opened the alcove and saw a woman walking in her plain white sleeping dress like a tired cloud and the little one in her arms wriggled and cried softly. I became the darkness and cloaked myself in the silence of the shadow I was, so much so that the woman started when she finally saw me beside her. She was an older mother; I could see that in the light of the one candle that burned on the table.

"I mean no harm," I said. "He awoke me from a distressing dream if that is any comfort to you and praise for him."

"I should not speak with you. They say you would put a spell on me and steal my child."

"I am no witch. I am only out of my way and shall leave you all tomorrow without leaving you an empty crib, with neither blasted crops nor dry udders."

"You are kind, I think, and though I have been warned, I believe you."

"Does he hunger?" I desired to hold him but knew this would be a great sin for her.

"Do not we all hunger in the darkness, even when the sun shines? No, he is restless; perhaps he shall make a journey soon."

"To where?"

A sudden grace—she handed him to me. Shocked at this, I could only stare at him, become wordless like him. He grew quiet and studied me. He pointed at my hair then touched his own: gold, so golden in the firelight. Then he declared in babbles the name of gold and black in the ancient newborn tongue wherein all things are wonders. "Soon he will speak, and join the race of men that utter wickedness, wrongs, and doubt the Lord," she said.

"You have great faith in his precociousness then. I doubt he will utter much evil for a while. He will grow strong and perhaps climb the cherry trees in Spring," I said, but she did not waver.

"There are no cherry trees here," she said. "The fruit and flower have gone. It all begins with words for us, imperfect though we strive, for only God can utter the Word, and so gave us His only Son. Would it not have been better for my Micah to be mute?"

The sorrow of Micah rose in my foresight, surrounding him and crushing my heart in the bleakness of his grey life. "Or never born then," I said.

"Perhaps. My name is Sarah. He is quiet now and will take to bed. I would like to thank you…"

"…Ada, my name is Ada."

"I understand you may come to our morning service, Ada. I hope you do not stay long." Her words crossed purposes with her plaintive face, a kind face, made beautiful with age and sorrow; as if she hoped I would not die or worse. "Forgive me." She looked away. "Our simple faith would no doubt bore you." She then leaned close and whispered, "the angel of the Lord may appear in a kind darkness to lead the Children to Light." I wanted to ask her what she meant, but she gently retrieved the little boy and retreated in hushed steps.

The morning came to leave darkness in the corners, and the slow shuffle dance of foot and board trailed out of the house. I could hear them leave in failed stealth, and I waited. I drank milk, a fading warmth of grass and goat, a bleak drink to go with dry bread left for me upon the table. My bones felt as cold as the old floor. I waited to follow them. I waited for the Sun to shine upon my arm, but She did not deign to burn through their somnolent guardian of fog.

In the grey morning of prayer, the church was not hard to

find. It stood in simple timbers, wattle and daub, once tree, straw and clay, but now crowned above the low houses by the Cross, made of temperance and temptation: at once deliverer, punisher and path: the beacon of borrowed Zion. Hymns filtered through its walls: plainsong homage to the Lord. What day this daily crush of wheat and adoration? I thought while I stood outside and considered my trespass upon them. The church door was open; I did not need to tap on the male womb of God for entry; the only sound was the whisper of my dress across the threshold.

Gazes down to Writ, their lips mummed under hoods and beards. They were all old, all save for Micah, the child in the front—one golden swatch amongst the black-cloth bolts. He spied me in the back, smiled and commanded an irresistible return; I had forgotten kindness, and yet found it in the gloom of the empty space furthest from the pulpit. I sat and was born upon polished darkness, for the pews bore no cushions, only the hard surface of supplication. The Elect gladly bore such ascetic formulas of contrition.

The walls were bare. There was no Catholic idolatry of paint and brass. A faint blue milk-light came through panes of frosted glass and bathed the congregation. The only ornamentation in the sanctuary was the careful inlay on the pews, made to look like hundreds of cherry blossom petals speckling the backrails, as if the first breath of God had stirred those trees in Spring and left the orchard of His thought upon the wood. The people sang, and I too longed to be away from this world where men are hung, beaten and butchered to salve unkind lusts: to be where redemption waits in honey, milk and apricots: the quiet of the desert and the nightly miracle of stars, the rich and undiscovered map of Time. The song gave way to a single voice in speech, and I could feel the rich consideration of venerable Mordecai who now preached the fulfillment of his covenant to the gathered. His voice spoke like a river in distant tones, so that the walls became the desert and the murmur of his waters marked the stones and falls of his meaning. Gradually, I left my reverie, the eddies of the Jordan and I heard these words:

By myself I have made this troth, said the Lord,

Because you have done this act and not withheld your only son.

And so I shall consecrate and mark your blood and shall multiply your blood,

As the stars move in the heavens and the sand waits upon the shores,

And you shall overcome the doors of the Adversary.

And in your blood shall you above the Nations of the Earth be marked

Because you have obeyed Me.

"And so did not Abraham go unto Moriah with Isaac as the Lord bid him? For He loved Abraham. Did He not give Abraham the chance, the door to see far ahead, to behold that Perfect Gift, so too slain in the misery of this Earth? Once so bright and fair, now corrupted by the Adversary and his servants, even when they know not what they do, nor where they go?"

The Reverend looked at me as he said these last words. His

gaze never faltered. After a moment, when he was sure I understood him he said: "let us pray and sing our praises to the Lord." I wondered, where was the honey or apricots? It was time to go, and so I left him a shrug and performed my silent departure. I gathered my few things at my sleeping place and left Moriah and saw no other beings except the perhaps of cat's shadows. Walking near the church, I heard the child crying, and heard it faintly when I passed the final house but it abruptly stopped.

"Silenced hunger," I said to the fog. Safely alone, I felt my desired rapport for Micah upon the far side of exile: the warmth of his body, his suck deep in my breast. Across the fallow fields, the old road lay under fog and lead to the broken carriage and cheerless onward, yet I harvested ripe grains of regret and prejudice along the way.

The driver, his horses and broken coach waited in the road.

"So they suffered you, or was it the other way?" He asked.

"Shouldn't we be ready? The next coach should be here any time," I said.

"A coach? Ms. Ludenow, there is no coach until tomorrow."

"No, the church elder told me a coach would be here at noon."

"He was wrong. Or lying."

"Micah," I whispered, and I wondered how many lies had swept away the steps of Abraham. Where *were* the children? I felt them in hundreds of silences and heard no more the driver's words. I ran, ran as best in a recalcitrant dress, ran like a scarecrow shambling across the wide graves of moments.

But their service was over. The Church was empty and quiet, left to the mice and crafty monologues of spiders. Afternoon sunlight poured into the chapel, yellow and tired. I walked through the valley of the pews toward it: their altar. The smell of iron was almost washed away and the remains of caught rain lay beaded and holy on the floor.

There upon the altar, was the basin filled with holy water's dark and crimson mirror. Beside it, lay a silver knife. I walked upon grapes invisible yet the wine of wrath was thick and rich upon my feet. Then I heard them: first amidst those cherry blossom seats, the shroud stamps short among the bloodless channels of grave and sapwood dry. Bereft of the darkness, their breath found its slow way, not fresh breath, but a fetid draft of lurid cold drawn to the hearth, the heart of carnelian stone: the red muscle home.

They came, moving mortifications of the flesh in that sanctuary. They came, not one aged past five summers of the Earth. They came with thin-line throat necklaces, thick beaded with bruised garnet and no wings to bear them away. They held out their bloody fingertips. It was only then I understood just what those blossoms were that made up the careful inlay. The church was a vessel of prayer, crafted of dead children's fingernails, a ship of doom, terrible in slain beauty.

I ran from the Church of the Hidden Children, and yet they followed me into the jaundiced fog. I begged a prayer: "Fly, in the light and memory of bones, live in the light upon cream neck homes undivided, unstained from the edge of silver and the blood swallowed by holy stone."

A wind came, wracked the fog and called to them. Mutely, they answered and held up their sanguine hands to the sky, to say that Cruelty wears the Face of God.

Let Me Fly Away

They whispered in the doorways and they held their voices low so the words could move along the ground like smoke. The words flowed quickly over the small town's square. Even the voice of the forest carried the news in the creaking speech of beech and oak. The ravens considered and remarked upon the news in scathing polyphonies. But it was the teamsters in the square who Mina heard:

"The Lord of the Mountain has been caught!"

Mina paused and listened. The words tip-toed like clumsy children and these children of the mind first gathered in supposition, then in declaration, and finally waited on the open window sill. As the bringers of gifts, gossip and hearsay, they enjoyed their borrowed magnanimity, and in that moment, a transubstantiation occurred, and flesh and rumor became a captured god.

He was not just any Lord. There were plenty of lords in the world, but they were men. The town had never seen the Lord of the Mountain, but they were all certain of his effects upon them and this indefinite power authorized the use of the definite article. The Lord of the Mountain was said to be fond of children and often took them in sickness and in health. Those that passed away beneath his fever were said to haunt the forest. Other children simply disappeared.

The town left gifts of food for him in the old grove of oaks, oaks so old and thick, torched and twisted from the hand of Thunder that they were holy, and no axe touched them. Few would venture beyond them, for they were the silent sentinels of the greater forest that crept down the slopes of the mountain and the realm of its Lord.

Mina cocked her head and turned away from the distaff. The winding wool and linen stopped their itching dance and seemed to listen with her. As one who had very little magic in her life, Mina supposed the man they held in jail was nothing more than some traveler whose luck and ride had turned and flung him to the ground. She knew the town was often quick and cruel in its judgments.

Mina then turned the distaff again. Until her older brother had married and started his family, and her younger sister Freda had disappeared into the forest, Mina had been overlooked and left alone. Chores were done, but seldom did anyone think of who did them.

Mina loved the turn of summer into fall: when fires burned brighter, their smoke drifted on the air. Mina could feel the nuance of the fall; she marked the cant of light that carved memories from leaves, conjured long shadows on the timbers of the town and made the sky a vaster shade of blue. The days were still warm and allowed for bare feet, yet in the night there were woolen shawls and apples bathed in honey on the hearth: honey from a year ago, hard and brown.

How much can change within a year, she wondered. In the year her sister had disappeared and Mina's time for womanhood had come instead, the honey had changed, and she wondered: how many threads had passed through her hands and how many eggs had she gathered, cracked and cooked?

Her father was the stablemaster of the town's chief inn, though he was not the landlord, and since the inn lay across the small square from the town hall and its jail, her father was the janitor and jailor of both; she often took meals to prisoners there and so figured she could decide for herself who this person was.

Much later, as evening came, her mother crashed in through the door, and with great excitement ran to Mina, shaking the distaff from her hands. Its wooden end clattered on the floor just as her mother's speech clattered in Mina's ears.

"They have caught the Lord of the Mountain!"

"The teamsters were saying as much outside. What does he look like?"

"Oh, he is very handsome: a tall dark man, with strong and hard cheeks. How like a wolf he seems, if wolves had black hair and walked around on two feet."

"It seems strange, Mother. Who caught him?"

"The Korder sons. They were on their way to the wars, you know, and cut through the south arm of the forest on the old Roman road. They found him standing next to his great black horse."

"If he is so powerful, as you have often told me, how could the Korder sons have caught him? You said he can come in the night upon the wind, or that he sometimes appears as a black butterfly that lures the children into the wood beyond the oaks."

"Why must you question everything I say? I have seen him in his cell, with bars of iron 'round him and you know his kind cannot pass iron."

"Nor can ordinary men."

"What would you know of ordinary men? The way you shrink from them or turn away that big nose of yours. You'll die with an empty womb, like an old puffball or a leather bag left along the road."

How many times? Mina thought. Her mother had never been a happy person, and she was set in her ways so that her remonstrations always took the same form. Listening to her harangue was like milking cows or spinning threads.

Just as chores placed Mina in the world, so too did her mother's regard. She did not need her mother to remind her of her scrawny body, or her nose, for she could always see it in front of her own face. In fact, her nose looked like her mother's, and Mina often had the shivering fear, common to most young women, that she would someday become her mother.

"You shall take him his evening meal later."

"We are feeding him?"

"Of course we are. He shall stand trial. The godmen from the City have been summoned and the Emperor's judge shall accompany them."

Later, after the sun had set, Mina fried two sausages and cut slices of bread for the prisoner. It was the best thing she could think of; she suspected the exaggerations of those around her for they were often given to exaggeration if not outright fabrication. She placed the meal upon a simple board and moved to the door. Her mother walked into the kitchen and up to Mina. She opened the door and then leaned close:

"Oh, you must find out what he did to Freda. How he raped her. He probably made a child upon her and then ripped it from her body and ate it in front of her." Her mother clutched at her breasts and stomach.

"The lurid way you say that, Mother, makes me not wish to ask him. If you are so certain..." but Mina could say no more for her mother slapped Mina hard across the cheek, leaving the five red prints of fingers and thumb. "I'll leave that as a warning to that rapist killer. He will know how we deal with his kind and you will keep your mouth shut in respect to your mother."

The sausage was still warm, and Mina could smell the mustard on the bread as it sat upon the board. It remained a warm and curious burden to bear across the square to the jail. The jail was nothing more than a large cabin without windows, made of strong timbers.

Walking in, Mina saw only a large beeswax candle burning on a table which suffered to collect the spoils of prisoners, writs and other detritus. The timbered walls retreated into the night as though they were not there. The bars of the two cells seemed like thin bones of the night descending from a starless sky and sinking to the dark beaten earth. One of the cells contained a man in a private booth of shadows. Mina cleared her throat.

"Yes?" the voice called from the dark. She could see his form in the faint yellow light. He did not seem monstrous, and not even very tall.

"I have brought you supper."

"A kindness I did not expect, and one carried by one so fair."

"Sir, whatever you are, your flattery will not work on me."

"I can tell by your tone that is true. Come closer." The man's voice was rich as crimson and stronger than the blacksmith's work that separated him from Mina. The voice passed easily through the bars and blanketed the room.

"What have you brought me? It smells like sausage: pepper and mace from the other side of the world, and there is also familiar caraway. That is also in the rye bread, and there is some friendly mustard, though I do not need so sharp a condiment in this prison."

Mina said nothing but set the board upon the ground within reaching distance of the bars.

"Bring us some light. Both the candle and your

conversation," he asked and Mina thought this was fair enough. She set one of the candles on the floor near the cell and then she sat upon a wooden stool at a prudent distance. The man huddled closer but Mina could not see his face.

His clothes were black, but richly made, although almost too big for him. In the faint light she caught a glimpse of a fancy collar, perhaps silk. There was a glint of silver in his hair, and the hands that reached for the food were deeply knotted, spotted, and possessed of thick horny nails.

"You do not look like the Lord of the Mountain," she said.

"Really?"

"My mother said you were a tall, dark haired man and handsome, of middle age perhaps."

He looked up at her then. He was old, with strong cheekbones and deep wrinkles lining his face as though he were an aged tree. His long silver beard was well-trimmed, and his nose was somewhat large from age but neither hooked with sinister experience, nor blossomed from alcoholic habit. Yet he summoned enough light from the candle to set a twinkle in his eyes and he smiled. He is a handsome old man, she thought.

"You are wondering why I am here?" he asked. She nodded. "That makes two of us then. I was having a fine ride upon my horse through the forest when I was surprised by those two soldiers-to-be. And now I am manacled and imprisoned." He held up the thick cuffs and chains Mina had seen before, but the jailor rarely placed them on prisoners.

"They said you are the Lord of the Mountain. You look like

an old traveler. I mean no disrespect."

"I hear no disrespect in your voice, child, and remember that even Our Father often traveled in this guise, so you can never be too sure. What is your name?"

"I fear to tell it to you."

"Why? Because I would put a spell on you?"

"Perhaps, but also you will either be set free when the Emperor's judge comes or they will put you to death." There was more she could say, but she felt it was best to keep quiet around the man.

"And so a connection of names would be unnecessary, perhaps even a dare to the Gods who would so quickly sunder us? I do not care. I am old and I will tell you my name is Friduric."

"That sounds like my brother's name, Friedrich."

"Then he is a good and trusty brother, and friend for you, which is even more important," the man said and then he ate in silence for a while. Though he ate with his hands, he did so with an elegance that Mina could only guess came from courtly life. She thought the Lord of the Mountain, if he existed, would eat more like a ravening wolfman whom her mother often glamorized. He simply seemed like a hungry old man, but one who retained his manners no matter what life threw upon him. This conclusion brought a certain bravery to her.

"My name is Mina," she said.

"And that is a pleasant name. This is good sausage and bread. Did you make them?" She nodded and he continued: "then you will make someone quite happy one day, for I can tell that you are an attentive and intelligent young woman. Somewhere in you is a whole secret world."

"You are flattering me again."

"Perhaps. You are pretty, though I doubt many here can see it. They would not choose to leave such marks upon your face if they did."

Mina had forgotten her mother's slap and the mark it left. "I am not beautiful. My sister Freda was beautiful."

"Oh but you must learn that treasures hard-won change people, and what is beautiful on the inside may rise and mingle with the outside and make the whole more beautiful. A hundred knights of the Emperor would clamor and fight to kiss that nose of yours if it can smell the way to future and peace. At least it is a wonderful nose for cooking, and this is very good."

Mina smiled at him, but then straightened herself on her stool. "I am not going to let you out."

"I should hope not. Inconstancy would mar your inner treasures. My only advice to you is that change is often a welcome visitor, though many curse and spit upon it."

"I will not let you out, but somehow I do not think you will come to ruin, sir."

"And why is that? Legal counsel is woefully underrepresented in these parts, I fear."

"I think I know who you are now. You are a traveler, a wise old man, but from your speech and your clothes I can see that you are rich. This whole nonsense about the Lord of the Mountain is some sort of ruse for the Korders, the innkeeper, and my father to make money off a ransom. I doubt very much that neither godmen, nor the Emperor's judge are coming. More likely they sent a summons to your estate beyond the Roman road. When your messengers arrive with some gold, you will be freed."

He sat silently and considered this. "As I said, you are intelligent and know your people well." He laughed a little and then sat away from the remains of his meal.

"I will say nothing of this," Mina said.

"And what is the price of your silence?"

"I do not wish for gold. They would just take it away from me. Be kind to me if our paths ever cross again."

"That I shall do, Mina. But let me add a story. Old men are full of them you know and it would cheer me to tell an old tale, and maybe you can then pass it along as well. It is about two brothers. One was rich and the other, as you can guess, is poor." He continued on and as such tales usually go, the poor brother made out well in the end.

"The important part is the last part. The rich brother, whose mind was so cloaked with gold and jewels, forgot the rest of the verse to get in and out of the mountain. When the trolls came back, they ate him. Mina, are you falling asleep?"

"I heard you. I remember: 'Simeli, Simeli, let me in, and when I'm done, let me out again.'"

"Good. Treasure and magic words are no use if you cannot keep your wits about you when you enter. Now tomorrow will be a very busy day for both of us, I think, so you should go to your bed and sleep well. Thank you for your kindness and attention."

Although he was a prisoner, Mina still curtsied to him, for he did seem noble. She returned to her house and was soon asleep on her thin straw mattress.

"Harlot!" Her mother screamed. Mina awoke under fists, scratchings, and shrieking words. "How could you!? That man had raped and killed your sister and you sure as much bend over for him. How much you hated Freda, and me!"

"Quiet!" Her father roared in the darkness. "Mina, get out of bed now and get dressed." He pulled her from the bed by her hair and threw her to the floor. "How could you?" was all she heard for minutes upon years as she pulled her old brown dress over her threadbare shift.

Outside some men and women were gathered in a circle before the jail.

"Out of the way, she's coming through."

"Slut."

"We do not know she did it."

"What else can you expect?"

Mina moved through this gauntlet of curses. She stumbled under their pushing, the gobbings of their spit lit upon her face and hair and she cried, "why why, why!?? I did nothing. Why?"

Through the early light and past the blurry angry faces she fell into the old jail. In the prisoner's cell was the town's chief guardsman waiting for her.

"That is enough!" he yelled. "That won't do any good. Where is he, Mina?" Pushing the spit-upon hair out of her face,

Mina realized the cell was empty save for the guardsman. A mass of clothes lay upon the floor. "You were the last to see him. What did he do to you child? Speak."

Mina looked at the fine clothes in their heap along with the unopened irons.

The old man was gone. "Your mother said you were late in returning. What did he do to you? Tell me. You may escape no worse than branding if you tell me what happened here. The door of this cell was shut, so if you let him out, he shut the door behind him like a gentleman. Or you did. Tell me."

Mina was unaware she was speechless. The blows of her mother stung, and the smell of the town around her was strong and fetid with anger. But what really took her tongue and hid it very far away was the empty cell. Finally, after she felt the dig of a fingernail in her back, so hard it drew blood, she spoke.

"He was here when I left last night. He was only an old man."

Mina's mother was given permission to cuff and beat her while the men decided what to do. In the end, Mina was shoved out of the town past the oaks and onto an old path the charcoal burners had used.

"Go and find him," the guardsman said. "If you wish to redeem yourself, you will lead him back here with whatever charms you used in league with him. If not, you will die or he will kill you and justice will be served on you at the very least."

Mina's tears and sobs were so loud she barely heard him, but she put one foot before the other, slowly, and touched the swelling of the eye her mother had blackened. A hank of hair was missing, and her scalp was bloody. She was bruised and exiled unto death and she would have given nothing more to return to cracking eggs and spinning her boring wool for the rest of her life.

She walked slowly for an hour or so, and then stepped off the path to sit in a clearing. She washed her face in the brook that ran through the clearing and tried to smooth down the hurts. Her name hissed out from the woods.

"Mina!"

"Who is there? Can't you see? I'm already gone. Please."

"It's me. Stop it," her brother said. He stepped from behind a tree and looked around. She wept again in the mingled strains of hope and joy.

"Here, I brought you this. You'll die otherwise. There is some cheese and water. Here is a blanket, a knife and a flint. And a Thaler. I don't have much else. What happened? Did you really sleep with the Lord of the Mountain and let him go?"

"No! Don't you even believe me?"

"I don't know what to believe, but I find it hard to believe Mother, of course." He smiled at her and while she did not return the smile, her frown grew less stern, her eyes less red.

"I suppose that is wise. You must not be seen. What will I do?"

"You could go find the man."

"But he is gone. I have no idea what happened to him or why his clothes were there. I took him his supper and he was simply an old man. He couldn't have done any of those things. He seemed so wise and sweet."

"An old man?" Her brother looked askance at her. "Perhaps he did put some sort of spell on you. You did not aid him?"

"No, he seemed very tired and resigned to whatever would happen."

"Well, if you go up this pathway a little more, I think there is another pathway that leads to the left. Go on that and you'll reach the Roman road. Maybe you'll meet your old man or maybe not, but you can maybe start life over again. I don't know any other way."

They sat in silence for a while longer. The birds were singing, and the fall sun seemed fresh and bright for Mina, but this contrast only made her more bitter and sad.

"I must go. No one must know you helped me. Thank you, Friedrich."

"You're my only sister now. I cannot let you just die out here. Go the way I said, and if things turn out well, have a scrivener write a letter to me, from wherever you are."

"I will."

Friedrich stole back into the forest. And having nothing else to do, Mina walked upon the path until she found another leading to the left, and did not notice it climbed up a gentle slope.

Unlike the threads upon her loom, there were no straight lines to follow in the forest. Even her hair, which was usually straight and unremarkable, seemed to bend and curl like the creek. It did not take long to know she was lost. The path had run out and seemed to turn right whenever she wished to go left. The trees had grown thicker and darker so that she could not see the sun and did not know where it was in the sky. She found another path and followed it for a while, but the forest grew darker.

Just as the sun was setting, the large trees gave way into a glade and Mina could mark the sky and early stars. There were trees though. They were gangly and small, but she could smell sweet russet fruits. Apples! Beneath a particularly welcoming apple tree, Mina sat down and drew Friedrich's blanket around her and ate some apples and cheese.

The dusk grew deeper and deer came and passed through the little apple meadow. Their grace and silence comforted Mina as did her simple meal. She lay down and tried to count the stars shine within the profound sky.

"Thank you, apple trees and deer, for welcoming me. I think this is the most pleasant place I've seen in all the forest." Mina closed her eyes to listen to the wind in the trees and they lulled her deeper into a dream in which she had become an apple tree. She sent down her feet and her veins into the ground. Near the surface, she could yet hear the careful steps of deer, rabbits and bears, and below them the deep groan of stone.

In the morning, something on her face tickled her awake. Mina opened her eyes and saw a single white petal on her nose. In surprise she sat upright, bespeckled and dazzled with apple blossoms.

How had they blossomed all at once, and in the night? And

on the doorstep of fall? Mina quickly rose and left the strange glade although she took pockets full of apples with her. She followed a path back into the forest, but the ground continued to rise with a subtle grade.

"A mischievous place," Mina said to no one, she thought. Yet there was a croak and popping sound. Then another. She turned and looked at her new companion in the forest.

"Hello and good morning, father raven," she said. Mina knew that is was never a good idea to ignore a raven in the woods, and a worse idea not to greet him.

"Tell me, father raven, this is your land, which way shall I go?"

The raven bobbed his head. Mina smiled, for she had not really expected an answer but her jaw fell open and her eyes grew wide and fearful for she would never have dreamed he would speak.

"This is not my land. I am flying through. You may follow me and seek what you're looking for. Why are you looking at me like that? Have you never heard one of my brothers or sisters speak? We do it all the time. Oh, I see. Never in your own mushy language. It's true, your terrible grammars and worse euphony are somewhat limiting in expression.

He waited for an answer but Mina simply looked at him in child-like awe.

"Hmm, so you see," he continued, "we don't speak to you much anymore because few of you has anything interesting to say in return. It wasn't always so, and there are virtually none of you who understand our tongue any more. Caw-haw! At times you even confuse us with those low-born criminals the crows. But I put no truck by that. You all look alike to us as well. Follow me!"

With two great beats of his wings, he flew forward and Mina, who was very understandably shaken, found herself stumbling along after him along a wide pathway. The raven stopped and alit upon a branch.

"This is the road, yes this is the road. Follow this and you will leave the forest," the raven said. He seemed correct, for Mina could see the lines of ruts of what was once a road, although now grass grew thickly in it.

"Is this a Roman road?" she asked.

"You wished to find a way out of the forest, a road, and insofar as this being a Roman road, of course it is, for all roads lead to Rome!"

The joke was lost on Mina, who had never heard the proverb in her isolated town, but the raven found it most hilarious and laughed as he disappeared upon his black wings into the canopy of the forest. She looked around her and noticed that the oaks and beeches no longer surrounded her: in their place stood tall fir trees. A single feather from the raven had fallen to the ground and Mina picked it up. She thought it would be good to keep the feather of such a wise bird, and she wove it into her now very tangled hair still flecked with apple blossoms.

But where could she be? She followed the road as the raven had advised, but again it seemed to gently climb the slopes of the mountain.

"Perhaps it goes over the shoulder of the mountain and then down to the Roman road," she said to give herself confidence and she continued on.

As before, the sun was hidden behind the tops of the trees, and so in addition to not knowing where she was, she had no idea *when* she was. The forest sighed in different measures for these trees and their needles had different concerns and there seemed to be other voices among the trees, like to her own, but highly pitched and soft, as though they were singing from very far away.

She listened as she walked and heard one voice grow clearer and louder, although it giggled and babbled in words beyond her understanding. It sounded as though it came from the trees, and as she gazed upwards, Mina walked straight into a small ford and so found the voice all around her bare feet: a stream.

Although this seemed to be an enchanted forest, Mina hoped that this stream ran downhill like other, ordinary streams. Mina knelt. She paused, for she knew that enchanted water was not to be trusted, but dying of thirst seemed just as stupid.

And so she said aloud, "please, I am very thirsty and very thankful to whomever set this water here."

She scooped up the clear cold water, drinking until her thirst had disappeared. It was certainly not wine, but it did not taste like any water she had drunk before, and she felt very sleepy.

Mina thought that perhaps forgetfulness would be a boon and closed her eyes. The water flowed into every vein of her body and she waited to sleep and forget. However, as in many turns of

Mina's life, she was somewhat disappointed.

The stream did not speak of forgetfulness, but rather filled her soul with memories. There was the first spring day she could remember, and then she saw her grandmother's hands sending the shuttle back and forth. Even further back, she looked and saw her grandmother as a beautiful girl dancing around a fire and she danced with all Mina's mothers.

The circle of women widened further until their count was beyond Mina's sight, and the fire burned higher. In the evening of this everywhen, Mina heard the voices above her again. They sang of pick-up-sticks and the corn-doll parade song. They sang of wicker baskets full of eggs and cherry-stone throwing, and Mina fell asleep. She passed into the dark purple realms of sleep below the ocean of dreams, but eventually Mina heard a voice singing. She didn't like what the voice said; she was certain she had heard this before. It sounded like something her mother would sing.

> *"The turner turns his lathe,*
> *The miller turns her stone,*
> *And Mina in her father's house*
> *Turns her distaff all alone."*

Mina awoke to only the sound of the brook, yet she was aware that she was not alone. Someone was watching her carefully, and she could hear breaths along with laughter so like the giggling of the stream she first thought she had not left her dreams. When she opened her eyes, the voice said very clearly and politely, "I am sorry to wake you. Are you lost?"

She rose and turned to see a young boy above her on the rocks. He was as naked as a baby and sat kicking at the air. He could have been no more than seven years old and no younger than five. He had a healthy shock of golden-brown hair and a tough wiry body with sun-browned skin. He smiled at her and leaned forward with obvious anticipation of her answer.

"Yes, I am lost. I have tried to find my way, but all I seem to do is get further lost."

"I was lost for a while. But I've found my way."

"Who are you?"

"I live here."

"That is not a name, but perhaps I will call you that. Do your parents live nearby, I Live Here?"

"They are everywhere, but not here right now. I am alone. But my home is not too far. Are you hungry?"

"Yes."

"Well, come along then. I have not met a pretty lady with flowers and a raven feather in her hair before. Come. It isn't far," he said.

Before Mina could question him further, he bolted up and began to run. Mina sighed, for he ran up the mountain and it was not a direction she wished to travel any further. But she was hungry and wanted something more than apples and the rind of cheese.

He moved quickly through the fir trees and bracken, but Mina found it easier to follow him for the trees thinned as they went up the mountain. The sun was easier to see as well, and the air was fresh and clear. In time, they came to where the trees stopped, and wide meadows stretched out and up the mountain. There was still no snow upon it; it was not yet winter, but the thought of fall upon the mountain unnerved her.

The boy ran ahead until he descended into what appeared a small dale at the end of which was an old stone edifice and some sheep milling about. The boy disappeared into a wide open door and Mina stopped. She realized he was only an orphaned shepherd boy and how strange it would be if he was the Lord of the Mountain. How stupid her people could be!

"Are you coming?" The boy had put on a ragged tunic and stood on the threshold of his cave. "There are berries and milk!"

Mina shrugged and walked down the dale, past the ordinary looking sheep and crossed the threshold. She saw a sheepskin and a crook on the wall by the door. She expected to see the rest of the low and primitive cave that the boy's parents had scraped out of the hill. They were probably dead and left him alone, she thought.

The sun had begun to set in the west, and she turned again to see the vast slopes go down away from her. She could mark the fir forest and where the green beneath the setting sun changed into the vague browns of distant oaks and beech. It was hazy, but she was sure she made out the flat lands where her home was. To the north, she could see a distant line lead out from an arm of the forest into vague fields: the Roman road she had sought.

Her stomach, unimpressed with the view, growled

wanting berries and milk. She turned to look into the darkness and felt his small hand.

"Simeli, Simeli, let me in, and when I'm done, shut yourself again," she whispered. The boy did not seem to notice.

"Come, it's this way, and it's still far, but we can see the moon rise from there." They walked into a vaster darkness than Mina could imagine. This was no small cave, but a deep tunnel, and Mina gasped as its length stretched before her.

Her eyes wrestled with the darkness as they walked deeper into the mountain, but she saw a faint light before her grow stronger. Eventually they came to the first of the silver lamps shining along the walls. She and the boy ventured on past glittering lodes of quartz filled with ore so rich Mina could only guess it contained gold, silver and perhaps metals undiscovered. A window cut high above them poured down the sapphire color of the early evening and it mixed with the silver lamplight.

The songs of birds filled her ears though she could not see them. They sang in rich modes and the notes made light in Mina's mind: like blue silk and yellow daffodils, sweet pine air and smooth glass upon her cheek and breast. It was then, still holding the boy's hand tightly, that Mina gave herself up to the wonder and delight of the mountain.

After a time, though Mina had no idea if it was a moment or a year, they walked out into the clear air. The rising moon scattered purpling light upon a terrace. In the middle, Mina saw a simple stone table was a bowl full of dark berries and next to it a ewer of milk.

She and the boy sat upon some logs near the table, but they could have been the richest chairs in the Emperor's palace, for all Mina cared. The berries and milk were sweet, and she soon felt something she could not identify, such an odd feeling, like a ball of gold amongst others of dirt or stone.

The boy ate and spoke of the adventures of his sheep and how the bears were growing sleepy. They watched the moon rise further and it cast the shadows of enterprise for those who lived at night within the forest. It was then Mina recognized the feeling: she was very happy.

"Why are you here?" he asked.

"I was sent to look for someone," Mina said. She then paused and thought about whom it was she had been sent to find. Perhaps it was not the old man after all.

"Tell me, I Live Here, have you seen my sister?"

"Does she look like you?"

"No, she is pretty, with golden brown hair and blue eyes. She is a little younger than I am, but I suppose that could be a lot of girls."

"I have seen some girls down below, like you say. But I can't remember. I am feeling sleepy like the bears. Will you tell me a story? We can then go to sleep."

Mina cautiously followed him back into the wondrous mountain, but this time they walked up spiraling courses of stairs until they reached a very great room. Bronze sconces glowed as though iron fires burned behind their thick forms. The walls were hung with tapestries of many colors and fabrics, with strange people and animals rendered in different forms and styles. The bedroom, more of a bed-hall, looked to the West and in the middle was a great wide bed spread with more fine fabrics.

"Where did all of this come from? You cannot live alone here."

"Yes it's strange. It was long ago I came here and it is as it is. The bed is very soft, but it is lonely sometimes. Can you tell me a story? What is your name? I forgot to ask. I'm sorry."

"Mina, my name is Mina," she said, looking out the wide window cut into the stone of the mountain. She wondered why it was not cold, and then turned to look at him. "I should think you can tell me a story."

"Well, I'm storied out, Mina. I'm young. You know more."

"Hardly. But very well, I Live Here."

They curled up in the bed together as the sconces somehow dimmed, though Mina did not notice it, so natural was the fading of their light. She could think of no other story save the one the old man told her and so she began.

"Oh, I like that story. The mountain in it is like this one, but don't worry. I'd like to hear you tell it. You can make it different."

Mina breathed deeply the next morning. She was very comfortable but still dreamy and half-asleep. The songs of the birds gradually became stronger, one voice at a time and she knew that the whole of her being was not in some dream but in the mysterious bed-hall. She sat up and looked around, but the boy was gone.

A very fine shift lay on the foot of the bed and Mina realized she was still in her old brown dress. The smell of rain suffused the room. Mina arose from the fine bed and wandered to the window. Rain indeed came from the west and the mountain seemed to sleep beneath it. She then heard a cataract of water nearby. It grew louder, from a trickle to a splashing as the rain increased.

She sought out the sound and found in a clever folding of the stone walls, a chamber. It was open to the sky, but it sloped away from the central hole like a great funnel. The water came down in streams, played upon the stone floor and ran away into dark channels. Holding her hand in the water, she found it neither too warm nor too cold.

She looked back into the bed chamber. Still alone and feeling somewhat soiled and bedraggled from her strange adventure through the forest, she shyly removed her dress and shift and stood under the water.

It flowed like all the rains of the world and spoke the secrets of oceans and lands upon her naked body and she remembered the apple tree and how she had sent her own dream roots into the earth. She imagined herself a tree in the rain until the rain ceased and the sun returned, but she spun and danced like a girl-top. Time moved either very quickly, or perhaps not at all, for she suddenly found herself dry once more in the rain and sun chamber.

Time was moving, for she was very hungry. "Thank you, I Live Here, or Whoever Lives Here," she called out loud, but only the chorus of birds resounded in the mountain.

The shift was dark green, or perhaps a light green like lily pads. Mina could not tell because in putting it on, it seemed to reflect all the shades of green she had ever known. Smooth on her skin, like curds on her tongue or lamb's ears on her fingertips, the shift clung to her and she noticed it bore no seams. Perhaps it is silk, she thought.

Except for the collar of the rich man in the jail, Mina had never seen silk, much less felt it. Silk had only been a fabric of stories. Only empresses and hierophants wore it, and they were always so far away.

But she was hungry. Of that she was sure.

Mina wandered back down the stairs. There seemed to be hundreds of passages, some smooth-cut and level as snow on windless nights, and others rough-hewn with gleaming crystals and fountains of rock caught like water in somersaults and dives.

Everywhere she found gold and silver cages containing the warblers, finches, thrushes and nightingales that filled the mountain with song. Peahens and peacocks even followed her in an iridescent parade.

At last she came to a room carved from stone but filled with books. Mina frowned. She could not read but surely such a place held all the books she would ever read, if she only could. A small doorway stood between two great pillars made of gilded folios, and light from outside spread across the floor. She peeped outside into a small garden. There was another table made of stone and the handsome old traveler sat at it, eating ewe's cheese and apples and drinking milk.

"Oh, you are awake, my child. Good morning, or perhaps afternoon by this time."

Mina curtsied and looked down, "Good morning my lord, I, um…" and she stood on one leg and could think of nothing to say. Fortunately for their conversation, this did not seem to be a problem for the old man.

"Come sit, child. Your name is Mina and you are welcome in my home. I hope that this humble food can return the favor of your sausage." Mina did as he asked and sat down. "You may eat. Please do, but before you do, ask your first question."

"Do I only get three?"

"Three? No, you can ask as many as you wish, only not with your mouth full. So ask, and then eat and listen."

"Where is the young boy?"

"Oh, him. I don't know. I suppose he is off wandering somewhere upon the mountain with the sheep. He is a wild spirit of the hills. You may find this strange, but I never see him. I see his footprints around here but he is always gone in the morning as you have discovered."

The old man told her of the mountain and its history, of how the Eldest Miners cut tunnels through it, and how the sun could find her way down distant shafts to the bottom galleries and the moon would follow with his own light.

"That is the best light for thinking," he said. "When I read too much and my eyes grow tired, I sometimes come here and watch the Sun carry out Her wandering course over the sky. We have many good talks, although I am the one who seems to do most of the talking."

"And who are you?"

"I am the Lord of the Mountain, Mina. You blanch at that, yet you must have some idea why you were watched. And you were always so polite: to my apple trees and deer, and you were polite about the water as well. However, the greatest kindness you showed to me was not asking for gold, but only kindness itself. Yes, the cheese is very good. I think the young boy makes it. You must stay awhile. You have nowhere else to go at the moment, do you?"

He leaned forward and Mina shrank back from him. He was right, of course, but somehow staying on the mountain had not entered her thoughts. She assumed that the fairy-feast would disappear at any time and she would be left upon a bare and windswept hill.

"And so it is for many who venture here," he said, as though he heard her thoughts. "But they don't know the magic words, do they?"

They went inside once Mina was finished eating, and she listened to him as he pointed at books and told her stories: of how the Romans came and cut roads across the lands, and then further back to when the Northern people came across the wide lands from the mountains in the east.

As the evening deepened, he led her to an old disused kitchen. Sacks of flour and mushrooms, a keg of butter, dry cakes, and all manner of spices and herbs were there, but left in an abandoned mess.

"The boy brings them. Your people have been giving me these gifts for quite a long time, although I don't have much of a hand for cooking."

"I would very much like to return the favor of your hospitality, sir."

"Would you? That is kind of you, and I cannot help but admit I hoped you would say that. It has been many years since a pretty girl cooked for me. It was in Russia. She was a skinny, pretty thing like you with black hair and she lived in a house that sat on giant eagle legs…" Mina cast her eyes about her, and then held up her hair. The raven feather was gone, but now her hair was as black as it had been.

She made him an omelet from peacock eggs with cheese and mushrooms and they drank elderberry wine that tickled her nose and feet. He never made a move to eat her.

Later they returned to the bed-hall and Mina sat on the bed near him as he reclined and continued telling stories. She then lay down as the night came and the bronze scones dimmed again until at last, she felt her eyelids grow heavy. *I will close them for a moment, so he thinks I'm asleep and then I'll leave when he snores,* she thought.

The next day she awoke alone again, and events occurred much the same. The old man was nowhere, and so she took her bath beneath the rain that came again. The only difference was a black shift had been left on the bed, yet with her eyes closed, it felt the same as the other. She even retraced her steps to the bookroom porch, but he was not there. She found only a pitcher of milk and some blushing pears. She had eaten enough of this weird food to bind her there, she realized, and so she decided to eat some more.

The boy never appeared, and so she wandered out to the bedchamber looking over the west. Perhaps she should go, she thought, but she looked down into the dark forest that separated her from her old home. It filled her with fear and dismay. How would she ever know the way?

As she watched, she saw that mares' tails began to stream over the sky and a dark cowl of clouds gathered over the horizon, shutting out the sun. The grass stirred in the wind and Mina watched the storm come, raining perhaps over her town.

The forest moved under the great heave of the storm and then a rhythm could be heard, pulsing up from the firs. She then saw a horse and rider break out upon the meadows and they thundered up the mountain toward her. Someone to save her, she first thought? But her doubts seemed to freeze her on the porch.

Mina could hear their breaths, distant at first, then louder as they came toward her, horse and man. They plunged into the dale and the horse's hooves struck fire and sparks as they careened to a stop on the stones before the entrance below her. At that moment, the storm struck the summit of the mountain.

The man dismounted and went inside, but it was not his presence that frightened her. Her fear came in an uncanny certainty, and it fluttered upon her hand: a single snowflake. It did not melt, but remained, and she wondered if it was a tear of glass or a strange, six-sided feather.

No, it was a snowflake. But what plunged Mina's heart, what sunk her insides after it was not the first snowflake, but the second, then third, and fourth and flurry of identical snowflakes that swiftly caked the ground and her arms. She turned and ran back into the mountain.

She ran straight into him.

He stood tall and strong, with a great mane of black hair. His skin as brown as the earth of the forest: his beard was black and long. The cold fire of his green eyes perceived her, studied her and the black shift she wore felt oppressive as though it bound her breasts and clung too tightly between her legs.

He came to her, and with delicacy and anticipation, removed his gloves. He ran his long muscled hands up her body. He said nothing but put his hand on her forehead and then ran his fingers down over her face, taking special care to caress her long nose. He paused and traced her lips, then her chin.

"You are yet here, Mina. In the Hall of the Lord of the Mountain. Why did you remain?"

"I am afraid, I..." but her words were caught in her mind.

"Good, Fear is but the first quickening of power, but power is made of other things beyond that. Come. I shall show you. Do not look for the others. They are not here. Not now. Come."

And he led her swiftly down the twisting stairwells, tumbling in the darkness until her legs felt scrambled and separate from her body, like flailing mistakes upon the stones until they passed out into the dale. The horse stood by, its mane fluttering in the uncold snow. In moments faster than the night or death, the man pulled her upon the horse.

"Who are you?"

"Do you not know by now? I am the Lord of the Mountain." He spurred the great horse and they thundered down over the meadows and crashed into the forest. The branches tore at her skin and shift until it was nothing but pennants streaming after them and the pain of the piercing branches gripped her, like iron nails in her flesh.

They rode through the snow and into a clearing, but as she held him tightly and looked down, Mina saw that it was a lake they rode across. But then she saw it was not a lake, but a mirror of the clouds and they were up above them suddenly, to where the moon touched them.

They crossed over a beach of onyx and over mountains and Mina felt a building pressure, like the ocean swimming within her, and she saw the Great Serpent in the darkest of the waters, turning and coiling in his scales. She wept and gasped at the thin air, so thin it never could seem to fill her lungs.

Her legs were weak from the holding the horse, whose sweat was thick upon her legs and belly like honey, but she felt comfort and surety in the strong course of the Lord of the Mountain and in her own arms around his body. She closed her eyes tightly and became the movement of the ride.

Mina did not know when the moonlight returned and lit the tunnels around her, but she felt him carrying her through the mountain and into the chamber of rain. It fell upon them both, and she felt his skin close against her and the gentle caress of his hands upon her hair. She did not feel the bed so much as she became a dream-sand woman upon the beach of onyx.

The sleep-ocean came, drawn by the moon, and it washed her beneath blankets of waves until she and the sand became one.

Mina awoke, but this time it was still dark. Her body hurt in strange ways, but stranger still was the arm draped over her body. She did not notice that this was the first time she awoke with someone. She was only happy for a long time until the dim dawn came and awoke the first bird. She then shifted in the bed and looked beside her.

Curled against her and as naked as she was, lay the beautiful boy. His hair glowed, even in the faint rose-light of the dawn and his eyes searched through thick forests of dreams beneath his lids.

And then Mina understood.

In time, Mina learned the Lord of the Mountain was mercurial in the temporal progression of his ages. One day he was the little boy, then the old man, and then the old man again, and then the next day he was her black-haired lover. Habit was a word not suited to him, at least as human beings were wont to use it, for it suggested a certain constancy.

And Mina began to change. First it was her hair, but after many nights, she could see her veins. When she looked closely, her skin was as tawny as ever, but the vessels of her blood began to stand out in clearer definition, as though blood no longer flowed through them, but rather the precious stones of the earth. "Porphyry and chalcedony, ruby and Tyrian sapphire," were the pretty names the old man said as he ran his fingers over her arms and legs, tracing them.

The old man taught her to read. The boy would take her over the meadows and into the forest to hunt for mushrooms and berries. The black-haired man would come and surprise her and they found other ways to spend the days and nights.

Save for the Lord of the Mountain and herself, almost everything seemed the same from day to day. The rain fell in the morning for Mina, and there were always apples and pears along with strawberries and milk. The Sun continued much as it always did in its course from east to west, but even Mina noticed it moved further south. Yet while the day seemed shorter, she could never count the passing of it, or the night and the air did not grow colder upon the mountain.

But the Lord of the Mountain became sluggish and tired. The old man would often not stir from the bed. The boy no longer walked out upon the mountain. Often, she would often lie upon the man, for he could only hold onto her hips and smile.

One day she asked the boy, "Where did the birds come from? Who brought them here?"

"I did."

"You did?"

"Yes, I hear them in the forest down below and I sing to them, and then they come to me and sit upon my hand. I bring them here because they are so pretty."

"But birds must fly free."

"Must they?"

"Yes. But I have noticed there are no ravens here."

"Oh no, Father would never let me keep ravens. They are unto themselves. But one does come by. Mostly he speaks about old times beyond the forest."

Beyond the forest? she asked herself. She had grown used to the lack of change, save in the Lord of the Mountain and the course of the sun, but her language had changed in describing where she lived. Beyond the forest. It was a there, and therefore, no longer home.

On the shortest day, the old man lay in bed watching Mina feed the birds. He began to sing:

> *"The turner turns his lathe,*
> *The miller turns her stone,*
> *And Mina in her father's house*
> *Turns her distaff all alone."*

"I used to not care for that song, but I somehow miss that world," Mina said.

"Tell me Mina, the why of things that change. Your pretty map of Tyrian time shows the courses of roots, the sap-blood ways of lives." He sounded senile to her.

"When I lived below, I did not notice things that changed," she said. "I did not know them. I thought I would always live in the same place. Now I miss the smoke of fires. They were different every night, but I did not see it. The birds themselves would come and go with the spring and the fall. You do not notice it, but these birds sing the same song: variations on a theme of 'let me fly away.'" Mina then opened one cage, and the warbler flew into the room.

"No," the old man wheezed.

"I'm going to change something here."

"But they are so pretty"

Mina did not mind him. She opened every cage. The birds flew around and around her in gyres until the last were freed, and then they flew up through a shaft toward the waning sun.

The old man sadly fell asleep, and Mina walked past him to the open window and porch. The cloud of birds descended toward the Town, until they disappeared amongst the oaks. But there was one bird who remained upon the mountain; he came of his own free will. Mina heard a familiar croak next to her. The raven eyed her.

"That was very well done. I'm sure the old boy wasn't expecting it. Shall you stay?"

"How can I remain here? Where nothing really changes? I cannot enjoy the smoke upon the air in fall. The strawberries are always in season. When will they lose their taste? The cold has even lost the allure and thrill of death."

"Ah but you have changed. Look at yourself. You are barely recognizable as that silly girl I found in the forest, but now your skin is rich with veins of memory. You are always free to go, the Lord of the Mountain said as much when he gave you the verse out of the mountain. That is a great gift, for you have given him change.

"In you I think he has finally found a spirit that can walk out upon the world and bring its news to him, in the smallest of things," the raven continued. "The creaking chirp of a cricket, and yes, apples and honey cooked in the turn of fall. And in winter you can hear the crunching feet of your brother's children upon the snow. Come, do you wish to hear them?"

"But it is far, and look at me. I fear the snow will grow cold below and kill me."

"Then fly."

"Fly?"

"Yes, it's the easiest thing to do. Come, just stand here and say…" and the raven whispered to her.

"Simeli, Simeli, let me fly away, and I'll return another day," Mina said and her hair grew wild and spun around her as her mind swam above the high mountain. "One step," the raven said and Mina walked out upon the air and flew.

Together, they flew down the mountain, over the snow covered firs and over the bare branches of the oak trees. They flew toward the few lights of the town. When they alit upon a windowsill, they looked in at children playing with wooden toys upon the floor. Freda sat nearby with Friedrich's wife, turning a fine ham on the spit.

"Where is Friedrich?" Mina asked.

"There, over in the corner asleep in his chair."

Mina peered closer but struck her face sharply against the

pane. "As your nose is long, so is your beak. You'll have to learn that." They flew through the town and saw everyone Mina had known. There was singing and there were tears. These her mother did not shed, she simply sat alone and angry in a stiff chair, glaring into a lonely fire.

"There she will be, and there she would be glaring at me," Mina said.

"And I imagine you had no idea you've been speaking to me in my own language. It sounds crackled and beautifully bent, as it should be on your tongue. Make your decision. Leave him now at the weakest point of his year, the strongest of yours. Or return to him. Or else…"

"Or else what?"

"You'll figure it out. You're a smart girl." He beat his wings and left Mina perched upon the sill. She looked at her mother for a long time. It was the darkest night of the year, and so the sun would be long in returning to the sky above the wide and secret world. Mina then made up her mind and flew away into the darkness.

Music on the Wind

I must write this all quickly. I cannot find any empirical reason for *how all of this works*. Perhaps I am already succumbing. I should say *how it endures*.

Three days had passed since I walked down alone from the pass.

I could not tell how many hours were in each day, because the Sun set behind different mountains of different heights. I had to imprint these thoughts and images upon my memory by speaking aloud, but the voice of the wind whispered beneath my words and confounded me. The wind spoke the subtle language of water, because in the mountains, water and wind have so much in common to speak about: rocks, earth, wearing and change. It is why I did not notice the stream until I walked into it.

The water was shallow, cold and fresh, but it felt

wonderful on my feet and I can seldom remember drinking so much of it at a time. Close by, I found a great mound of ants. They seethed out of their little fortress. Unlike most ants these were different hues. Some were white, some were red, some were blue, others brown, some amber. They did not seem to know one another and scrambled without purpose. There was no queen, fat with eggs, for I pawed at the ground to find her. I ate as many of them as I could.

A path ran by the stream upon an embankment. I sensed that many people had lived here long before: the stones of the pathway seemed purposeful, like a road but the old walls on either side had melted back into the earth. I grew tired and decided to lay down just off the road in the shade.

The music awoke me. The notes moved in twinkling lights, behind which deeper bass notes of sapphire turned black until there was one last cadence of orange and red sunset. I opened my eyes and crawled up the hill to marvel at the walls of a city. The music came from it.

The servants of time—the wind and water—had rendered the stones to look more like the mountains from which they had come rather than masonry. But the wall remained unbroken and before it was a group of people packing up their businesses amongst multi-colored booths. I quickly tried to pick out this place from the catalogue of cities I carried in my head. The brushstrokes for this place were not in the cartography of memory. Half starving, in need of shelter, I resolved to go though I was unsure of what sort of populace I would find.

I found faces, skins, genders, hair, (and lack thereof) from all over the world. I understood scraps of their talk it seemed, but consider how focused you would be in any new city at listening to the speech of new people. What did feel familiar—was it an ambience of home I had never listened to properly before—was the strange music drifting over the walls. In a moment, it was not familiar. It was a foreign secret that yet suggested enlightenment from around a corner.

I approached unnoticed, or perhaps I should say, unregarded. There were glances, but they were quick and moved away from my gaze quickly. I cannot say they were unfriendly, but they were not welcoming either—not exactly the same thing. Perhaps it was the fact I was dressed as a eunuch. With my height, shaved head and mannish features, I can pass for one quite well and am usually left alone. The merchants finished their business and I followed many of them toward the main city gate. Upon passing through the stone archway, I stood and breathed deeply, as if my long nose could take in the first experience of the city better than my eyes.

Save for one aroma, it smelled like many cities: camels, smoke, the vague smells of people ranging from delightful pubic arousal to unwashed skin, to scabies-flakes to feces. But the one commanding aroma was that of camphor, which cut through the stinks like a brilliant ribbon. But this scent lost its novelty when I opened my eyes.

The city was a massive colonnade, almost like a forest. It stretched off into the vanishing point of converging lines and disappeared. The boulevards and columns formed a regular grid, but the columns themselves varied and were covered in scripts I could not decipher. There was no roof or any other sort of overarching structure. At the feet of the stone bases there were houses, halls, jakes and other shelters, without any sense of order: the more recent hodgepodge of a fallen civilization made of wood.

I asked several times for directions in all the languages I knew. The people smiled, awkwardly averted their eyes and tried to concentrate on something else. I finally found a man selling fried grasshoppers with honey and it sounded like he spoke a language I understood.

"The claptrap of hegemony, no it rains often on the 20th design," he said.

"I only have this." I held up the smallest coin. He eyed it, nodded and took it and handed me a huge paper cone of grasshoppers. I began to eat them. He smiled, faintly.

"Kibble. The bank frog. Appropriated."

"Thank you, these are delicious."

He shoved a small copper coin across the counter, sighed and looked away. "Krebbs. The gerund can and battleship today." I couldn't understand him, save for the weary tone a shopkeeper affects at the end of a day.

Did I really just have that conversation? Could I really call it that? I thought my hunger had toppled my reason so I smiled and bowed as low as I could and scuttled away. Then it struck me. We had not haggled at all. Then again, how could we?

I found a stone bench and listened to the music coming

from above. Oh yes, the music. I should describe it since it appears to be the only communication here that makes sense.

I said that the columns do not support a roof, but they do support musicians. The City does not have a hold on me yet. I am not being figurative or obscure. The music comes from the musicians living near the tops of the pillars.

I listened to a melancholy pentatonic song; there were no words—only zheng and huqin. At the end, I looked up and saw the musicians, both men and women, considering me with fierce blue and green eyes.

Throughout the City, they sit upon platforms or in rope-nets strung between the columns and play. At the end of a program, they chatter amongst themselves. They point this way and that. They argue, then agree, after which they strap their instruments, things, and children upon their backs and swing away into the night upon the cords, ropes, and cables that form a network for their transit. None have legs, as we would call them, but rather shriveled, leathery sacs were legs should be. Bones rattle in them like pebbles in a pair of maracas. The rhythmic possibilities are eerily explored in rumbas and bossa novas.

A veiled woman sat next to me and said: "Considering precipitation, the run market toward Hillman." She then smiled wistfully. This is my best exact translation. I knew the words, but her syntax was bewildering. I returned her smile and then quickly looked away.

I wandered through the columns for a while until I found a kind of plaza, a wide space, really where no homes or shops had been built. A broken fountain gurgled water and I drank it. The air was warm, and I thought a fast nap would be safe there.

The Next Day

I awoke in the plaza, listening to a frighteningly virtuosic Roma arpeggio played on a viol. It was on this second day I was able to buy some paper and ink and I am writing it out now.

I still cannot understand anyone although many of their words remain familiar and yet I can gain no sense of usage from overhearing others. They do not speak to one another much. I spent much of the day listening to music and eating; my money seemed to go a long way here.

There is always the music playing above. It is the strangest feature of the place. I have heard chants alongside flute music. Sometimes there was only a busker playing a guitar, yet swaying a hundred feet above me, and at other times an entire symphony orchestra arranged themselves in a dense web of cargo nets.

The musicians' arms had grown huge from brachiating along their rope-streets. I saw one young woman leave her trumpet behind and in a remarkable flash of gymnastic perambulation, move off to accompany a singer with a huqin not less than 200 yards away. The musicians moved, had sex, ate, defecated (they would often blare out with ill-tuned trumpets to warn pedestrians below) and played, yet the instruments and themselves remained aloft, never touching the ground.

I found no exit from the City and no clue of exactly where I was. I looked at the sky and realized that the Sun still appeared to move in its usual way. But then I remembered, while the earth went around the sun, how would I really notice the difference if the Sun began to go around the Earth?

Eventually I found an urban farm: a large stucco building with openings for livestock occupied the center of a yard enclosed by a fence made from whatever scrap was at hand. Some cows, a few goats and several chickens moved around. Some eyed me with the desirous gaze of any domesticated animal (even well-fed ones). At least I knew what *that look* meant: "can you give me something to eat?" A woman burst out into the yard and scurried around, trying to gather eggs and firewood, and shovel shit.

"The astrolabe than you could antiquate the catheter," she shouted. "Because snow, turbulence and Rococo Tuesday, always Antipodes. Fruit rots aggregate. My is fruits June man. His stapler tastes funny."

She looked at me imploringly. I could not understand her—like all speech of this place, it was utterly clear and completely opaque. Never before had the irony of those lucid metaphors been driven into my mind.

She gestured at the sky several times, and gathered her laundry. "The are pigs last summer, repointing and conducting" was all she said with a shrug and went inside.

I felt some rudiment of connection with her and decided to

take a chance. I swept the yard, cleaned up the chicken feathers and milked a cow. I had done these things in many places and hoped my actions at least let her know I meant no harm and remuneration could be simply sleeping under an eave in relative peace. It was all I wanted.

A man looked out the upper window and said: "the polyps bulbous multitudes." The woman came back out looked up and told him simply "pus." He shrugged and disappeared from the window. Later, she handed me a bowl of broth and delicious steamed bread with an egg in the middle of it. Without speaking, she showed me to a loft above the cows.

"I can sleep here?"

"Pus."

Later, I went outside again to better hear the music. Most of the players above me had long swung off to somewhere else but a young girl struggled with a violoncello much too big for her. A boy clutched at the naked stone and played some sort of small crystalline instrument one-handed. The music was beautiful, simple, and it was a joy to listen to sounds that did not have some meaning obscured through usage and syntax.

I thought about what the woman said. *Pus* could have meant *yes* in her particular dialect. But it may have meant *a place to sleep.* I couldn't be sure of what she meant. Then again, perhaps there are queer complexities of language. The time of day may affect declension. Gender to gender communication (and I was technically neuter there) could also be different.

When I returned to the urban farm, I found the man and

woman copulating. The man kept saying "French sidewalks, French sidewalks." The woman simply groaned and looked down, her face obscured by her hair. Even when they came, they had the expression of wild animals who set to business during the rut. She said "Considerable wave magnitude" afterward and lay on him.

I don't know if they took notice of me or cared. They spoke a few words in low whispers. "Freight berries, yes, the way of cooling towers." "I sort of knew him back in high school" and other such gibberish. Was this pillow talk?

And now I can see the full moon arcing over the columns, the musicians and the roofs. It gives enough light to write this by. I can read what I have written just now. I am safe. My hosts drifted off to sleep, neither listening to the other. There is nothing extraordinary about that. What if they are as unintelligible to each other as they are to me?

The Third Day

I awake this morning in the manger. I lie above the sheep and am comforted in that I understand their movements, the soft sounds they make to one another that indicate contentment. There are no signs of wolves, at least.

I can write in the bright sun.

I go over possibilities. Explanations.

I am mad and this place does not exist.

I am dead and this place is a hell of some sort. It would explain the seemingly endless rows of columns and pillars when I remember the place had finiteness when looked at from the outside.

It is some other place that is outside my normal world. Then again, there are many such places and I am not sure where their frontiers overlap.

I consider my reason: to see if it is still intact. René's *cogito* appears to be functioning as usual. I am here, and I am questioning this enough, suspicious of not the universe but only my own grasp of causality. If I am not mad, then I am somewhere madness may not matter. I suspect that this may be the most philosophical City I have ever visited. Or most normal. Neither are comforts. You see, it causes thoughts such as that.

History may teach me something. I search over all of my thought for such a place but an annoying koan keeps returning: "the Universe is only where you think you are." I have no time for koans since they only lead back to Philosophy which, while operable, is of no use to me—like having a beautiful paddle when one is trying to get a horse-drawn coach moving. I could hit the horses with it, but I doubt that would have the desired effect.

I am now thinking of striking animals with an oar. Perhaps that crippled metaphor could pass for communication here, if I said it in Latin or Japanese. Then again, given the uncertainty here, I might be insulting. I am off my course of thought.

Where do I start? Herodotus, of course.

But I don't remember him mentioning this place. I run over other texts I have studied and remember something from the *Enmerkar and the Lord of Arrata*. Enki, a somewhat quarrelsome deity confused the languages of some place. Babel. I remembered the Abrahamic God was fond of such mischief as well. Perhaps it was not Babylon, but this City. The pillars perhaps once supported a much larger architecture and are all that remain? There are many such places in this part of the world. Shambhala and Khandormand are frequently confused and equally remote if not legendary.

I shall go explore and see if I can find an egress, before it becomes an egret and then incomprehensible. I do not have such a tail.

Later

Yes, I did write that.

I am afraid I am becoming one of them. Perhaps the initial slips are dim, etymological traversings: moving in metaphor across the face of a mountain. *Comprehend*, and its negatives are related to the curling tails of howler monkeys. Both grasp. In Latin.

I listen to the music. It is rhythmic drumming now. If I close my eyes, I can see canoes paddling across an ocean toward a horizon as wide and vast as it always is. But the music tells the paddlers the way across: when the current turns warm and it somehow describes the sidereal movement of the Southern Swan even during the day. I understand this clearly and for a moment the camphor smell, and the pong of the sheep are gone and I can smell only the salt water of the pure, landless ocean.

The music communicates something here. It is the only communication that makes sense. The musicians agree. Perhaps theirs is the only form of navigation? Perhaps the dialogue of the People Below, like me, becomes merely decorative phrases. We are not even poetry, which usually freights some meaning in its words.

I sip warm, weak tea with butter in a bazaar and notice again that the people do not actually speak to each other. I was right, they are all mutually incomprehensible. They have given up trying. But pancakes, is it really any different from other places I have lived? I remember one City in particular—a cold and dreary place that lived under rain for most of the year. Its populace was equally leery of friendship. The only dissidence is that here there is no pretense at understanding one another.

Corsairing through the air are the musicians. Of them many a for tuning and performance. I am not sure, but it could be another symphony of cats. The woman with the veil I met earlier smiles and sits down Friday to me. In this we stand under.

Only then jars fandango turn. Once again before it completely April and jest. It has caught Erickson's fattening lark crotch. Correlatives of caps of move calico. Four? Elbow swallows, party in the greenest song?!!!

Instruments of Wonder

As with most days of destiny, that Wednesday showed itself as no different from other Wednesdays in the Free and Hanseatic City of Hagen. It's true, the weather was somewhat changeable, but that was usual as Winter and Summer fought their pitched battles for supremacy. Ships came into the long wharves as they always did, laden down with salted herring and cod, silk, spices and tea from the far East, timber from Finland, iron ore from Sweden, coal from Newcastle, and people everywhere in all the colors that skin and textiles could imagine. Bread rose in the central bakery and none of which did so in portentous shapes. Dogs did not howl, except in their usual manner, and there were no flocks of ravens circling the skies because The Free and Hanseatic City was not beset by war but only prosperity, one that could almost be considered embarrassing. Few in Hagen would ever want some profound omen bursting in the sky to announce changes to a stunned populace. This was a business city and stability and surety were the foundations of a much-loved mercantile economy. Many even embraced a certain measure of inertia, worshipping a religion that eschewed any sort of change excepting the kind which rang with delight in tills, strong boxes and coffers. The downtrodden and the disappointed, like an old man looking out his greasy window at a dead tree in the park, took a cynical approach to change, regarding it as the wearing down and decay of everything beneath the Sun. But still, for some, Fortune might sneak into their beds at night like a lover, or into the bank account, like an unexpected investment windfall. Change could then reset the course of life in unexpected ways. Change could even be a tree root which has grown enough to upheave pavement and present enough of a profile that one day a toe finally catches on it and the walker goes sprawling.

Perhaps that is why Fritz Dettin didn't think of anything but the fact he was late for work and taking the unpaved shortcut through the City's South Forest to get to the Griebenbad Agricultural Inspection station. The shortcut was well known, perhaps too well known. Crimes had occurred there: robberies, mostly, but there were a few stabbings, one shooting, and upon a time a massive and correspondingly bloody knife-fight between criminal factions. The South Forest was planted to be a store of wood and timber for the City in case of emergency, not a place for robberies much less a place for respected City Burghers to engage in dangerously rough trade with the apprentice sailors on shore leave, nor was it a place for clandestine meetings that artificially set the price on potassium nitrate and thus controlled the City's lucrative and famous ham and sausage industry and it certainly wasn't a place for impromptu rehearsals of dubiously English plays beneath the more romantic skies of summer, although this non-sanctioned, non-guild activity supposedly occurred in broader stretches of the wood.

Fritz looked into the shortcut way like it was a tunnel, and remembered he was late and Heinz Kalbenski, his supervisor at the Agricultural Station would be furious. Perhaps it was the thick alders and hawthorns, or perhaps it was the aural image of a roaring, Kashubian mouth in the middle of Kalbenski's face uttering oaths about Fritz's mother—how her alimentary canal served as the place of Fritz's gestation after a French donkey or Dominican friar had made water there upon a time, (and why was it always a *French* donkey or a Dominican whose country of origin remained unknown?)—but whatever the distraction it allowed Fritz to run into one of the aforementioned common crimes occurring both in the right of way and right in Fritz's way.

There was an old man, bent from age and the blows of his three assailants whimpering: 'No, no, no, I beg you, I will give you whatever you want." His hair and beard were long, and his tattered clothes had perhaps been blue once, but their own age and battered condition beneath the shadows of the forest made them look gray. The thieves were a spread of manhood, one was skinny, one was fairly midsized, and the other was fat, but they all had on the traditional hoods and scarves that thieves wore in a particular manner to avoid identification. Like the old man, their professional outfits had seen better days, and perhaps these three clods were out in the South Forest because they had been shoved out of the City proper by better practiced or connected thieves. They had outstretched hands in the universal demand for money: palms open to the sky and matched with cudgels raised on high. The man pleaded with them, but they merely laughed in the callous manner of the inverately stupid and pushed him back and forth.

Who knows what may have happened at this point had Fritz Dettin—scion of a remarkably undistinguished family of mid-level bureaucrats and lesser grade civil servants who pioneered newer and duller ways of synthesizing sublimity and mediocrity; the Fritz Dettin who had a belly full of Mackeslaut's herring (with sour cream sauce and beets along with a poached egg); the Fritz Dettin who had just passed his 15th year in the Service of the City's Agricultural Inspector Guild—not stopped in his tracks and shouted: "stop that!"

It pains me to write that he did not even think of enriching his shout with some embellishments of thoughtful pronouns or at least creative profanity. The thieves momentarily paused and looked at Fritz. So did the old man. One the thieves laughed, and the others smirked. But you may be wondering, who is Fritz Dettin beyond the sketch I have written above, and why did his appearance result in mirth rather than fear?

Friedrich Karl Heinrich Dettin was an inch or so shorter than average: not enough to be very small for a man and perhaps exercise that opportunity to over-compensate for such short comings. Such a Fritz could have been a little giant or some other paradoxical metaphor, and he would have struck fear in the three thieves owing to the slightly crazed expression that revealed no sign of fear. Our Fritz often practiced such a look in the battered mirror his wife had left in their modest home, but such a performance was strictly limited to his domestic theatre of one. He had what they call sky-gray eyes—it's frequently overcast in the Free and Hanseatic City of Hagen—and they were his most striking feature, for his nose was not distinguished and he lacked a chin beneath his thin lips. He rarely focused his eyes in an intense gaze of remorseless defiance or visionary leadership although upon a time they suited mischievous glances that bespoke camaraderie and deft complicity. Fritz had pale, blotchy skin, as though his own blood had arguments about where to collect in his face. The hair beneath his agricultural secretary's cap was neither blonde, red, or brown, but an indeterminate muddle between the three. It hung in straight hanks around his head of a longer than usual length, for after his wife left him, he had no one to cut his hair and was too frugal to see a barber, so Fritz took to cutting his own hair with predictably poor results. He was neither fat, nor particularly thin, but rather average. To complete the picture of what the thieves beheld, we must remember to include Fritz's plain blue, single-breasted secretary's tunic, and his equally unremarkable trousers (black). Lastly, there is the matter of his hat: a blue felt affair that did not fit him all that well, with a thin brim that was useless in warding off the sun or rain. But its most preposterous feature was the regulation issue peacock feather sticking out of the band—the plume was supposedly there to mark out Agricultural workers during fairs and amongst crowds while they went about their holy work, but most often it was simply embarrassing and most of them did not wear the cap, much less the feather.

But Fritz followed the rules and so now we can see him: his right hand outstretched in a familiar gesture of "halt;" his uniform, which did not inspire obedience nor even much respect; and his ordinary face upstaged by the absurd, iridescent panache waving in the spring breeze upon his head.

One of the thieves laughed. Another made an obscene gesture, the other picked his nose and the old man shrugged and looked down at the carpet of last year's leaves moldering in the mud. Fritz was recognizably alone, and probably possessed more money than the codger, so by this simple calculation the thieves quickly moved after Fritz and the chase was on down the alley of trees. Glancing over his shoulder, Fritz saw one of the thieves cutting off to try and get through the brush.

Fritz ran through the forest as quickly as he could. It was early in the morning, so he did not stumble across male lovers going at it, nor did he upset any cartel meeting about saltpeter, and he certainly didn't plough through the blocking out of *Pyramus and Thisbe*. The only ass's head to be found remained on Fritz's head, figuratively speaking, and the only heretofore mentioned activity was a robbery, and even that undertaking was somewhat enterprising given the hour. Fritz neared the end of the wood, that much he knew, but the thieves followed him so closely he could easily count their footsteps had he the inclination. Fritz also knew the shortcut the third thief took was about to let out into the path.

"Stop now, you little shit, and we won't rape you," "I'll smash your skull in if you don't stop now," the two behind him shouted.

Although these pronouncements certainly set an agenda and mood, their effect did not result in Fritz stopping and letting them go about their business. Rather, the thoughts of a crushed skull and violated rectum gave speed to Fritz's legs in remarkable ways. It's easy for me to tell you this and for you to read it. We're both likely sitting down in some comfortable place, although some of you may be standing on public transportation and laboring under the duress of uncouth smells and interminable distance to the end of your commute. Nevertheless, you don't have two thieves calling out various forms of injury to your person and you likely aren't facing a third thief stepping out proudly (but huffing, the run wasn't easy) and holding aloft his cudgel.

And although you don't share the danger Fritz faced, you may share the surprise of the thieves at the secondary result of their shouting. Lumbering out behind the thief were the three Wünchi brothers, Rolf, Tolf, and Golf: the three sons of Old Man Wünchi, who owned a smithy along with a farm not too far from the agricultural inspection station. Primarily differentiated by their hair lengths: Rolf possessed long flowing blonde locks, Tolf had short thick brown hair that stood out like boar's bristles, and

Golf had gone prematurely bald, the Wünchi brothers were imposing men. Not one of them was under 6′5″ and it was said they ate a whole sheep for breakfast. They were not fat, but thickly muscled from working the forge bellows at their father's smithy, or carrying pigs of iron around, or ploughing their own land and others as well for wages. Golf was also actually quite good at crochet, but since that talent does not come into this tale, I will elide over his more intricate accomplishments in doily-work. Of importance to us, and especially Fritz Dettin, was that he knew the three brothers fairly well, for they often drove livestock through the station.

There was no request to desist as Fritz had done: Rolf only said: "no you don't." and did not wait to bring down his fist—about the size of a fair-sized cabbage—onto the head of the thief blocking Fritz's way. The second thief, with knife drawn received the wrath of Tolf and even managed to slash him across the arm, but this was an unfortunate, yet understandable mistake. How would the thief know that Tolf wrestled full-grown boars in the stys and was used to slashing tusks? The stroke did not even slow Tolf down and his uppercut caught the thief squarely on the chin and drove his jawbone into his brain. The third, who wisely attempted to turn and flee, felt Golf's left cross bash in his temple and he too fell in a heap at the feet of the brothers. As quickly as it had started, it was over. Fritz, between his huffs and puffs showered the brothers with gratitude. They indulged him for a moment or two, but then, being sensical men of few words themselves, they asked him what was going on.

"They were beating an old man up the path there and I told them to stop."

"And they chased you. Yes. Well, they won't anymore." Rolf said. The four debated their course for a short while, with Fritz adding: "I don't think they will do anything but run off with their tails between their legs."

"These three won't be doing much of anything anymore unless it's being food for worms…"

Neither Rolf, Tolf, Golf, nor Fritz said that, yet they all looked at each other quickly wondering where the rich dark voice had come from. It was the old man walking down the path, hobbling a little on his ash cane. His he wore a hat pulled low over his face, to hide the scarf bandaging an eye. "I must thank you all," he said. "And I will, but especially the young man in that silly coat." He was old, but Fritz took the insult like he did every other slight.

"Now what do we do?" Golf asked.

"Let me take a look at them," the old man said and stooped down to the pile of robbers. "Why don't you four keep a look out. We don't need the City Guards getting involved in any of this business." He bent down close to the robber Tolf had punched and looked at his head for a minute, a rivulet of blood ran from his dirty ear. He then put his hand on the chest of the robber Golf had given his left cross to, and shook his head.

"Mmmm, well, these two are done. The lice and fleas are beginning to pull up stakes and looking for greener pastures already. They know when the wain has left the village better than many doctors I have known. See, there's a lousy family crossing over to this fellow, who will be a simpleton at best." At first, they thought he was crazy, but Fritz thought he might be right all the same. The Wünchis stood back looking knowingly at each other. They had lived in the country long enough to recognize a cunning man when they saw one, even down on his luck. "You're the Wünchi brothers, aren't you? I thought so, well your work was a bit too thorough, but not thorough enough. I'll tell you what. I will take care of these three for you now that you three have done the hard part." The old man stood up and looked around as best he could with one eye. He sniffed the air and Fritz did too.

"Whew, what is that smell?" Fritz asked.

"Oh, this one shit himself in his last moments," the old man said, and gave a kick to the man Tolf had flattened. "There is no paperwork for what I need to do, young man. But…" and he paused and looked at Fritz with a strange twinkle in his eye, then gave Fritz a quick up and down once-over with his gaze, but returned his stare to Fritz's hands. "…but, maybe that's something you'll learn. You have clerk's hands, naturally, but suited for something better than shuffling paper and stamping out the Hansa's seal and your life. I don't know what it is, but you'll figure it out with a bit of help.

"Now, the lot of you need to clear off. Get to work. I know what to do. I'd forget this happened and don't mention it to that Kashubian blabbermouth you work for," the old man finished. Fritz was a bit taken aback, but realized that his own distinctively silly costume would naturally be recognized, but who was this man? Fritz had no idea; he had never seen an old man like this around the agricultural station.

"C'mon with us, Fritz, let's forget this happened." Rolf said, somewhat unimaginatively, it's true, but he was bothered with what had happened as were Golf and Tolf. They weren't killers of men, after all, although perhaps the physical needs and habits of the stockyard manifested themselves in a too complimentary way with what had happened. They all looked back at the old man who was whetting a Finnish *pukko* knife on his belt. The knife looked sharper than a razor and well-used in taking apart problems, and this last grisly vignette gave speed to their steps as they left the forest.

"I really must thank all three of you. I don't know what I can do to repay you."

"Repay you for what?" Tolf said. "I don't know what you're talking about."

"But—"

"Yes, we just shared the path a bit on our way to work," Golf said.

"Pleasure to see you today," Rolf said. "We might be driving some stock in later this week, Fritz. Good day." And Fritz, who was perhaps a bit still too excited by the morning's events finally understood.

"Yes, a good day for a walk to work," he said but he thought to himself *drat it all, I wanted something to happen to me, but that? That was awful.* We could blame Fritz for not considering the full implications of any wish, but there was no spirit around tempting him with riches, love and power and even if there had been, it is doubtful that Fritz would have had thoughts articulated enough to ask for even something in the vague realms of those pedestrian desires. He merely wanted "something different" which is exactly what he found.

He contemplated this as he walked across the fields to the agricultural station, a brick building near the last of the City's salty heath, where the shepherds would drive their sheep to their penultimate resting place. Mossy-backed on its thatched roof, the building seemed to sag and scowl there, with small windows, and a muddy stone pathway that had never been scrubbed and certainly not lined with flowers. The office inspected agriculture bound for the City, on a lesser-known drive.

"Dettin! Do you know what time it is?" Kalbenski roared "What were you doing, probably off..." and the speech degenerated into human-donkey relations which I have already told you about and don't need to rehash here. Heinz Kalbenski had originally grown up in Hagen's sister city of Danzig, which perhaps explains his earthy manner and lack of tact. He escaped incompetence at the station by extraordinary acts of creative accounting and an uncanny sense of what the monitors would look for when visiting the station. "Kalbenski's skeletons are buried deep" was a common enough phrase at the station, but while he was somewhat coarse and given over to ludicrously improbable narratives of cursed figureheads and unconfirmable tours as a circus performer, he was generally good natured and protective of his crew. His dark hair had only begun to turn gray even though he was north of 50, and the twinkle in his eyes could not be obscured by the manifold wrinkles which, along with old small pox scars, left his face resembling an old saddle that had been soaked in the Baltic and then dried out in a brick kiln.

"Lay off of him, Kalbenski, you know he's never late. I'm usually late." Makurken, an Irish Immigrant roared back at Kalbenski, and the two of them set to arguing about their respective pedigrees conceived in the beds of unlicensed prostitutes: by dwarves, Cathars and when they got really insulting, sunk to the depths of accusations of parentage by attorneys.

Even the profanity is the same, Fritz thought to himself. He duffed his silly hat and coat and went over the ledgers concerning pigs. Fritz cut such an inconspicuous form, even in the office, that it took Kalbenski three hours to lumber over on his thick legs, settle on a stool and ask Fritz why he was late.

For the briefest of moments, Fritz's tongue stood on the precipice of spilling the beans of his entire morning's misadventure, but then the image of the blood running out of the robber's ear and the *schick, schick, schick* of the *pukko* knive's stropping on the old man's belt brought him back to his senses.

"Overslept, that's all."

"You're lying Dettin. You never oversleep and you're blinking like a schoolboy whose been caught jerking his gherkin. But whatever it is, it has nothing to do with us here or the station, correct? Yes, that's what I thought and it's too much trouble even to write down the report. Just stay late if you can. I have a card game early tonight and I don't trust Makurken to shut the door."

And that is exactly what Fritz did. You may wonder if he was addled all day at work because of his misadventure, but it would be difficult to tell, for one would usually need a goldsmith's assay scales to measure the minute difference in apparent workload of a violence-addled bureaucrat from the ordinary workload of a ennui-addled bureaucrat and such instruments were nowhere near the agricultural station. It is true, toward the end of the day, the concomitant associative creations of his mind began to constellate into scenarios wherein the thieves' friends would hound him, or perhaps their headless-yet-undead bodies would pursue him through the gloaming wood. He splashed water on his face and dismissed such nonsense for he was going to take the long way home along the main drive which was well-peopled and generally devoid of mischief. But the thoughts of *what's next?* still troubled him as he locked the door to the station and walked home.

The turn of his days proceeded that way for several more risings and settings of the sun, until gradually, his old habits of thought returned. No word of the events appeared in papers or even the rumors of the stock drovers for the next five days. Finally, he was able to return to his traditional sulking subjects.

If only he worked downtown at the City Rathaus, listening to the councilors and giving them his erudite and surprisingly practical opinions. If only someone knew he existed, for he felt very alone, and the permanency of that condition was a great weighty box. Inside the box was a beautiful soul, like a golden candle burned in secret and after long years of bearing this burden, his candle would be gone and his own wraith would wisp and wind up to the air, to be taken on a breeze to the West and oblivion. He returned home the standard way and the hawkers sold smoked eels and herrings on slices of fresh rye bread just as they always had, and Fritz ate them but perhaps without his usual relish. Flowers had begun to sprout in pots, the air smelt fresh, cool and rife with possibility. One night, a young couple stood on the bridge he usually took, kissing and caressing, and he sighed in anguish and a little bitter jealousy as he always did when he saw people in love. After his meal of plaice and potatoes at Granghoffer's, he had one more mug of beer, read his newspaper and still could not drive out the image of the three men, their lives running out onto the packed earth trail. He went back to his modest home in a row of equally unremarkable half-timbered homes housing unremarkable people who went to bed early, did not travel, and did not even get in great yelling fits of passions. He turned in his hallway and remembered the sight of his wife holding her son's hand and walking out the door to go to market. That was the last he saw of them. The crib he had carved for the child was still in the corner of the bedroom. The toy duck, and a wooden pig he made were still there, forgotten by everyone save him. The marriage bed was small by most standards but still felt unreasonably large to him and he would lay in the darkness listening to the city breathe in sleep around him, like his wife once did. She was breathing different air now: the thick, perfumed wash of Adriatic air, the smell of her lover's hair. He could hear the night songs of Venice: lovers speaking in whispers, sex cries through open windows and pigeons cooing in Italian.

If you are concerned at this point that I'm not "getting to the important part" and I will labor you with more trivial insights into Fritz's quotidian existence, such as his day off spent moping in a library, or about his not entirely unreasonable fear of eels invading his person while he was at stool in the jakes behind his house (Hagen's plumbing being a thing of caprice and mystery), then stop fretting because something *did* happen.

A week after the attack, the chase, the battle, and the denouement in the forest, Fritz was still walking the long way to work. He was leery of seeing the strange old man, for Fritz suspected him of possessing fey powers, and yet Fritz didn't trust them enough to stave off an attack by vengeful and greedy thieves who no doubt waited in the forest. That day plodded on like any other, and the foggy morning sky slowly burned away to reveal the flatness of the horizon. Bleating sheep came, the same in their sameness. He cut quills for pens, crushed soot and glue into ink, wrote out reports and invoices and appended useless notes to existing files. And if you think such work left his mind roaring for a clear sky and a pleasant lunch beneath a tree, then you would be right. The day became quite fine, and Fritz had already decided to skip the dice-game and profanity of the usual lunch and instead struck out across one of the fields of the local landowner, the Graf von Dietzen. There was an ancient, solitary and vast oak tree in one of these fields and on nice spring days Fritz would avail himself of the tree's shade and solitude. Fritz liked trees and even preferred to burn coal rather than wood. He had missed trees since he had sworn off the forest trail. Fritz had never wondered why the tree remained there, untouched and full of valuable old growth timber.

He grabbed his satchel of lunch: black bread, blood sausage from Hannauer's, an onion and an apple along with a bottle of Kalbenski's home-brewed beer, with which the old man was liberal with his employees. He walked out in the fresh sunlight and was at the tree in a short time. The oak was in the full flush of Spring: green oak blood filled each leaf, as they voluptuously stretched out to catch the sunlight and the wind. Fritz ate his lunch, drank the beer and was just at the point of drifting off, imagining the crystalline wings of naked oakgirls fluttering in the breeze, when he noticed something high up in the tree. *What is that, a child's kite?*

But no children were flying kites yet. *A monkey, escaped from a sailor, dangling by its tail and contemplating the view? What could that be?* It was an unusual dangling thing, a tangled thing hanging in the tree and swaying in the slight breeze. The oak leaves had obscured it, and still occluded the mystery of its true line and definition, confounding Fritz until a raven squawked and an eyeball came down bouncing from twig to branch to limb and to wetly plop on his forehead.

Other than the moist eyeball, no other drop of blood from the three heads fell on him: they had been there a while and were drained of blood. Six (now empty) eye sockets looked up at the heavens in rapt misery: beards, caked with browning blood and open mouths stuffed with little bags. The heads were all strung up together by their hair to an old knotted ship's rope that had been expertly bent upon a tall branch. Each one looked out in a different direction—Janus's older three-headed brother, and Fritz immediately remembered the old man whetting the *pukko* again: *schick, schick, schick.* He stared at the thieves' heads for a long while, feeling frightened and awestruck, but not really wanting to leave. The wind moved again over the earth and kept them swinging gently. He looked around and noticed that in four places the ground had been overturned—four spots of clots and clods at North, South, East and West. There was no sign of the bodies: just the heads. The ravens, considering Fritz to be neither a pestering boy with rocks, nor a guard or body snatcher calmly resumed their luncheon. He walked away, shaken by the mutability of life and the callous skill of the ravens. He had not gotten far when he saw two vehicles approaching the station.

This is where my part comes into this tale. Or deposition. Or narrative.

In the morning prior to Fritz's *dejeuner sous le chêne,* I read a summons in my mailbox. Three heads had been found hanging in the venerable Oak Tree on von Dietzen lands outside the City proper—an act of Fundamentalist Wodenism was suspected. For you must remember that while Hagen remained a "pagan" City, a bulwark of the Saxon Federation who had fended off the attempts by Charlemagne to make us love Christ and the Pope by killing us on Frankish swords, it had long become moderate in its religion.

I was to accompany Investigating Surgeon Gudrun Sigurdsdottir and three City Guardsmen to question the station men and take depositions and sniff out anything paranormal or at least irrationally religious. You may think that religion is inherently irrational, and I would usually argue with you on the fine points of that generalization, but this isn't a philosophical critique of theological beliefs.

I sighed, when I read the summons and already felt tired. Investigating Surgeon Sigurdsdottir was Swedish, fairly tall, uptight and lacked any sense of humor. At times I detected sparks of humanity glowing in her, but she was careful to extinguish them before they gave out any substantial light much less igniting the vast reserves of desire that dwelled in her heart. I didn't have the patience to elicit them from her. But she was intelligent, relentlessly thorough and possessed a vehement distaste for Fundamentalists.

I had only finished reading the summons when I heard her knock at my door. "Adjutant Inspector Secretary Ludenow, we must be off now. This is a bit of a drive out and it will be a long day. Are you prepared?"

We took a trap from the Wolkenhaus Yard. Gudrun snapped the reins from the hands of the driver and told him he was unnecessary and would be in the way. Before the little man could say anything, she shoved past him and held out her hand for me. Now, I am just an inch over six feet tall, so I brushed her hand away as I got in. What a pair we made, riding through the streets of Hagen. The three City Guards had a hard time keeping up with us.

"Are they still there?" I asked to pass the time.

"What? The murderers? I very much doubt they would have stayed around."

"I meant the heads, but you bring up a good point. I assume this is some sort of inquest into Fundamentalist activity?"

"I don't need to tell you that," she said. She drove the horses fast enough for her thick Valkyrie braids to flutter in the breeze, which made her unspeakably picturesque if not a little absurd.

"Then whoever did this may very well be out there somewhere close by, if the oak is a local spirit."

"Spirit? Don't tell me you believe in any of that." Frau Inspector Sigurdsdottir was of the new Gnostoscient faith, in which she showed the same zeal as her grandfathers did in the bloody worship of Thor. For Sigrid, religion was garbage, superstition was childish and only that which could be empirically understood and falsified was the truth. I didn't bother to argue with her about this because anyone whose faith is so deeply rooted in induction is about as hopeless as any Abrahamic or Freyist. I, on the other hand, simply couldn't pretend to know, and I didn't really trust a faith whose greatest prophet (so far) was named after cured pork belly. I just used language appropriate to the situation.

"Sigrid, it wouldn't be a deity, and therefore it would be a spirit. It's simply easier in the nomenclature"

"Why don't you just say *stupid superstition*? That is more efficient and covers all of the ground you mention. These farmers and cowhands are all stupid, but I am gracious enough to blame it on their lack of education." I could only hope that something extraordinary was in store for Inspector Surgeon Sigridsdottir, and now that I understand something off the events that were about to occur, I can only look back in hindsight and wish that like Fritz, I had been a bit more particular in my wish, and yet it's very difficult in the past to know exactly what to avoid. But I will always include eels on future lists.

The Guards in their green coats and wide berets arrived behind us. All three of them had grim, granitic jawlines: handsome albeit clichéd perhaps. I don't believe any one of them was under six-foot-four, and they dwarfed the station workers, but there was no question who was in charge.

"Good morning Frau Surgeon-Inspector, to what um, do we owe this special visit?" Kalbenski asked, being as deferential as he could.

"You mean you don't know? Or you are lying?" Gudrun said and stepped off the trap and walked up to the station workers. "There are three heads without their owners out in the oak tree." Gudrun said this without any shred of irony, and I rolled my eyes. Kalbenski noticed this and smiled but said nothing. His employees did not stay silent. Yet I saw one of them walking in our direction from under the old oak tree.

"What? How'd they'd get there? Who? Why didn't we see?" They all asked questions, proposed answers, exclaimed explanations and debunked one another's debunkeries. In short, they were excited because against all prognostications, beyond all hope, Something Had Happened not too far away from their place of employment and they all forgot their manners save for Kalbenski himself.

"That is not City Land, Frau Inspector and you know that very well. I doubt any of my crew here would know about it."

"Oh really? What about that one walking here from the oak tree where the very heads are hanging?"

"Oh, him. Well, I apologize for Dettin's trespass, although it's a well-known spot for a bit of luncheon and peace. If you are here to question us, and I doubt the good Lieutenant here and his chaps are out for a nice drive in the sun, then I would like to see a warrant."

Kalbenski was simply following procedure and policy, like any good middle manager faced with the enormity of the uncertain and possible danger. But as careful and experienced as Kalbenski was, I don't think he was quite prepared for the full experience known as Gudrun Sigridsdottir. She reached into her double breasted robe and pulled out an Inquest Warrant and held it aloft, much like Thor would hold aloft Mjøllnir, or perhaps a Calvinist Preacher would hold up his right hand in the proclamation of his own Election to the Eternal Glory of God. "Here is the warrant, you impudent Kashhube. I trust you can read it since you are so obviously employed by the City and literacy is a requirement for the position."

"Indeed! My dear Surgeon Investigator and Chief

Agricultural Inspector!" I yelled. "It's obvious something has happened here, there is the warrant, enough of this arguing. It's wasting your valuable time. Let us begin with that man over there." I pointed (as dramatically as I could, because the situation seemed to warrant a flourish of theatricality) toward the person you now know as Fritz Dettin.

"Thank you," the Lieutenant said under his breath.

"Fritz, there you are. What's this all about? What do you know?

"Nnnnuthing. I went to have some blood sausage and beer,"

"What kind?" the Lieutenant asked.

"Oh, um, some Schonspaten and the sausage was Hannauer's"

"Not Viskund & Sons?" the Lieutenant countered.

"No, they oversalt it."

"I don't think so."

"Vssikund does that to sell more beer," the second guard said.

"Oh, shut up about the sausages," Gudrun said. "Why are there three heads hanging in that oak tree?"

"Perhaps he was thirsty, or lonely for company," Makurken said.

"Shut up, Patrick, they're not fucking around," Kalbenski said.

"I doubt these shit-shovelers and paper shufflers know their asses from elbows sir," added the third Guard.

"Point taken," the Lieutenant said, coming back to his senses, for Gudrun was glaring at him. "Herr Kalbenski, has there been any persons here, drovers, teamsters or so forth?"

"No, the week's just started. We haven't even seen a farmer selling off rabbits or millet."

"No one suspicious… come on you clods, I have to ask that."

The Station men, including Fritz, shrugged and mumbled their answers which the Lieutenant obviously expected: "Nevertheless, we have a situation here obviously. None of you knows much anything about it, I can see that from your faces."

As the Lieutenant said this, his gaze passed right over Fritz who was pursing his lips, fearing the worst until he remembered his unremarkbleness and silently thanked the Gods for it that time. He looked up as the Lieutenant then harangued them about the need for an investigation and that dispositions would be needed, and that the Investigating Surgeon and Adjutant Secretary were here to ask deeper questions. That was when I knew Fritz was my man. So to speak.

The youngest guard was sent aloft to cut down the heads, which Gudrun rather unceremoniously snatched up by their hair when they hit the ground. She then took them and her leather satchel containing her various implements of dissection and study, and a notebook and requested a semi-private room from Kalbenski.

"Sniffin' out a bit of the old Wotan worship, eh Mistress Madame?" he said

"My name is Surgeon Sigurdsdottir."

"Of course, and you are?" He asked me.

"Secretary Inspector Ludenow, assistant to the Surgeon...." Kalbenski was not an obese man, nor was he svelte. He was somewhere in between, but more on the obese side of the fence, but he had friendly brown eyes and thick dark hair. He affected an easy manner with me but was shorter and so I knew his game at once... "but *nazéwóm sã Ada.*" I said to him.

"*Gôdósz Gôdajã pò kaszëbsczi?*" He said with a widening smile.

"*Gôdajã kąsk pò kaszëbsczi.*" I answered in Kashubian which was all I really needed for he proceeded to show us around the station and gave me a bottle of beer. I actually couldn't speak Kashubian all that well, (although when you know any of the West Slavic languages, the rest of them are easy to fake), but it didn't matter, because I knew the Free and Hanseatic Sister City of Danzig well enough and that was good enough for Kalbenski. He set aside a table for Gudrun to do her grisly work and I took dictation of the autopsy.

There isn't really much to say other than what you already know. Gudrun knew how long they had been dead by the progression of maggotry, and she also knew they had been killed by something before they were separated from their bodies.

"The blows that killed these two were committed by some blunt instrument, perhaps even a blow from a fist, but such a fist would need to belong to a particularly powerful man or woman. Look, the jaw has been driven into the brain case on this one. And this third fellow, he was knocked unconscious, but had his throat slit to bleed."

"What direction?"

"From left to right across the carotid artery. The blade that did it was sharp. It was… the same blade that cut the other heads clear."

"It was done leisurely?" I asked.

"It appears to have been done with skill and not too hastily. We can assume the knife wielder knew his or her business."

"An expert?"

"Yes, the cuts through the spinal column discs are well done. The raggedness of the heads' appearance is a secondary decomposition owing to post-mortem feeding by divers and sundry beasts, although I would hazard many of the mutilations came by the beaks of ravens. I would also say—and take this down, Ada—that the three heads were detached by a single hand."

I wrote this down and walked over. "Can you tell if there was a gag, or anything else?"

"Ah, a good question. It does not appear so."

"This was made to look like a sacrifice."

"But it wasn't. Not precisely, no." She said. "You should question the men here and see if they know about it. Use your mentalist tricks or whatever, but it would be nice to wrap this up. I have a feeling it's nothing more than a thieves' squabble and these three bought the chicken-house as part of general hostilities."

"You mean they bought the farm."

"Whatever the idiom is for "they were killed" in the language you speak here."

"Actually, Gudrun, I rather like *bought the chicken house*. I don't know why but it has a more comical…"

"…that is enough, Ada. We have work to do and may I remind you I am *Surgeon* Sigridsdottir?"

"You may remind me, but it won't matter. That's too much of a mouthful to say and I know you don't like it when I call you Gudrun, so I will stick with that."

"I would rather you didn't. Think of how insolent you will appear and look."

"You're the officious one, Gudrun. I can call you Swedish Honeyhole, if you'd like. It's what I call you on the other side of your front, as I think you would say."

"I will have you reprimanded for this Ada,"

"I'd like to see you try." I looked down at her. Gudrun was tall, and she was very pretty when she was mad, which was often so you could say she was generally a very pretty woman. But I was taller than her and she resented this. I was taller than most men and many of them did too, except for agreeable chaps like Kalbenski and, it turns out, Fritz. Gudrun straightened up further, snorted and turned around to further deconstruct the heads. I wasn't sure if I was bluffing. I knew that the Dispatcher was partial to me because I had solved some rather delicate problems for him, but Gudrun was smart and capable. But she was too stuck up to be generally liked by the boisterous crowd of Guards and Health Inspectors from the Juttrock. Besides, the Dispatcher was in the Hallward's hansa which was a sister-hansa to the Clerks which I belonged to and we held our own against the Surgeons who had just recently emerged from simple haircutting and bloodletting into a semblance of profession. It is too bad. Gudrun was rather attractive, and I make no distinction between women or men for bed mates. I have to admit I had a bit of a crush on her in a feral, sexual way, but it usually disappeared after a few minutes of conversation. Still, it drove me to tease her at times as I was now doing.

But she was right, I had work to do, so I went to interview the men. I didn't have to use any "mentalist" tricks. It's true that I have learned, over the course of my years, many interpretive techniques and conversational means to get information out of people that are akin to the elegant forms of manipulation that fakirs and magicians use in performances where they guess what sort of vegetable you are thinking about and card-guessing tricks so numerous I won't even go into them here.

Nearly all of them had no idea how the heads found their way into the oak tree, but they all had theories ranging from the Gods, to Old Religionists (the majority), to Carmelites (Kalbenski). There was only one reticent fellow among the lot.

"Friedrich Dettin." I said, writing down his name.

"Yes."

"Herr Dettin, you know why I and my esteemed, albeit brutal colleague are here." He nodded and swallowed. "Did you know the men whose heads adorned the oak tree?"

"No."

"What do you know of the murders?"

"I have no idea how they got in that tree," he said, then he realized what he had said, and not said. "I mean, nothing."

"Yes, well, as you know, I did not ask you how the heads got in the tree, and I'm not particularly interested in any theories."

"I think it was Old Religionists, sir. I mean ma'am. Maybe a single one, acting independently."

"A single person usually acts independently, but that does not matter. How would you be sure of this."

"None of us saw him put the heads there, and he must have done it silently, after we had all gone home and when none of Graf von Dietzen's workers were around."

"How do you know it was a him?"

"Oh. I'm just guessing. Women don't usually do that sort of thing."

"Don't be too sure. The Bacchae were quite capable of such work, although they weren't quite so careful. My colleague thinks it was perpetrated by someone with some skill in butchery. You must know some butchers around here. Care to implicate anyone?"

"No. I don't know of anyone around here who would do that." There was a banging, pounding noise coming in from Gudrun's makeshift workshop. Fritz swallowed hard again. "What is she doing?"

I took a small leap and said: "oh, I would think you're

familiar with that sound, or one very much like it. I think she's opening up a skull. She has this project: measuring the brains of criminals. These men were well known thieves around here, correct?"

"Yes, well, I suppose so. Not decent folk around here. I know decent folk pretty well, and these fellows weren't any of them." He blinked.

"Very well. What took you out to the Oak tree that day?"

"I wanted to get away from this office. It was a nice day and I used to like to sit under the oak tree."

"I see. A pleasant place to read or nap?"

"It was."

"I'm sure it still is. The heads aren't going back there."

"Where are they going?"

"We'll haul them back to the City. Unless there is something unusual that she wants to preserve in a jar of alcohol, I suspect they'll be thrown into the Elbe for the eels." Fritz grimaced. "I shall have more questions for you, Herr Dettin."

I decided to wait for the next truly beautiful and sunny day.

I didn't have to wait very long, for the weather remained agreeable. The oak in question was a magnificent old tree with a span of three hundred feet. Lightning had struck it at some point—an oak of that age and size nearly always has felt the touch of Donnar at some point— but it merely left a bifurcated aspect of growth, as if two tops decided to grow out of the old wound which was so ancient that the scorching was completely gone and only the twisting convolutions told the story. I won't go into the lessons of arboreal biography I have learned, but I knew them well enough to tell. An oak that is touched by lightning and lives is considered a holy tree, even by our relatively modern standards.

Insofar as Wodenists, I thought about the situation on my way out to the agricultural station. There were a few old sects—the rural folk almost always lagged behind in theological "progress"—but I didn't know of any that would actually go to this length. The men were known thieves: of the Black Crane Group, a large syndic of criminals headed, supposedly by Klaus Hunser, an intimidating businessman whose main income derived from wholesale seafood processing. No one had ever definitively, or at least publicly, linked him to the Black Cranes, but it was widely assumed he headed the organization.

Once, a rival crime lord had even gone so far as to leave one of Hunser's men, gutted and cured, in the great smokehouse where they processed eel and cod: hanging up there with the fish instead of sleeping with them. A crime war broke out after which eventually caused some damage to commercial property and the Guards were called in specially to put it down. Gisling Forbar, the rival, was found murdered in the botanical gardens with a rare, exhumed dahlia stuck in his ass. The dahlia had not been picked, so by careful removal, the rhizome was saved and still blooms in a prominent spot in the southwest corner of the gardens.

While that marked the end of the war, I was concerned some newcomer was trying to assert power: it would make sense to blame it on Old Religionists.

This entire potentiality stirred in my mind as Milly, the cab driver, let me off half a mile from the station. "Miss Ada, it's no trouble to take you there. The Office of Investigation's payin' for it anyway. Besides, how will you be getting back?"

"No, I wish to walk and think a bit, Milly. This one's a puzzler and I need my feet to think." I stepped down and took off my shoes. Milly scratched her head and I knew she always wanted to ask me why I went barefoot like that, so that day it seemed somehow appropriate to tell her.

"I can feel what the earth has to say a bit better this way and it's a lovely day. I will have my shoes and I suspect I'll be wanting a long walk home to think this all over. Besides, when was the last time you felt the grass between your toes?"

"With my work, Miss Ada, it'd be horseshit, so I'll keep my boots on, but you have your ways and I wouldn't question them. Besides, you have lovely feet," she said and winked.

"Thank you," and I blushed a little. Milly was my age, and plainly rugged. I mean this in no hurtful way because she appeared born to deal with horses. She was thickly set, with short hair and a keen gaze that had spent years observing both the emotions of her horses and fares: an important skill in her profession. I suspected I was a problem for her because she, in spite of her best maneuvers of sublimation, liked me in a Sapphic way. Her own "little missus" I had learned was a short spitfire who kept house for them in the Køpping District and would brook no rival. But I still greedily appreciated the flattery and glances.

I walked toward the station. It was nearing noon, and I hoped my quarry was out by the tree. I cut into one of the Von Dietzen fields of barley and easily made for the oak. It was a bit of a landmark in that flat land and taller than most of the alders and maples that formed windbreaks in the fields.

What a fine day to be working, I thought. The breeze was just strong enough and the weather was bright, clear and yet not too warm. As I neared the oak tree, I saw a man dozing underneath it. I did not have to engage any skills of stealth; he was dead out asleep with his mouth hanging open. It was Fritz, and I was glad he had returned to the scene of the… disposal, I suppose one could say.

I stood for a while, studying him. He was fast in the sleep of dreams, for his eyes darted and rolled quickly under their lids. I wandered over to the station and told Kalbenski that I had to question Dettin further. He smiled, we chatted about the weather and the case, which appeared "to be a real mystery, eh?" And then I returned to the oak tree and Fritz Dettin. I looked around again at the ground and the tree. Aside from its massive size, (it looked older than most of Hagen), there was nothing terribly unusual about it at first. At first, mind you.

A sleepiness came over me, even though I had drunk plenty of coffee that morning. That was my first hint. The second was the memory of voices deep in my body. The chorus of voices had not risen to the point where I could *hear* them with my ears, but I felt the trills and bass chords reverberating in my long bones. My heart quickened a bit, my stomach seemed to turn over and fold itself from a kind of strange hunger and my sex became noticeable.

"Ah, so you are awake, aren't you?" I said to the tree. The tree only answered in the whispers of leaves in the wind: I thanked the tree, for all its work in putting on a new language (which deciduous trees do every year) and as I nodded my head, I noticed Fritz was beginning to stir out of sleep.

There are many kinds of sentient trees. Young brash trees full of vigor and ambition, older trees that long for simpler days, lonely trees, hungry trees, and malevolent trees that will grab and drown you when they can: willows especially, as is well known. One could say *all* trees are sentient, but that would be like saying all humans are sentient. I am not sure a generalization such as that is entirely accurate and human behavior usually validates me, especially when it comes to matters of history and learning from the past, abstracted and distant though it may be. This tree had something to say, but it couldn't come out and say it. That much I sensed.

"Mistress Ludenow, I..." Fritz said this in the clumsy furbles of speech one makes in the first moments of movement from the dreamworld to the daylit world. I held up my hand.

"Do not speak. Not yet. And quit fussing." I sat down next to him. "This is a pleasant spot for lunch. The heads must have been a bit of a shock."

He blinked at me and I took a leap. It was not a great leap, and since you know what happened, you might even think it was no leap at all, but remember, at the time, I had no clear idea of

Fritz's previous adventure. "But the heads themselves weren't the surprise because you had seen them before, perhaps alive and breathing."

"I don't know how they got there." He said. A good thing to say, since it was the truth, he did not give up any tells of lying.

"I believe you, Herr Dettin. I can see there is no lie in your eye, but the truth is hiding that which could either be a lie, or the truth—depending on how you look at it."

"What do you mean?"

"Something presumably happened that resulted in those three men losing their heads. The Surgeon Examiner tells me that all three died before they were decapitated. That is interesting. I doubt very much that they were killed, strung up in the tree and then decapitated. That would be too much work. Are you a Wodenist, Herr Dettin?"

"Of that kind? No!"

"I did not think so. You seem to be the sort who goes to Temple once or twice a year, at the Solstices, perhaps. Maybe there is a shrine to some lesser God in your household."

"To Freya. My wife prayed to her."

"Prayed? I am sorry."

"No, she's not dead. She ran off with an Italian saffron merchant. Took our little boy with her."

"Oh, then I am doubly sorry. Death is somewhat forgivable, but that sort of thing…"

"Thank you. I don't see how that has anything to do with your interrogation."

"This isn't an interrogation. It's more of a cajoling conversation, perhaps even an interview. I don't think you really had anything to do with the killing or disposition of our friends, but I know you know far more about it than are letting on. I have a report to make. I simply want to know whether this was the work of Wodenists or not. But before that, I wish to know something else."

"Which is?"

"What were you dreaming just then?"

"Oh. That's strange. They say this oak is old, but you know what?" He looked around, perhaps by habit for there was no one near. "I think this tree is alive."

"Well, it's not dead."

"No, it speaks. In dreams. It just did, but the strange thing is, it never has before."

"Before what?"

"The, um, heads. Do you believe me?"

"About the tree's sentience? It may be of more assistance to me if you tell me the dream."

"I didn't murder those men and the dream has nothing to do with it."

"Oh, I wouldn't say that exactly. For one, you would have to tell me your dream, truthfully, for me to ascertain whether there were any kernels of information that might better describe what happened to our three friends. Yet even then, I am intrigued by this idea that the tree hadn't spoken until the heads were offered up as a sacrifice."

"So, you think it's Wodenists?"

"No, actually, I suspect the act was supposed to look like Wodenists, but there is a deeper import to it all. Then again, I could be wrong. But I will need to hear the dream to know."

"Oh, very well. This wasn't the first dream, but it was the strangest."

"So far, you mean."

"Yes."

"Do the dreams only happen when you sleep here?"

"I hadn't thought of that, but yes, I suppose they do. I don't remember my dreams at home all that much."

"Few people do. Go on and tell me more about this dream."

"Well, it was about music, all the dreams have been about music and I'm afraid you'll be wanting more from the story at the end and I'm not lying."

"Why?"

"The heads aren't in it. Nor are the men who killed them. It was all music at first, and nothing to see. The music first made itself into taste, actually, then the touch of sound."

"Taste? Really? That's fascinating."

"Yes, sort of a strange flavor of radishes and dirt, with some kind of red berry. I couldn't tell you that one precisely. Then there were also smells. Violets, shoe gum, armpit, both nice and nasty. Then something like the fresh wind of the sea. That smell always happens in the dreams, you know when it smells fresh and healthy like the day it first rained out of heaven. And then I was on a cliff. Something, oh I don't know, like what you see in pictures of Dover. A big cliff."

"Cut from chalk, bone white and very tall."

"Exactly, and there was one lone tree on the cliff, an oak of course and a skeleton hung in the tree by a thin silk chord. But it wasn't an ordinary skeleton. It had been made and was banging and bonking and kedonking against itself in the breeze like a..." he paused and searched for the word, "...a skelephone, playing his own bones by dancing and kalonking in the tree's swaying arms. That was when I heard a voice. It always sounded just behind me, although I turned around and around on the cliff."

"What did it say?"

"*You see every house is a mirror of its maker, master carpenter, board, and joist, the timber framing joints the elbow mortise and femur tenons. You are an old house, Dettin, and one fallen into disuse, as though you were forgotten when the other houses moved away. The whole music of the world was there in oak bones and speaking in oak tones, sound like color—what is brown and green? Carve me the bones of English yew.* It was something like that but in fancier words, the sort you use."

I looked at the tree and back at Dettin. "Well, the houses moving away is a fairly obvious one, Herr Dettin. But it made a specific request, and that is interesting. Was the other dream a request as well? I can tell by your look—you know you don't lie very well. You may as well tell me what happened. But... later. I want to hear this other dream."

"I should get back to work."

"That's not an issue today, but… I suppose you do have things to do. How do you get home from here? Do you walk back to your home in Stockdale?"

"I, uhm, I guess you would know where I live."

"Yes, and I could have visited you there with some guards and the Surgeon, but I don't think that will be necessary. Very well, I shall accompany you and we'll dine at Makeslaut's."

"But I have to go back to work."

"That's fine. I shall be there when you are off the Kashubian's clock. Now be off. And if he gives you any trouble tell him you were speaking with me on official business and the less he knows or cares…"

"…oh, he'll get that for sure. What are you going to do until then?"

"Isn't it obvious? I'm going to take a nap beneath this tree of yours and see what it has to say."

I had a wedge of Harzauer cheese, a small flask of Rhine wine, some rye bread and sweet pickled onions from Juntermann's. I took up Fritz's place beneath the tree and listened to wind, ate and watched the shadows course across the barley. It was a pleasant place and maybe that is why I didn't notice it at first: a leaden feeling in my fingertips. Not unhealthy or alarming as in a stroke or paralysis, but merely the suggestion that Not Moving my fingers would be more pleasant than Moving them. This laziness spread up my feet, calves and thighs, so that they practically locked in place. It felt as if some invisible, highly skilled hand were slowly painting my eyelids with gold and my neck grew weak and nodded.

It's true, the cheese was delicious, with that sharp tang that reminds you of aged Gouda but with the smoother texture of Comte that I always liked about Harzauer cheese, and Juntermann's pickled onions are simply the best in the city because they don't over-sweeten them. The wine was simply to wash it all down with and wasn't that strong, but I suspected it was in league with the tree, because this sort of sleep usually means a tree is at work, making one feel as though the particular mixture of dappled shade and sunlight, the specific breeze, the spring day, the memories of long ago, and destinations in Elsewhere are all too irresistible. I thought about how good a cup of black coffee would be but the sleepy thoughts pushed the demitasse right off the table onto a pillow of honey clouds, and when I think of honey clouds, I know that I am no longer "thinking" as we use that word but dreaming.

The clouds were the bright sunlit color of clover honey deepened through melismatic gradients until they bore the color of deep amber, the color of honey collected from richly pendulate flowers and the air was heavy with the perfume of vermillion and violet. Sunset came instantaneously as it only can in dreams. The clouds moved through the purple sky as moon shadows moved of their own accord, separating themselves from the templates of trees and bushes and the wandering legs of night beasts beneath the clear bright stars. That was when I noticed the ocean of barley had disappeared and a singing came through the forest surrounding me. The notes moved over the forest like swallows and under it, digging deep into the earth like jewel nosed moles. No ugliness tainted any note and each one seemed to play upon the whispering speech of the oak tree standing like a king in front of me, for I no longer rested against it. Silver ribbons and gold chains moved in the breezes: tinkle, kalinkle all finkling jingling music and the pure notes of a bird wrapped them and danced with them. I knew the birdsong all too well, and still missed the depth of its sweetness, the empyrean of its sadness. I listened to sheaf and leaf, root bark, and raindrops disappearing in the labial folds of the earth. How cool the earth felt, how delicious. Crowny blades of grass and cool earth and the air a blanket on my body, fletched now in iridescence. The notes did not end, nor did they begin, but folded upon themselves like the silent treasure of a yolk within the shell.

"You have not been here before." It was a rich baritone voice, neither male nor female, but well versed with the tenderness of summer nights.

"Of course I have," I answered. "I was here the other day, when you were festooned with heads and ravens."

"No, I mean here now, with me. Isn't the singing beautiful? We can remember this night which passes like so many summer nights when I was younger and surrounded by my siblings beneath the stars. There were less of you then and no ships to craft—the ocean was a terror unknown and not just a larder of clams, mussels and articulated lobsters."

"Yes, and the stars are brighter for looking on them," I said. "I could live here."

"But you don't. And I don't any longer save when I am alone and thinking. But they are good to remember. I think I can help you, if you help me. I would like a souvenir of those days, something in the daylight of the Sun to remind me of these summer nights when I was barely grown from acorn and the earth."

"What can I do?"

"I came sailing across the seas, I wandered far before rooting here. The lands were wide and unknown to you as they still are. Far to the north they sang into the dawn of the world and the trees grew beneath the old poetry. Wings outspread and yearning for that lover in the night, a lovely form hidden save for the magic of the song. *Make for me a nightingale of Finnish birch and hang it here in my boughs. You will know where.* Help that silly clerk from the office. He has skill unknown, perhaps even to himself."

"And how will you help me?"

"Well, I gave you the nightingale's song again, didn't I? Perhaps a way to keep a memento of that moment in the Harz mountains when you saw into forever?"

"How did you know that?"

"Oh, I know someone's who's been touched by the Waterpeople when that someone crosses my shadow. But you probably want more than that. Very well, I will help wrap up this business of yours. But you know the rules, I can't really do that directly."

"And you can't really tell me the future."

"You know as well as I do that's absurd. It's always in

motion and far too complex."

"Do I get three guesses?"

"Do I have whiskers or beguiling breasts such as your kind possess? And do I possess the legs of a lion?"

"You are no sphinx."

"Or is my ass made of smoke, my ears pointed, my head topped off with a decorative knot?"

"You are not a Djinn."

"And I don't have a pint of water in my forehead you'll spill through my ludicrous adherence to manners?"

"You're no Kappa, either."

"Then does that answer your question?"

"About the questions? Well, not really, but I suppose I'll have to infer a lot… oh, I understand."

"Ah, you're not so slow are you… Ada? A pretty name. It sounds like a birch tree growing in the Taiga."

"So, you have no advice?"

"Watch out for thieves of the Black Cranes. Like I said, you are on the right track."

"Yet you cannot tell me when they'll assail me?"

"No. I just know the three buffoons whose blood woke me up were in that gang. I heard a couple of them the other night looking up my skirts, as it were and talking about it all."

"Oh. Is this the point when I wake up?"

"I suppose, but what are you going to do? Remember it has something to do with …"

"A nightingale made from Finnish birch. Yes, yes, yes.

Does this have anything to do with the skeleton marimba that Dettin was talking about?"

"Perhaps."

And the last word trailed off back into the whispering leaf-talk and I awoke. It was much later than I imagined for dreams usually don't take all that long. The nightingale's song was fresh in my mind and the ants were there making merry with my lunch. Dettin was looking at me.

"So what did the Oak say?"

We walked back through the light evening, for it was getting closer to Midsummer and the sun would not be down until nearly 9:00.

"A very talkative old fellow," I said to Fritz. "He seemed to go on about a desire for a wooden nightingale."

"Was he specific about the wood?"

"Yes, Finnish Birch."

"I thought so. In the first dream I had, it asked for something similar. It was like a song at first. I don't remember seeing anything. Like brooks of water in old mountains or maybe the currents in the deep sea. I can't remember honestly if those were words or how I felt."

"You were in a proto-linguistic state, which means they meant the same thing, but go on."

"Anyway, I did see something. I was walking across the grass, but on a path made of green stones, not jade but…"

"Beryls?"

"Yes, that's the word. It was strange. The land was

beautiful, and the beryl road lead into a row of yew trees. The song changed and grew sad: 'oh, mother, why have you gone among the yews to dance among the mounds to sleep.' I reached a mound. It must have been one like in the song. Nine women carried harps and played upon them and I heard a voice. It was a woody voice, old and young at the same time if you understand. It sang to the notes of the harpers."

> *Tune to the ripples of the pond,*
> *Tune to the laughter of a girl,*
> *Tune to the rattle of the dying man and silent march of clouds,*
> *Hew me a wind harp of maple, it shall be the counterpoint.*

"Now what do you think that all means?"

"A lot of death, but death is always change, transmogrification. Whether a stillborn, a fevered child, a stupid adolescent, a suicide, murder, or old age, all deaths pass beneath the earth marked perhaps by blades of grass. Or beryls."

"How do you know?"

I shook myself. I wasn't even really thinking of those words or rummaging in the library of my memory for words. I suspected the Oak was at work, even at this distance. "I don't. It just seems that way to me. I am hungry. We're close to Makeslaut's. You're welcome to come with me."

"I told you I don't know how the heads got there."

"How did they become just heads in the first place?" I asked, but Fritz said nothing, so I smiled, and we walked through the South Gate into Stockdale and through the winding streets to Makeslaut's, known primarily for fish soups, lobscouse, and beer.

"I may not lie very well as you say, but I know when to keep my mouth shut instead," Fritz said, and put a wad of rye bread in his mouth as though it were a gag.

"And why is that?" I waited and he realized I wasn't going anywhere.

"Because, people will use whatever you say against you. They always did and they always will. Sometimes it's not much. 'How's the weather out there?' That's not too bad, they're just using you for what you've seen and if you're dripping wet it's a bit of a joke. But I don't know why you're asking me all of this. I have to think: what happens if I tell you what I know? How are you going to use that against me, and if it isn't you—you seem kindly enough—then who? A judge? The surgeon? My boss?"

"I don't think Kalbenski will really care as long as you keep showing up for work."

"Well, you're right about that. But you see what I mean."

"Oh, I do, Fritz. I do. And so, I can only say this, and it won't be short or kind. What if you don't tell me? Why would that be? I'm no fool to think that you're not hiding something from me. Let us consider old saws. For example, the old syllogism that says:'if you have done nothing wrong, then you have nothing to worry about' is more fragrant with worms and flies and stink than the biggest pile of shit a champion bull can leave on the stable floor. Why? Because how do we know what is wrong? What is wrong and what can cause worry *are not the same thing.* Now, the what we know? That comes first because it's the easiest to dispense with: it is what we have been trained to know, either by ourselves or others and there are so many little things we can be uncertain of, yes? Especially as you grow older? Especially when you get surprised? Especially as the generalizations of youth, the most heuristic of our claptrap become unwound and turned to garbage. But perhaps I am speaking of knowledge of the heart. If nothing else that knowledge is the most mutable, most suspect because the heart has been hurt more often than loved. Yes, there is knowledge of this table, these glasses of excellent beer. The sun will likely come up tomorrow. But they aren't what we're talking about, aren't they? No, it's something *someone else can hold against you* and you never really know what that can be. I believe that's the heart of your argument, is it not?" Fritz looked at me and was silent. A really tough case.

"I don't think I really understood what you were saying. I'm feeling the beer a bit and you're kind of wordy."

"You really don't know what I can find wrong, correct? Because you're sure I'll find something wrong." He swallowed loudly. I made my stab: because it's what had always gnawed at my own soul: "Because there was *always* something wrong? No matter what you did that was right, no one gave three shits and a cough about that, did they?"

"No. How do you know?"

"Why do you think I talk like this? We have at least two paths, perhaps more, two strategies: we hold our mouths tighter than a clam at low tide or we talk till the stars fall from the sky and hope no one notices and it becomes such a part of us that we don't know what else to do. Oh yes, I found I was good at living behind walls and what's better I could cut the stones myself with skill that came to me as flying comes to a swallow."

We sat silent for a while and sipped our beer. Finally, Fritz furrowed his lips three times and then began to speak.

"Very well. I was late for work and decided to take a short cut…" And he told me about the 'poor old man,' the thieves, the flight, the fraternal *deus ex machina* of the Brothers Wünchi, the brief battle (which did fit with Gudrun's diagnosis of massive, blunt trauma before the decapitations) and the old man whetting his knife. Fritz included many recursions, inversions and repetitions.

Did I mention the excellent beer? We were not drunk, but socially lubricated to the point where he felt safe with me, and I felt strangely safe with him. I believed every word he said, but I wasn't sure about the backstory he apparently didn't notice. Why was the old man in the forest? Why did the brothers show up so conveniently? Did the old man really do them in?

Fritz's house was not too far away. I felt compelled to visit the place, simply to discover more of what the Oak had been talking about. Perhaps there was a clue lying about, and yet my eldritch-bullshit sense did not indicate it would give me any notions to solving the "crime." Like many living spaces in Hagen, the building Fritz lived in had originally been a small warehouse of timber-frame and brick. Schming-Alley could have been any such alley, so narrow as to avoid the title of 'street.' He was trepidatious about letting me visit, but I insisted, somewhat lamely, that to clear him I would need to understand his living situation. He had a small set of rooms, really only one large room that had been subdivided into a sleeping alcove and a living area where he cooked and… carved.

As I alluded to earlier, nearly everything in the place had been touched by his carving knives at some point. The dining table, chairs, the small bed, shutters, armoire and toys. A child living there would have no need to visit a farm or modest zoological garden; there were ducks, pigs, a dwarf Percheron draught-horse, a hippo, giraffes, and even an articulated Chinese dragon that remained unfinished. What most struck me was the empty crib in a corner.

He sheepishly looked at me. "Now I understand," I said to him. "You see what I mean about knowledge, it is ever changing. Mine certainly has. Do you have any brandy?"

"Only some gin"

"That will do. May I have a cup? You don't say many words, Fritz, but now I see that you speak with your hands. These carvings are beautiful. The Oak wants some decorations and you must carve them. It's plain as the day on my face. Or nose. You know, I wouldn't have believed you at first, except the Oak gave me a dream with fancifully carved wood as the central symbol, and at first that's what I was disposed to think of the nightingale as, but now it's... literal, an actual thing. Why on earth are you wasting your life in that clerk's office?"

"My father was a Hanseatic clerk, Frau Ludenow. I am following in his tradition." He sat in a chair and looked into his own cup of gin, then drank it down with a wince. It wasn't very good, but by that point I didn't care. I drank it sitting on the edge of the bed and running my fingers along the vine-work of the headboard.

"But surely he should have apprenticed you to a carpenter or joiner or someone who works in wood?"

"That was not to be."

"I see. My mother wanted me to be a weaver. It's what she did to make money and thought it appropriate for me although she didn't think I was very good at it. Tried to marry me off to some fat tapestry merchant that my uncle knew."

"But you're not doing that. It must be quite a tale."

"Like any tale, it grows in the ears of listeners because the teller isn't really paying attention to it when it's going on and then it tends to grow a bit in the telling. I suppose it is a long tale. I've circumnavigated this silly globe, which is something even most men never get around to."

I think I will draw a close on the drunk ramblings of myself at this point. It does nothing for the narrative and seems to paint a picture of myself as some kind of boasting mountebankess intent on making poor Fritz blush several times and gulp down his gin as I did and until we both fell asleep.

I woke up in his bed with my feet sticking out over the end—a common enough posture for me. And no, before you think the wrong thing, I will report that Fritz snored gently in one of his marvelous chairs wrapped in a blanket. Fritz has his charms mind you and I still wonder what he can do with his hands, but the night didn't go that way. My immediate thought was of alarm, even though our surroundings were quiet and calm. How could I have gotten drunk and passed out like that? I was getting old, I told myself, and couldn't really handle my gin anymore. True, I had been somewhat lulled by encountering a kindred spirit of sorts, but I had let my guard down, *almost* and I could not afford *almosts*. I took my chance to snoop about a bit and found nothing extraordinary. I was struck by the bust of the Lady, in her scintillating Freya-guise, by the door which I had missed on entering at first.

I knew Fritz had to go to work, so I rousted him up and we blindly parted ways, but not before arranging a further meeting to discuss our plans.

"It's obvious you have to make these things. My part is to help you somehow."

"What if I don't want to?"

I thought about this for a moment, my head craving the blackest coffee on earth.

"I don't have time to reason with you, but I will say that life has already plucked something away from you. Don't squander the rest of it in that damned agricultural office. That pathway shortcut may have been difficult, but it could lead to better things. I will meet you at Hannauer's later for dinner, or I will bother you at work."

"Alright. I will meet you there, Frau Ludenow."

Fritz was good to his word and we met again at Hannauer's for dinner and mostly to figure out what to do. There was not much to say about that night, or the short few that followed that week. We had decided on our plan. Fritz was going to carve the three instruments the Oak had asked for. I say instruments because it was obvious to Fritz, and then me, that they were not just decorative carvings but had to make tuned noise—to echo, or perhaps even perform, some of the wonderous music we had heard in our dreams.

A skeleton made of yew.

A wind-blown, or Aeolian, harp made of maple.

A nightingale made of birch.

All of these items could be made to play in the wind, although Fritz admitted the aeolian harp sounded the most difficult because he'd never seen one. I thought the nightingale would have been more difficult, but Fritz maintained it was a glorified whistle that was oriented by the proper placement of the wooden wings and tailfeathers. We also agreed that the birch wood and maple would probably be the easiest to procure. Given this, I gave Fritz my Secretary's pass to the Central Library of Hagen where he could look up the proper books on making Aeolian harps, and I would handle the procurement of the wood.

"I don't think that's actually for the best," he said.

"Why not?"

"You know a great many things, Frau Ludenow, but is wood quality one of them?"

"You have me on that."

"It's got to be just right. You know the luthiers in Cremona only use certain trees for the violins. They have to be facing the right way, the right age, and everything for the grain to be right. The same was true of the Old Fathers who carved the longships…" and here was something Fritz could *talk* about.

In the end we agreed I could scout out some acceptable merchants, but he would have to be the authority on the purchase. Fritz seemed to brighten at the whole arrangement; it gave him something to do with purpose, which I realized was a novelty in his life.

I had other issues to attend to. For one, Gudrun had been pestering me about what information I had gotten out of "that surly clerk. I know he knows something."

I was standing in her office at the end of the week. Gudrun looked lovely, with her hair free of braids and spread out over her white and black cassock. The red, crossed razors embroidered on her wide white collar sparkled in the sun almost like rubies. I was simply there in my old black scrivener's dress. She was writing out a report of the disembodied heads and my pile of autopsy notes lay nearby to attach. She was expecting some sort of an answer from me about what I had been doing.

"Maybe the clerk's just fooling us. He claims to have seen nothing at all until he was sitting out there."

"How are you sure of that?"

"How sure are we of anything?" I answered and she slapped down her pen so hard it splattered ink across the page.

"Ada! Now look at this mess. We don't have time for your contrite and pointless philosophical games."

"I am not playing one with you right now. It is another

kind of game, but one that is serious, since you…"

"Why can't you just answer my question?"

"…and since you interrupt me, I will have to back up a bit on the board and say that since you are one of those people who think games are silly and childish, I will have to consider some other term. But now I don't think so. So let me put it to you in words and phrases you can understand.

"There has been a murder. I suspect that Dettin knows about it, but I don't believe he was actually there when it happened. And how do I know this? Dettin told me so himself. He was walking through the forest that morning and met an old man, but he was a strange fey old sort of character. The man had three assistants with him, and they were moving through the forest with some purpose. Ah, no! I am talking here. When I asked Fritz if they bore any resemblance to the murdered men, he said no. The assistants were much larger and had close cropped hair and I believe all of those wonderful guests of yours had long hair?

"Disgusting, with elves' locks."

"They all had elf-locks of tangled hair on their left sides." I said. At this point I was making it all up to keep her off the trail. Much of what I said was true, but I was tying a bend on it that would serve the knot I wanted. "But that was all Fritz said. I suspect he knows more, and I'll get it out of him."

"I could have him brought here and the lads will beat it out of him. Much more effective and quicker."

"Typical. I'm not surprised someone adept at bleeding and purging would resort to a physically brutal and rather unreliable form of information gathering. There will be no need to torture him."

"Why not? He looks strong enough for it."

"Because, you Swedish pratt, I can just get him to talk about it by being his friend."

"Make it quick, Ada. This is a minor affair and I don't want it taking up our time."

"Our time? Your time. My own is my own to spare."

"I don't have time for the insolent little girl right now. Just tell me this, how were the men dressed? Did he remember that?"

"Oh yes, now that you mention it, he did. They had mostly gray clothes on. Dettin said it was hard to see them in the forest. The three assistants had blue hoods, thrown back. The old man wore an old style robe, I think he said. It sounded like an old Rus merchant's gown."

"Ah, I see. That's interesting. I would expect it almost, but you may go now. Ada?"

I had left as soon as she said 'see.' I figured if she got angry at my insolence it would throw her off the trail a bit. According to an Inspector's Bulletin, blue and gray were favored colors among the Wodenists. They typically wore old style clothing as well, so I thought the old Rus merchant's robe would help with that.

My truthful ruse with Gudrun bought me some time. It wasn't difficult to find suppliers of maple and birch wood in Hagen, for it was a great and powerful seafaring town, although, perhaps owing to its incipient problems with humidity and changeable weather, it was never known as a great place for making instruments. Besides, the culture of Hagen, like Bruges, Amsterdam, Lübeck, Riga, or Danzig was more interested in selling things than making things.

Nevertheless, I knew there were luthiers there to work on repairing broken or misloved instruments. The first two I visited got suspicious at once. "Why would you want wood? What are you going to do with it? Why don't you just get out of here" and other variations on that theme.

Ah! Human Secrecy! I could write an entire monograph on it, but it would probably bore you unless I was able to add a dash of fictional sparkle and pleasure to its all-too familiar subjects, reconciliations, counterblasts, apologies, satanic advocacies and preemptive self-criticism designed to shut you up before you can even question this analogy or that research source.

In this case, professional jealousy, the delicate coddling of a 'competitive edge' was to fault. But then I realized I was going about it all wrong. None of these toads would sell me any wood, except at exorbitant prices. I would have to speak with someone who had a good knowledge of the commercial underbelly. Not the criminal one, although they often worked in league and with a fair enough dash of plausible deniability, but rather the secretive commercial world that avoided the grasping fingers of the City's bureaucratic stewards, whose Holy Badges should have been a visage of Mammon surmounted by a crest of a pinching hand and supporters, sable, of two dung beetles rolling up piles of money. I knew with whom I had to speak, but he was never easy to pin down. Yet a note sent through some mutual friends was all I needed in the end.

"My dearest Ada. What do you want? You never summon me for a friendly meal, or an idle time spent shooting at pigeons."

"I would think that agreeing to this preposterous location would have been enough to satisfy you. Do you know how much this takes me out of my way?"

We were sitting in the crow's nest of one of his ships, moored at the great commercial shipyards at Stook, on Hagen's northern side. We had an elegant meal of cold pheasant, raw Holsteiner steak with egg and caper, Fischinger's knackwursts, pickled tomatoes, horseradish, French style croissants, white wine from the Loire, and a hunk of Harzauer cheese because Kanute Eldredsohn knew my appetites.

The Crows' Nest could barely contain us and the food, but we managed it all somehow.

"Yes, but it's a beautiful day. Besides, this way I could climb up behind you and watch those beautiful legs mount from deck to the topmast. Also, it was inconvenient."

"Thanks. Yes, you old goat. If it was a look up my skirt, we could have taken care of that in less gravity defying ways."

The problem with Kanute was, he was one of the richest men in Hagen and he was also very attractive, even if he had been a porter living on a pfennig or two a day. I would hazard him to be about ten years older than I was, and yet possessed of a rugged, deeply masculine strength that made one wet when you spoke with him. Or terrified.

I watched him elegantly slice the sausages, spread the raw tartare steak on biscuits baked with a delicate touch of asafetida and sesame. When Kanute squeezed a lemon wedge over a dish, he did not miss a drop. That will tell you what sort of man he was. His beard was closely cropped, well kempt and clean. His eyes sparkled when he thought there was some plan afoot. I had to be extremely careful. We both knew each other's strengths and weaknesses, intimately.

"I simply need to find somewhere around this city where someone will sell me some wood."

"Some wood? Why don't you go cut down a tree?"

"No, it has to be instrument grade."

"Ah. Who is this for? I shall not ask 'What,' you'll get to that, I'm sure. Is it for that little clerk you've been seeing?"

"Alright, yes, it is. We've known each other for far too long for me to be surprised at you knowing that. And I also know that there is no eldritch power you are using. You seldom have need of that."

"No. This Pinot Gris is quite good, don't you think? It shouldn't be."

"Why, is it a 32?"

"Yes, a miserable summer, but evidently not in the Haute-Pouran vineyard. I'll have to remember to get more of this. A real steal."

"Isn't everything for you?"

"No, I pay for things, but I like to take advantage of things when I can. So do you. Our interests are different. Mousy clerks at the agricultural station doesn't exactly seem like your style. I would have thought you'd be getting kicked out of the Inspector's office by now for a torrid affair with that insufferable Swede. Very well, when you contacted me through Theresa, I had you followed a bit, just to be somewhat acquainted with whatever it is you got involved with about those three heads in Von-Dietzen's oak tree.

"Perhaps you have solved the mystery then and you can save me quite a bit of trouble."

"Far from it. At least I don't know why you need some instrument grade wood. The heads? Fah. Three thieves from the Black Cranes. No one will miss them, but I can tell you that someone will be insulted by the act."

"We both know who that is. But if you know about this, then Klaus Hunser knows about it, obviously. What I am curious about, is how. Have the loose lips at the station already been wagging?"

"Yes, I won't waste your time Ada. You must have been in a hurry. There is certainly no great power at work in letting the information slide. At least I never considered *The Freeman* a great power." Kanute slapped down a copy of the morning broadside and there was a small article about my three arboreal friends and the location.

"Wodenist mystery…" I said. "Hmmmm. I doubt it."

"Of course you do. You know more about it than most people do. In fact, I'm willing to bet you know all about it. To a point."

"I know where this is going. What's in it for you?"

"Rather this time, let us say, what don't I want. I don't want another crime war carried out by Klaus Hunser and his idiot followers with some other crime boss and *his* idiot followers. Makes for bad business."

"What about the Wodenists? Wouldn't that cause some… oh of course it would. No wonder you want to buy up all that Loire wine on the cheap. Mazarin in France has a trade bargain waiting to be signed but the most holy and Pederastic Catholics in his country don't want to have anything to do with it. And the trade embargo will make all that Loire wine, even the '32s more valuable. I understand."

"Ada, you're such a smart girl. I still think you should enter my employ instead of this freelancing business you're doing for the City. I could use you in my organization."

"We tried that before. It didn't work, remember? It wasn't you, Kanute. It's those damned other employees of yours."

"Pity, we made such a great team, in and out of the sheets, but you're right. Well, the deal is, I'll give you the sources for, what is it you need?"

"Maple, Birch, and Yew."

"Yew? Well, the market's recovered after all these years. The English have so much of it they export it now."

"It was rare?"

"Yes, all those longbows were made of yew, Ada. At one point the English actually made you bring yew to them if you wanted to trade there. But guns have made that commodity not as valuable. I'd prefer you wrap up this business with the heads quickly and blame it on the Wodenists. That's what Gudrun Sigurdsdottir wants, isn't it?"

"Yes. And for all I know, you could both be right."

"Indeed. We could."

The next day Fritz and I were standing in front of an old half-timbered storehouse.

"Are you sure this is the place your friend said to go? It doesn't look like anyone's here. And why am I here? I'm sure Kalbenski wasn't pleased...."

"...I told him you'd make up the work tomorrow on Friday. Besides, you were the one who said you needed to check the quality."

"But that's my day off."

"You're in the thick of it now, Dettin. Fritz. We don't really have "days off" in this business. You have days when you do less than others, and perhaps have a measure of free time. I suspect you can get to work on the carvings at the Station if no one is around."

"I suppose. Who is this friend of yours?"

"The less you know the better. He's very rich and well-connected in this town. He simply said Steinman here was a wholesaler of fine grade instrument wood. At least the birch you need for the bird and perhaps the maple for the skeleton. Do you have any plan yet?"

"Well, the bird's easy, like I said. But I don't know anything about skeletons."

I knocked at the door as Kanute had specified: four quarter notes, two halfs, and two more quarters in three-quarter time so it sounded disjointed and strange. Fritz said I wasn't doing it right and I was rushing the last two notes and adding one to make it fill. He rapped out the rhythm and we argued for a bit until the door opened. A middle-aged man with a long beard and forelocks looked at us.

"You must be the two Master Eldredsohn said would come."

"See, he knew the knock."

"There is no special knock. He said there would be a tall woman unmusically banging on my door with a short man. They would probably be arguing."

Joshua Steinman let us in through a characteristically small door set in the greater door where wagons and teams could be brought in. The whole shop lay curled within its own embrace of wood. The walls were plastered over the typical brickwork you see everywhere in Hagen, so that wasn't it. Instead, neat orderly bundles, stacks, faggots, assemblages, concourses, cords, and packages of wood lay everywhere and each gave forth a different scent—rich camphor, the redolent memory of dry lands in cedar, resinous pines—one merely had to hold one's nose over a part of the warehouse to feel lost in the olive groves of Rhodes, or the vast birch forests of Karelia.

"Karelian birch! Fritz, this is what we need."

"What are you going to be using this for, exactly? Kanute said something about instruments. I have some fine grade maple over here."

"The birch is for a whistle. This is fine grained. Do you think it'll warble correctly?"

Before I knew it, Fritz and Joshua were jawing back and forth about the various grains of wood, what they did in terms of resonance. I remember two millers arguing about flour once, and I suppose the same is true of any two experts whether the subject is the tooth of a particular paper, or, worst of all, two brewers talking about beer. French vignerons dispense with these formalities. They know they will categorically disagree from the outset, and one either dispenses with niceties and makes immediate use of the rapier, or they talk about their mistresses' talents and skills with their *levator ani*. I know. I've been there. Sometimes they fight and then, prinked and bleeding but honorably upholding a particular approach to malolactic fermentation, they talk, usually about the same thing, but according to a precisely arranged set of rules that ensures a triple *entendre* to save face and further bloodshed. The best course of action is to drink the wine with them and allow Dionysus to effectively smear the difference between words so that you aren't sure if they are talking about managing a hood or a cap. Ahem.

Fritz and Joshua were hot at it, in their own way.

"Yes, see the burls on this one."

"I'm sure it's too expensive."

"We haven't even discussed price yet. But that doesn't matter. Your money's no good here."

"What do you mean?" I asked walking up, being able to

understand the first thing in a long discussion of boles and ring density.

"Heh, I've always wanted to say that," Steinmann said.

"What?"

"Your money's no good here. Here, hold it out and I'll slap it away like I saw at the Kanser Theatre last year." Joshua said, rubbing his hands together.

"Oh gods, let me guess, Kanute says he'll pay for it all." I said.

"Well, yes. I already have his letter of mark."

"I see."

"Dettin, this would make a beautiful lute," Joshua said. "I'm sure it'll make a proper aeolian harp. Besides, you're still getting this at wholesale."

"I don't know. Maybe throw in that ebony over there." Fritz added.

"For what, you don't need a fret board. The wind doesn't have fingers."

"I know, but it'll look nice. Besides, Ada's friend is paying."

"That's true, he won't miss it," I said. "Do you have any English yew by any chance?"

"I'm actually fresh out of yew wood. The Chanson Daughters bought up the last of it. Seems they're going on a big push for viol bows."

"Where could we find some?"

"Well, I don't know, usually there's a fast ship, the *Jenny*

O'Neil that comes into the Stook docks. It comes from York. Maybe they would have some, or you might as well sail there and chop one down.

We walked out of Steinman's shop with a wheelbarrow full of wood and began our walk back to Fritz's house.

"Well, this is a good enough haul. I can start the nightingale tonight."

"Hmmm. You may not get a chance."

"Why."

"It seems we have some friends." I said.

"Friends?"

"There are two men who have been following us. I wasn't sure until we left Steinman's, but they are back there again."

"What will we do? We can't run away with a wheelbarrow."

"No, but we can split up. This plaza is a good place. I want you to turn and face me when we get to the crossroads. I am going to kiss you and then I want you to look past me at the two men on the left curb of the street. See if they follow you, me, or they split up. Then walk to Gansestraße where the Carrigolianos's Shop is.

"I'm not going to give this wood to them."

"Just pretend you're dropping it off. A porter carrying wood to a viol maker won't be suspect. Look for me there. I will figure out something to throw them off and get you back to your house, although doubtless they know where that is.

We reached the square and Fritz turned to look at me.

"You can say something. Mouthing words like that makes

you look like you're mouthing words," I said.

"I love you my dearest. I will take this wood to the Italians for to make sweet music instruments…" Fritz said.

"Oh shut up and kiss me!" I said, although I sounded as fake as Fritz by that point. I didn't expect him to be a left-hand kisser because he cocked his head the wrong way and I fumbled to adjust. "Grab my ass or something. Make it look real," I said, and he did, and I then understood just how strong his fingers were.

"You have a very muscular ass, Ada. You must…"

"Shut up. Are they there?"

"No, just Dr. Sigurdsdottir."

"What!?!" I turned and looked. Sure enough, where the two men had been, stood Dr. Gudrun Sigurdsdottir.

"Secretary Ludenow and Clerk Dettin. A lovely day for a stroll. With a wheelbarrow full of wood. Or perhaps love?" She was wearing her officious white robes and the thick plait of her hair looked like some angelic and therefore entirely untrustworthy *challa*. Gudrun smirked, and so perfect was the pinch of her right side, the languorous lolling of her left cheek that I remarked it must have been an expression she was born with: perhaps the result of forceps.

"Hello Gudrun. We are simply out, gathering some simple things for Fritz's hobby."

"Which is what? Carving toys or something?" She looked at us head to toe. Fritz was not wearing his silly clerical administrative vestments that day—he simply wore brown trousers too big for him, a simple black coat and a much-worn old fashioned bonnet, the sort you see in Holbein portraits. I was in my black scrivener's dress, which flounced around my booted feet, but drew in sharp and tight around my thighs and torso. I did not wear it to present the world with a fine example of womanhood untouched by children and yet much touched by men and women in circumnavigations both of her person and the globe. It's true, my breasts have always been small, but they have an indefatigable perk that the rest of me (and a few others) finds childishly optimistic. But my dress was simple, you must understand, and the tight cut and color was common because it kept us from wetting it with ink, the purple blood that flowed in our veins. In perhaps more benign and simple language, we looked like any other lower-middle class couple out on "their day off." Except I was taller than Fritz, but that didn't matter.

"Frau Doktor Sigurdsdottir," Fritz said and bowed, not knowing what else to say.

"Well, do not let me detain you from your wood gathering, but Inspector Secretary Ludenow, I expect to see you in my offices early tomorrow morning. If you can pull yourself away from the distractions of *amor*."

"French? I wouldn't have thought it possible. Well, Fritz, come along. Let's go home and fuck."

We did no such thing of course, but I carefully looked up and down the lonely street—I've already described it before, and that day its desolation was welcome albeit momentary I feared.

I was fortunate that day to watch Fritz at work. For my part, I entertained Friedrich with stories of my travels. How I left

Hagen, how I had been a scrivener in the Harz Mountains, how I had been whisked out of that place by an impossibly beautiful prick named Modran and was abandoned in Spandau to my own devices and further adventures which resulted in stints in England, France and the Western Continents and then an unplanned circumnavigation. He was especially enchanted by my travels through Japan and China.

"I bet you saw some wonderful carving in Japan."

"I did. It's the product of many aspects, but especially their skill with bladesmithing."

"Really? Hm. You know, it's nice to have a woman's voice around here, even if yours is a bit low and mannish."

"You can be awfully frank and specific, Fritz. Did you know that?"

"I've been told before. I just say what I mean. Everyone else never really means what they say anyway, and I get tired of translating it," he said.

"It must be a welcome state of affairs at the Agricultural Station."

He grunted.

"See, how many of your daily exchanges consist of nothing but apelike expressions such as that. I imagine you and some of the farmers use nothing but grunts to carry out your task."

"Sometimes there are numbers you know."

"Oh yes, there is no one so unlettered so as to not know how to count thalers and pfennigs. Besides, I am sure you are using math all the time out there."

"It's not just that," he said whittling away at what would become a wing.

"How so?"

"You've met Kalbenski and Mukurken. They do enough talking for the lot of us there. They're the ones I first didn't get. But I do now because I've been there so long. They're a lot like you."

I looked at him and raised my eyebrow—something of an unfortunate, but adorable reflex I developed over the years. I leaned forward. I even tried to emulate Gudrun's delicious smirk but finally I had to say something. "And what does that mean, Fritz?"

"You sort of talk to talk. I still don't understand what there was about all those cherry blossoms in…?"

"Kyoto."

"A good name for a city. I think I would like Japan."

"They would love you there. But what do you mean about the *sakura*?"

"The what?"

"The cherry blossoms."

"Why don't you just say that?"

"Because *sakura* is the Japanese word for it."

"But I'm not Japanese. Ah, see that is what I mean. You can't just call it an oyster, but a 'sea-rock of moist promise and concuppial potential."

"Concupiscent."

"Whatever. You can't just call something by its name."

"A name is meaningless, Fritz. Surely you know that."

"I know I have one and you have one. Even when someone has a secret name like the Roma fellow who brings the sheep in from the Dietzen estate, well, that's understandable because he…"

"Why?" I asked and continued, "if he has two names, and one is "secret" and the other not so, do they both not work? One is important perhaps in a different context, that is all."

"But it isn't meaningless."

"A name is just a particular sound for something that we agree on. We put it in line with other sounds through the articulation of speech and thereby have language, but we must agree upon it to work."

"That's not really my point."

"That's very beautiful. I cannot believe you just carved that with a knife this quickly."

"I carve well, and you talk well. Anyway, I see what you mean. I guess it's when people use two meanings for the same word, and we haven't agreed on that. That's where it's hard."

"Precisely."

"Oh, if only the world were so precise as people seem to say it is."

"I do not particularly care what you do with your new man, but I hope it has something to do with finishing up the examination. Have you bedded him to find out? He doesn't seem to be your type and not nearly worth the effort." Gudrun, in a different set of robes, but equally pompous, was writing out some kind of report.

"How would you know what my type is?"

"Do not get me wrong. I am not casting aspersions on your boyfriend, even though *I* wouldn't call a man you would have to stoop to kiss in the Peerman's Square a boyfriend. I have lived here a long time amongst you mongrel Hageners but I still don't seem to understand your customs."

"I suspected we were being followed and it was a way to check and see, you Swedish clod."

"I see."

"I doubt it."

"No, I do see, impudent slattern. There were two men following you. Who were they?"

"I don't know."

"I do. They were minor servants of Hussman, both known in the Black Cranes although no one has charged them with that publicly. I'd be very interested to see where this is going with Wodenists."

"It wasn't the Wodenists," I said. I had to think quickly. "Fritz bought that wood. He does carve toys and such you know and we bought that wood illegally. I'm sure they're looking to run some protection racket on him."

"Do you know this or are you making it up?"

"I am inducing, sweet *challa* (she looked confused by this). Like I said, we bought the wood on the shady side of the forest, and so I'm just assuming we probably crossed a line we shouldn't have."

"Don't get mixed up in it. Just get the confession out of

him. Or statement. Or whatever. Dietzen isn't very pleased with the attention you know."

"I didn't."

"You can read about it in *The Freeman*."

"May I go now mistress?"

"Yes, you may leave, but I do… you little bitch." I heard this as her door snicked to, because I always left before she could answer. Petty, stupid, and worst of all predictable as you've probably noticed by now, but it was my only way of 'tweaking her nose' and I had to keep her on her precious pursuit of Wodenists.

I had already read in the paper how some were Arguing for the Right of Worship (sort of a religious right of way) to the Oak tree with Old Man Dietzen, who professed a disbelief in jumbo of the mumbo, the wooing of chakras and runic rigmarole. After one particularly effective Sitz bath and the greater part of a bottle of Thüringian Schnapps he loudly denounced at the City Council, the allowance of certain mischievous superstitions to rise again and taint the flower of a City the world looked upon for reason and sense. He said the allowance of such barbaric custom would no doubt bring the whole of Christendom down on us, complete with its hypocrisy, absurd fasting rituals, fondness for cartels, egregious attitude towards the rights of women, and a general lack of hygiene.

When I left Gudrun's office, I saw the two men again, but this time they did not notice me slip away onto the running board of a barouche bound most likely for the fashionable strip of Langhaller. Inside the barouche, some old rich woman was patting and sighing and clutching her pearls while her younger lover was working on a more singular pearl. They were both well-dressed and as we got out of eyesight of my followers, I could only imagine the Old Dame was taking him to Langhaller to buy a new set of lace cuffs. I wasn't particularly interested in the occupational skills of the gigolo, and wanted something to distract me from their frictional niceties. We passed a viol maker's atelier and then I remembered Fritz, probably plodding on his way to work and wondered about the men who were following him. There was much to consider.

Both of us were being followed, of that I could be sure, or if it weren't the case, it was still safer to assume it was the case. They may just be sussing out his habits. I had told him no more short-cuts through the forest and to stay with large groups of people even if they lied and laughed and pissed and farted their slow way to the station. I didn't doubt he would, but I could see him getting distracted by some finer point of detail on the beak of the nightingale—which was coming along nicely—and being late. I looked behind the barouche, wished the passengers a good days 'shopping' and jumped off at the great circle and then back tracked to Stockdale.

Along the way, I caught up to our two followers. One of them was non-descript. He had a long elf's lock of muddy-brown hair, but the other had a shock of neatly cut blonde hair, so blonde it was almost white, and his skin was pale and pink. We made our way back down to Stockdale along the side streets and kept to the shadows through the seemingly endless rows of homes converted from old warehouses, until we arrived at the residence of Fritz Dettin.

Never have I been so ill-prepared. Actually, that's not really true, but I felt like it at that moment for many of my other (mis)adventures had fled to unreachable nooks in the eaves of my memory.

The only weaponry I had didn't seem up to the job. I had my small Schmeitzer hand-pistol which I kept concealed, but its accuracy at anything but shoved-into-the-stomach or held-right-against-the-skull rendered it problematic. Its larger sibling remained at my abode, but I realized while it would have easily handled one of the louts at range, it was loud and would have rendered me an object of comment. My crossbow would have been better had it also not been at home.

I had a couple of knives of course, but they were more for self-defense. My sword cane was doubtless still by the door and my beloved katana was luxuriating in its case.

I saw two men waiting on the other side of the street and I remained incognito behind a hay wagon. But I couldn't stay there forever. I had to find some way to answer Juvenal's immortal question and watch the watchers.

The road behind me curved, so I could silently move backwards until the tangent finally eclipsed the two men outside Fritz's house. Candles began to be lit in some of the other occupied places and I cursed myself for being too much in the open. Alas, I looked above and understood that I had to follow the cats.

It would not have been a hard thing to bound up the half-timbers and shoddily pointed brickwork of that place if I was attired correctly, but I wasn't so I had to pull my skirts up between my legs like a diaper and scamper as best I could. Ordinarily, I like the tightness of my dress, but at that point I wanted a pleated skirt.

I was in the middle of my preparations when a voice behind me sarcastically asked "madam, what are you doing?"

It was a Hagen Guard on patrol. He eyed me suspiciously.

"My husband is up there cleaning chimneys and it's well past his time. I'm going aloft to fetch him."

"That's a terrible lie, but entertaining."

I was losing my touch.

"Look, I… oh here." I produced my badge and charter of warrant.

"I beg your pardon, Frau Ludenow. But this does seem a bit… irregular."

"It is. Look perhaps I don't even have to do this preposterous roof-top exploration."

At that point the pale man rounded the corner and looked me straight in the eyes. His gaze narrowed, and he smirked, put a long meerschaum pipe in his mouth and pulled a generous draw of tobacco smoke.

The Guard looked at him, then me. "Ah," he said, then whispered "trailing Pinky Schmitz. I wonder what he's up to now. If you will explain…"

"Why not simply escort me to the premises I was observing?"

"I can manage that."

Pinky Schmitz moved off and gathered in his friend and we all shared that awkward moment of realization that our dance was to be deferred—they had done nothing wrong of course and it was just the Guard and myself. The détente was established; the evening was over. Guardsman Kief said he would send a few regular patrols around the street to keep them off for the night, but my friend may want to find other lodging until things evidently "cooled off."

The next day I awoke and looked out Fritz's window. He was busy trying to show me the finished nightingale.

"Yes, it really is beautiful, but Fritz, you cannot stay here."

"How do you know the men were Black Cranes? Did you see their tattoos?"

"No, but it doesn't take a lot of guesswork, oh shut up, I know what I'm talking about. I don't even want to stay here for breakfast. Gather your carving things and clothes. We're leaving."

"Where? This is my house. I'll bolt the door."

"And they will burn you down in the lovely house." He stared hard at me, like a child. "And all these lovely carvings. Believe me. They are quite safe here."

"But what if they break in?"

"I doubt very much they will do that."

"Why not?"

"Fritz, I will grant that you know a thing or two about estimating the edible pound-weights of pigs, sheep and cattle. You probably know a cheese that wasn't licensed and how old the milk is that some charlatan bought off a poor farmer for a steal. You know a great deal about the growth and grain of wood, what makes for a delightful timbre and how to carve a bird's beak to catch the wind. But I know criminals. You don't have anything they want. There is no secret satchel containing stolen gold, an incriminating letter, or contraband jewels. They know that. If these men are Black Cranes they are looking to do one thing."

"Which is?"

"Separate you from your mortal coil in retaliation for killing their brethren, or else punish you by hurting those you love. Usually by dismemberment and some humiliating sexual assault."

"But I didn't kill anybody."

"Do you really think they will believe that?"

"No."

"Did your wife leave any of her clothes here?"

"Yes, but she was shorter than you."

"I just need a pleated skirt."

Again, we found ourselves at Mackeslaut's only this time we were burdened with a loaded wheelbarrow. We had to eat outside and sure enough, Pinky and his companion were there as well.

"Do you all know each other?" Fritz asked.

"An excellent question, I am not familiar with these men, and I don't think they know exactly who I am. Do you want some more mustard?"

"Yes. So, what are we going to do?"

"You may pray to the Gods while I think of something."

"Hmmm."

In the course of our meal, I got to know the men. Pinky seemed to get to know us quite well, while the other mostly breathed through his mouth, eyed the breasts of the waitresses in their dirndls and occasionally glared at us to maintain his street credibility. Pinky was smoother. He knew he had me caught, the next play was mine and I was running out of stones.

I supposed the easiest method was to merely leave and try to find opportunity for giving them the slip on our way, but Fritz's wheelbarrow was an obvious problem. Still, there was nothing for it and we couldn't sit at Makeslaut's eating herring and drinking beer all day.

"Fritz. Are you finished?"

"Yes."

"I will go pay the bill and see if there is any way out of here besides past Our Good Friends there. I doubt it. But be ready."

"For what?

"I don't know, just be ready. I'm afraid this won't end prettily."

We walked past the men and smiled, and they immediately got up and began to follow us. We walked for a mile or so, away from my residence which was my general plan. I had no intention of leading them there. We cut across several streets, each of us taking turns with the barrow. "How much further?" Fritz asked. "They are going to catch us." We walked through less and less populated streets, until finally we heard their feet catching up to us. By this point Fritz was a bit winded. I feigned exhaustion myself to keep my pace with him.

Finally, I saw the sort of alley I wanted. I had to test them. Fritz waddled along on my left. At last a pale left hand came down on Fritz's shoulder and began to turn him. The were no words.

The other man grunted as he grabbed my hair.

"Now see here! Fritz managed to blurt out as he turned around.

I shot out my right hand and caught Pinky's right hand which held his knife and I kicked backward into the grunter's balls. I spun to the right. The three of us tumbled that way, and Pinky's knife went into the grunters right arm. I missed his gut which was my true aim, but his knife arm was a good substitute. I wrenched it free and flung it out of the way.

"Ada! Guards! Help!" Fritz ran off yelling, which is what I wanted him to do.

I rolled away from the men, grabbed Pinky's knife and flipped up onto my feet.

"Oh, this bitch wants to play a little, Pinky" the grunter said.

"Shut up, you stupid fuck!" Pinky said followed with a "stop" but the grunter was too furious with me. I tucked Pinky's blade back against the inside of my arm.

I know, timing is really all it's about. There was shouting from somewhere, perhaps Fritz but my chi was on now and as soon as the grunter got close enough, I spun and wheelhouse kicked a blow on his temple. He crumpled but Pinky was on me at that point. One blow I threw off Garden Viper style, the second I let him grab my wrist with the blade up and then punched forward so I cut his hand open across the palm. I aimed my open palm for his nose at the Kirin Stroke angle, for I meant to kill him by driving the bridge of his nose into his skull, but he was too skilled.

Master Chang taught me many things in the Wudan Mountains. Actually, we were outside the Wudan Mountains because they wouldn't admit women, especially foreigners into the enclave. But he was retired, and thought I was interesting, so he left Wudan and we traveled west together. The point is, he was always careful to describe:

"Theory and practice fighting are wherein you can be assured your mind and body are one, Ada. But then there's street fighting where you better just kick ass and take names."

"Why names?"

"I don't know, it's part of the proverb. It doesn't make much sense, one of those Koan things I think because if you've sufficiently kicked ass, they probably can't tell you their names."

We had puzzled over this awhile in between practice fighting, calligraphy lessons and sex. I don't remember that we ever really got to the bottom of that one, but Master Chang did teach me a lot about streetfighting, but with the advantage of deep Kung Fu conditioning.

Thus, I knew that I merely gave Pinky a bloody nose, and

as I was bringing the knife back in a slash, he warded it off with a fairly decent Brookhauser dodge. He was a good streetfighter. I knew that meant he'd go for my legs, but I was too fast, and switch danced back away from his kick. Grunter was a bit more robust than I thought and started to rise but it was no matter, my backward motion was already there, I already felt him so I merely let the angle carry through and brought my heel across his throat and broke his larynx. He fell backward coughing like crumpling paper, while Pinky looked at me with eyes that ran red from fear, rage and bewilderment. I simply then started walking toward him and he ran off bleeding from his hand into the darkness.

Fritz finally arrived with two City Guardsmen who did not expect to find us disposed of in such a way.

"So, you left her, you little cowardly shit…"

"But you don't understand, I think you know her."

They did. It was Schmitz and Ferdinand and they actually stopped and laughed.

"Ah, up to the old tricks again, Ada?"

"Shut up Schmitz. I think this man is dying. You may want to do something with him before he does."

"You're the one with all of the old wizardry. I'd say you bunged up his throat pretty bad. Where's the other one?"

"Ran off."

"As well he should if it was just you and him. I take back my words, sir. You couldn't have a better protector in this City than Frau Ludenow," Ferdinand said. "Frau Ada, if you'll be so kind. I think the Chief Inspector would like some words with this man. Perhaps not very well rendered, but he'll die if we don't…"

"Oh, get out of the way." I knelt down. "Fritz, you have that French carving knife? It's sharper than this pig-sticker Pinky tried to use on me. Give it to me." While Fritz looked for the knife, I looked up at Schmitz. "do you have a Pipe? Erwin?

"That I do."

"Give it to me."

"I don't see how having a smoke right now will help with anything, Frau Ludenow." I smirked at him and took the clay pipe he handed me and snapped off the end of it.

"Hey now!"

"I don't have time, Erwin. Thank you Fritz." I took the knife and I didn't have time to heat it over a flame as I would have preferred. I reached up inside of Schmitz's coat and grabbed the flask of brandy (he always stank of it, so I hope he had some and he didn't disappoint.)

"Frau Ludenow, I… hey you could have just asked for it." I cocked an eye.

"Well, alright. First my pipe and then my brandy…

"I'll get Gudrun to buy you a new thorn pipe and a cask of brandy for this information." And I tapped the head of the man who was by now, dramatically clawing at the air and his throat. I uncorked the brandy and splashed it on the knife, the man's throat, and lastly for good measure, I drank the rest of it. I then took Fritz's knife and pressed down on the man's trachea. The knife was sharper than a razor and easily cut him open. I then took the pipe and shoved it into the hole before the tissue closed back up. Suddenly the man's eyes opened wider and the sound of his breath through the pipe could be heard, whistling almost.

"Ha! Well it seems everything that knife touches, learns to whistle, Fritz."

We couldn't escape Gudrun that day. I knew that Schmitz and Ferdinand, who had been of help would have gotten in a lot of trouble to haul in my bedraggled tracheotomy patient without me. Ferdinand didn't ever really have to ask, I just said.

"C'mon Fritz. We're going up to the Rock."

The Juttrock was the massive old basalt promontory that had been heaved up in some undreamt-of ages past. The popular story was a giant had thrown it there, for it stood up above the largely flat area of Hagen by a good 300 feet. It was originally, unsurprisingly, a fortress commanding the outflow of the Elbe. Gradually, the rest of the City grew up around it, but it retained most of the main governmental buildings and the big guildhalls that ran the city, such as the Hallwards and the Engineers. The Guard Tower was there as well, made up of several different keeps and dungeons plunging into the rock below.

As we arrived, Ferdinand gave the now unconscious thief to another Guardsman and he quickly bolted up a stairwell nearby the main Guards Gate. I knew which way he was going and sighed. Fritz and I followed Schmitz and the other man, whom I did not know, turning this corner and that, and I helped Fritz with his stupid wheelbarrow, which actually wasn't so difficult owning to our difference in height and the incline of the stairs. We probably looked "cute" doing that.

We were just about to one of the main interrogation rooms when who ran into us, faster than a starving cow to pasture, than Gudrun, there in her white robes clutching a large book. Too fast in fact. She crossed the T of our pathway and sailed into us like a brilliant white cloud, like a piece of the Dover cliffs broken off and moving over the water like some angry Norse goddess, and Fritz and the wheelbarrow and Gudrun went sprawling all over the dingy, depressing stone floor of the Guard Tower.

For some strange reason, I was on the opposite side. Perhaps it was the intuitive awareness I had long ago developed at the side of Master Chang, or perhaps dumb luck, which I have a large and well-developed hoard of it seems, but I avoided the general crash and falter, the wheelbarrow going over, Gudrun slipping and falling over Fritz who was rolling under a pile of books and wood. I was worried some of his carving knives would cut the two of them to shreds, but the tightly bunched form he rolled them in followed function and harmlessly rolled out into the middle of the hall. There were quite a number of books that were splayed open and compromised, so I quickly moved to their rescue. Gudrun was punching and slapping at Fritz as they wallowed together with the barrow and it was then I conceived my plan.

"Get off of me you Swedish whale."

"Darling!" I said and picked Fritz up and stood him up as though he were my boy. "I am so sorry."

"You stupid ignorant fuckball curdshitting…" I can't actually tell you what the Swedish was, but a literal translation is all I can manage. Gudrun stood up, looking at us in fury.

"And you! Of course it is you! Gods damn ye, Ludenow! They have brought in a prisoner and I understand, oh give me that." She snatched away the book I had in my hand. I withdrew from her fury and clutched at my "lover" a bit more closely. He didn't seem to mind.

"How is it that this happened."

Fritz began to collect the rest of his spilled possessions and I began to explain where I had left off the other day, through Makeslaut's, the herring, the mustard, the beer, the alleyways, Pinky and the recent fight. Not my best work, but it did the job. I suggested she interrogate the fellow we brought in, once he was capable of communication.

"To tell me what. That he's a member of the Black Cranes? That he was dispatched to trail you and find out what you knew?"

"I think it would be very interesting to see who is guiding him and why."

"That sardine isn't the shark, Ludenow and you know it. Get out of here before I have you and your man arrested."

"But..." Fritz said.

"Darling, let's do as she says."

I clutched his hand and led him away.

"I know, but why do we have to do it tonight?"

"The moon's full you idiot, that's why."

"Oh, for some special magic."

"No, it'll be easier to see when you're climbing in the tree."

"I thought you were climbing the tree."

"I'm not going to climb the tree. I'm staying down here to keep a look out. You're the carpenter. The Tree spoke to you first, you get to climb."

"Alright..."

Fritz and I had escaped the lovely confines of the Guard's Tower (never a paragon of interior decoration and bereft of anything that spoke of welcome, warmth and comfort). We disposed of the wheelbarrow and I was able to procure a Guard Wagon to take us to an undisclosed location in Stook. It meant a longer jaunt to the agricultural station and the Oak Tree, but it was also my place, a lair if you will, in one of the lofts above a warehouse.

This time I had a gun and a sword with me and felt much better as we wound our way through the City in Milly's cab and she expertly navigated those roads convenient for avoiding the attention of the Black Cranes.

It was well past 11:00 when she dropped us off at the Fair Gate, which was a mile or so from the Southern Gate most frequented by Fritz and his colleagues. We had a bit of walking to do, but in our black clothing and keeping as stealthy as we could, it wasn't difficult to walk unnoticed across the farmlands leading to the station and the Oak.

Fritz awkwardly clambered up my back and into the lower branches.

"Where do you think I should put it?" he asked.

"I don't know. You know this place better than I do. Which

way does the wind usually blow?"

"From the North and the sea."

"Then I would put it somewhere efficacious for the wind."

Fritz disappeared up into the branches, but at times, I could see his form, like a timid monkey clambering across the face of the moon as it crossed the sky. Then I heard something. At first I thought it was some magic summons from the tree, or an ordinary atmospheric occurrence I simply hadn't noticed, but then I heard the melodious trill from up above.

As we walked back, this time to the Southern Gate where Milly waited for us, I asked him:

"How is it that it makes such a melody. Most whistles blow only one note."

"Oh, the wings you see. I made them movable so they would open and close and depending on the way the wind is blowing, they open or close note holes on the body of the bird. The wind actually plays it. I didn't make a music box that only plays one song."

"So the wind, and perhaps the tree are really playing it. It's quite beautiful."

"But someone will know we put it there."

"I think someone will know someone has put it there, but who amongst your esteemed and cultured associates around here know that you can carve that way?"

"Nobody around here."

"Not even Kalbenski?"

"He might. But he's never been to my house."

"Hmmm. That's for the best now, I think. We still need to put the other instruments in the branches."

"I still need to, you mean."

"Of course."

"Frau Ludenow?"

"Fritz, you may call me Ada. I don't know that we're friends exactly, but we're on a first name basis now."

"Alright, Ada. Won't Frau Surgeon Sigurdsdottir think that Fundamentalist Wodenists are behind all of this?"

"More's the better. It will take the suspicion off you."

"That's true. But aren't a lot of people counting on that treaty with the Kingdom of France?"

"Yes, perhaps some of your charges going through here, but they're doing fine on their own right now, aren't they?"

"Yes."

"To be honest, I wonder what stake the tree has in all of this. I would have ventured we should spend the night there under the tree and then tomorrow morning compare notes on dreams, but it doesn't seem entirely safe to me."

"No, it doesn't. The Tree's branches spread wide though. Maybe we don't need to sleep there."

"You're probably right." We walked a bit in silence, Fritz had more questions I could tell.

"What else, Fritz?"

"Won't Frau Surgeon Sigurdsdottir be angry about the book?"

"That was her fault for practically running through the

halls and into us and upsetting your wheelbarrow. And she didn't bother to check when I handed her that library book on Aeolian harps."

"She'll be angry, and I would have liked to have it handy for when I make the harp. Won't you get in trouble for not returning it?"

"We'll get it back and we'll give her back her Vesalius. Besides, I suspect other powers, perhaps that Oak had something to do with it. Imagine, we practically had a beautiful anatomy book given to us so that you could make the skeleton."

"That's true. It is a beautiful book."

Milly drove us back skillfully and I didn't notice any followers, although I was sure that condition wouldn't remain in place for very long. Inside the carriage, he looked contemplative and curious.

"Frau… Ada. May I ask you another question?"

"Yes, but I have my price."

"What?"

"I am going to ask you a question."

"Alright, well, something I don't understand. Why is it so important that we look like lovers to Frau Surgeon Sigurdsdottir?

"Because it bothers her, that's why."

"I don't understand."

"You will."

"What did you want to ask me?"

"Does anyone call you Friedrich?"

He thought about this for a while. His expression changed

from one of surprise, to contemplative and finally, as I thought, to sad.

"No."

"It's time we change that, Friedrich."

The next few days went without incident. Friedrich agreed it was best to remain at my lodgings and he would work on the various instruments although I did arrange for him to return to his work so as not to stir up any suspicion. I watched him like a hawk, of course, even though it meant putting on a disguise, which was his suggestion. "You cut a rather distinctive figure," he said.

I can't say how very effective it was. Something I did know was that while women were certainly freer in the Free and Hanseatic City—we could own property, we could have professional occupations beyond the oldest, we did not have to take a husband's name, and even Sapphists were allowed a certain measure of peace within certain confines of the City—we were still second class citizens. That meant the oldest of us were largely ignored, especially those poor souls without homes. So, I dressed as one of them: an indigent collector of rags for the paper-makers. It was a disguise I had long perfected and it offered me a measure of protection during my surveillance of Friedrich.

During the next two weeks, Friedrich would return to the secret entrance to my lodgings and I would wait an hour and return via a way he didn't know about. And we soon settled into a fraternal-sororal pattern. Mostly he spent the night making the harp, which I was fascinated with. I don't have a musical bone in my body, sadly, save the mournfully jealous kind that wished for what it hasn't got.

Finally, the harp was finished, and we repeated our late-night trek to the Oak.

I should mention at this point that the nightingale had caused a bit of a local stir, at least according to Friedrich, since there was usually a crowd of people there.

"We had better watch out this next time."

"We'll go even later."

And so we did. Milly was not available at such a late hour, so we had to come up with some other plan. This time I had to make my way alone, in my indigent rags with the harp under my blanket like some monstrous hump. Friedrich made some excuse up to remain to "lock up" the station and then remained there, frightened out of his wits, I later learned, to wait for me.

It took much longer to get there and occasionally, I thought I espied a shock of platinum blonde hair in the faces around me as I plodded through Hagen to get to the South Gate. I hadn't gotten very far down the road toward the Oak when I finally determined that someone *was* following me. The man didn't make any pretense about it. When I stopped, he stopped. When I went on, he went on.

We wakjed on for a couple of miles. I grew petulant and angry. The damned harp was most uncomfortable on my back but I had to treat it like a fragile child made of glass. The last teamster passed me as the night deepened and he even threw me a couple of pfennigs. Not wanting to disclose myself, I reached down for them and I heard the tramp of boots even closer behind me.

The lantern on the teamster's wagon grew smaller and smaller in a gulf of great darkness. The light from the City was the only light cast up into the sky, for the stars were veiled behind clouds and the moon was new at that point.

I tried a peak from under my hood and sure enough the silhouette of my follower, shapeless mostly in the darkness, grew closer. He threw off his hood and there was a flash of light off his hair. I reached in and cocked my pistol.

The figure heard this quite sharply and stopped. And we waited. I was sure there was going to be an answering click of his own wheellock, and as dark as it was, I had no idea how or when I should make my move to fire, or if he was doing the same.

"Standing here waiting for me won't do at all, little swallow. Don't you have some errand at the Station?"

I breathed a sigh and uncocked the gun. That voice belonged to one man alone in all of Hagen although I then grew cross.

"Why are you here and why are you following me, Kanute?"

"Oh, a lark, I suppose. Or a swallow. Like the one tattooed on your hand." He came up to me then smiling. "Don't you think this beggar woman get-up is a bit old by now? I could tell it was you all the way back at the Temple."

"But most people haven't been behind me when I was hunched over like this. You have."

"Ha, I suppose you've got me there because I had you

there. What are you doing? Does this have something to do with those instruments? I understand the oak tree has a new adornment."

I scowled in the darkness. I had forgotten about Kanute being "in on the know" about all of that.

"Perhaps, but I have some strange sense it's of interest to you. Or else you wouldn't be out here waiting to follow me."

"Oh, you are always an interest to me. But you're right and we know each other well enough to try and fool one another. But you should be careful. I understand the Authorities are interested in that nightingale you put there because a lot of Wodenists have been going there in the daytime to listen to its augeries. It's being watched."

"Thank you for letting me know."

"So, are you going to tell me what you are doing?" He said this with a blasé tone that already anticipated my answer. I laughed.

"It is a pity you have so many other entanglements that make things difficult. We really would be a wonderful old married couple…"

"…Finishing each other's thoughts and sentences. That's true. I know you won't tell me."

"Then why are you here?"

"The reason is in what you just said. We are sort of an old couple and sometimes, Ada, I worry about you. Don't shrug that off with some cynical 'isn't that sweet.'"

"I won't. I know you do. I am grateful for it although…"

"…it's hard to say. That's why I like you. Let me at least accompany you to the agricultural station where your friend is. I'll feel better that way. And I'll have a carriage sent for your return to the Swallow's Nest. Since it's too late for your usual driver?"

"Of course it is. Thank you." And we walked together in the night. With Kanute, I knew I was safe, so I stood up straight. "Anything else?" I asked.

"Yes, I was also going to tell you that a shipment of yew should be arriving two days from now. Conveniently, the dock isn't very far from the Swallow's Nest, so it should be easy to get to it."

The 'Swallow's Nest' was his term for my lodgings, which were really owned by him. He made it up for me when we were lovers so that I wouldn't have to worry about his wives and girlfriends or other people bothering us, so it remained quite secret and safe. I pestered him about granting me title to the warehouse, but it was mostly a formality. Even though he and I no longer regularly shared a bed, chairs, the intricate copper tub, he still liked to drop by 'like he owned the place.' Sometimes we made more than nostalgic use of the silken swing and I didn't care to argue; it wasn't very different from most arrangements in the City. A few rich burghers like Kanute owned most of the city anyway, so the rest of us were a city of Tenants. In Kanute, I had a benevolent landlord so I calculated that my arrangements in Stook were the best I could manage and I left it at that.

Friedrich was non-plussed when he met *the* Kanute Eldredsohn and kept obsequiously bowing and scraping the floor with compliments and ludicrous formalities of speech.

Finally, I could take no more: "Oh Friedrich, knock it off. He hears that all day. We have work to do."

"I am impressed Master Dettin. This is beautiful work." Kanute was gingerly handling the harp in the station. We only had one candle, but even that seemed dangerous, so I said so.

"Yes, but I wanted to see it for a moment before it goes aloft."

"My lord knows?"

"He's nobody's Lord, Friedrich. This is the Free and Hanseatic City," I said.

"That's certainly true. I don't have a drop of noble blood in my veins, that I know of. The accident of birth is no reason to fawn over someone who might as well be a world-class idiot. But it certainly isn't a meritocracy here, either. Anyway, I've taken too much of your time. Ada, I would be careful walking back. My carriage will pick you up about half-way at Dornhauser's Corner. And let me know about the third trip. Somehow I don't think you'll keep the Cranes off you for that one unprotected."

He then smiled, kissed my cheek and left.

Again, Friedrich had clambered up into the Oak and after a while, I heard that strange mixture of string voices, underlaying and flowing around the notes of the nightingale as if its melody were a series of stones within a swiftly flowing river between banks of deep healthy green.

I assumed Kanute had set some men to watch over us. We made it back to the waiting carriage and "the Swallow's Nest" without incident.

I woke up on the next morning, or nearly afternoon quite tired, but a dream had come across my mind and gently lifted me into the day. A soft sound, like a viol, or perhaps even a hurdy gurdy droned across a wide land of trees and grass. The day in the dream was bright and sunny. For some reason I didn't have any clothes on save for an old coarsely woven blanket. My feet were muddy and of all surprises, I felt a child moving around in my tummy. Or what I thought would be the sensation, for I am barren and childless in the daylit world.

The long single note kept on, as though it were part of the sunshine or wind. The Oak Tree was there nearby, festooned with bright strips of linen and wool gently flapping in the breeze and then I knew what it was.

"Thank you, well done." These words came late, as I was coming out of sleep but there was no mistaking their source.

The sound of the harp was a pure note in my dream, and yet its variance and tonal surprises were deeper, as though I had heard one note played upon it and it was all my mind could grasp. I lay in bed for a while thinking about this green. Off in the other rooms I heard Friedrich whistling to himself.

Since I could not trust Friedrich to go out and not get seen, I went myself to gather food, drink, supplies and most importantly: news. I did not need to avail myself of my usual roster of informants. The Hagen *Freeman* had enough. Word had spread about an old oak tree away south of the City on the Von Dietzen land that had been attracting worshippers owing to some ingenious musical instruments that had been placed in its boughs. As I have said before, Von Dietzen had not been happy about people trampling over his fields until he realized the monetary value in the situation and had roped off the area and was charging admission. This wasn't good. I had wondered all along if we shouldn't have just put them all up at once, but evading the Black Cranes was chief amongst my concerns at this point. Although I dreaded the thought, I surmised that perhaps Kanute could make himself useful for the final installation. However, that was a last card to play when all other hands had failed, I told myself. While the *Freeman's* story did mention the dislocated heads as starting the whole affair, it did not dwell on them.

I told Friedrich about all of this as we walked silently through the night toward where the English Cutter *Jenny O'Neil* was moored. She had arrived that evening and Kanute had given me an introductory letter for the Captain so we could get first crack at the wood.

"Von Dietzen will likely have a guard there at night, but I don't think that will be too much trouble."

"It won't?" Friedrich asked.

"Well, it might. But we'll figure something out." I explained various subterfuges and stratagems for night-work. Some were more elaborate than others and all had a measure of danger and dare I say a dash of bold criminality about them. That was when Friedrich asked me:

"Maybe we should just pay admission?"

"I hadn't thought of that."

We approached the dock were the ship was. Everything was quiet under the light of a few lanterns on the dock. The moon was waxing again by this point and helped me survey the scene.

"Stop," I said, and pulled Friedrich into the shadow of a doorway.

"What's wrong?"

"This seems too easy. Don't you feel it?"

"No, but I've learned to trust your instincts."

We waited there for a while. I looked back at our path and caught a brief glimpse of a shape, a man-shape, move off into the shadows of the street.

The Black Cranes were a large organization from what I knew of them, but I had been meticulous in using the hidden passageways that left my residence and found no evidence of being followed. Still, had they cast their net wide enough they may have learned of our general whereabouts. Someone may have tipped them off as to where I generally lived and as Friedrich said, I cut a rather noticeable figure when not in disguise.

The other possibility was that Kanute had posted some men to follow me.

"Well, what do we do, Ada?" Friedrich asked.

"We can't go back that way and we certainly aren't going to wait for daylight. My vote would be to make straight for the ship and see what happens. Do you have that concealed pistol?"

"Yes, but I've never even shot a gun before."

"It's very simple. Wait until they get closer. Then wait some more. Then point it straight at the man's chest and pull the trigger, here." I reached into his coat and cocked the pistol for him. I then took out my own gun and cocked it.

"What if they have guns?"

"Don't get shot."

"May the Gods preserve us."

We then proceeded out into the moonlight. The ship was perhaps 300 yards away. For the first 100 yards nothing happened, but then I heard footsteps behind us. As we drew closer to the water, two men stepped out of the shadows, hooded and cloaked. They carried cudgels. They would be easy. Then another came forth, walking swiftly toward us. He was cloaked as well and carrying a sword. That made it a bit harder. When we were 25 yards from the ship, the two following us stepped up their pursuit.

"Stop right there, you Hunnish witch." Pinky had also stepped out of the gloom and stood in our way.

"Come no closer, or I will blow that pink face right off of you."

"True, but you'll only get one shot off and your little boy here doesn't even seem to want to hold that pistol."

"I will take all of you down."

"I don't doubt that, Frau Ludenow. We know who you are, and we know who he is. We can make this easy. You just come with us to talk."

"Why not right here? It's a fine evening and it seems there's no one around but us."

"Very well, Kacker!" Pinky turned as he said this and one

of the men produced what looked like a long gun. "Shoot the bitch. The clerk won't be any trouble after that." I heard the click of the wheel-lock and at that moment I turned and shoved Friedrich down and rolled away toward the edge of the dock. The shot blared out and I heard the bullet skip off the pavement. Luckily there was a groan behind us. Evidently, one of the followers had gotten too close and took the ricochet. I did not hesitate—cut off the head and the snake is helpless—so I fired at Pinky although it was some distance and the shot caught him in the shoulder. He spun around and fell to his knees.

The remaining crook behind me took this chance to rush at me but I was back on my feet and had the katana out before he realized it. I didn't want to kill him, but it was still difficult to check the stroke I had been trained for. Still, I had to parry him first and let his energy do all of the work. His cudgel went wild and struck the pier piling to my left and I counterstruck down low, slicing off his kneecap.

"Get the clerk and shoot her!" Pinky yelled. The swordsman standing next to the rifleman then ran straight at Friedrich. I thought it was going to be all over until Friedrich lifted his arm, without a moment to lose and unloaded the pistol at the man who stumbled and fell.

By that time I saw the rifleman had reloaded, a quick bastard and all I could do was run into the fray, dodging and lunging to avoid the shot when another blast roared out above me and the rifle clattered to the ground and the man who had been holding it reeled backward.

"Avast ye buggerlugs! What are you doing?!" It was a loud voice, an English voice from the deck of the ship.

Pinky staggered off to the darkness in the same direction as the rifleman. The man behind me with the cut leg was screaming so it was difficult to hear what came next, but I turned and could see him hobbling away with the other follower. They too moved off into the darkness, hobbling slowly but away.

"I won't have your Hagenish fighting or dancing or whatever it was you were doing near my ship!" The voice spoke in the curious, combobulated form of London English, so I answered him.

"We were being attacked, and thank you for your attention and timely arrest of their further endeavors." Clumsy, perhaps but it was all I could manage.

"Throw down your arms then, or I will empty my ship of its men upon you."

Friedrich dropped the pistol and scrambled to his feet and went over to the lifeless body left crumpled up in the lantern light. I did the same. The man wasn't lying; he and ten English sailors came down the gang plank and surrounded us.

"You two should verily explain yourselves here ere I call this City's Guardsmen."

Captain Edward Farnsborough was the skipper of the *Jenny O'Neil*. We made our introductions and explained our visit and how the sudden appearance of our dancing companions was not an expected part of the evening's progression.

"This man's not dead Captain. There's a whole blown through his right side but I daresay the little man here didn't hit anything important. I think the fellow's just got a nasty shock and hitting the stones here knocked him out."

"Very well, bring all of them aboard."

We stood on the deck of the ship with lanterns in our faces while Farnsborough examined the letter from Kanute. "I see. You're associates of Master Eldredsohn. Well, that changes everything. Had you not been in possession of this letter of mark I would have held ye here until the Guards had come anon."

"Do you always speak in iambics?" I asked.

"Oh, bit of a habit, picked it up at the theatre."

"And so you trod the boards in addition to the planks of the stage upon the sea."

"Why yes, with Kit Marlowe's boys until the light that led fell extinguished."

"In that bar fight. Yes, I remember hearing about it." I said. "You must understand, Captain. My friend and I here had simply hoped to come and bear away a faggot of yew."

"For what purpose?"

"Viol bows," Friedrich said. He looked defiant, almost angry, although I was unused to that emotion from him and wasn't even sure if it was that. "The mark-up here on yew is ridiculous and these are for a special occasion. Master Eldredsohn's daughter is to be wed in a fortnight and I have been charged with making replacement violin bows," Fritz added. He was using some of his facial acting practice now.

"Really? I can't imagine they would need to be that special."

"Ah but they are. They have to be inscribed with the right runes for a propitious marriage and not just anything will do. I'm not a superstitious man, myself," Friedrich continued, "but Captain, you and I will both agree a customer is a customer and while this request may seem a trifle, it is important for a man of business to keep his word about a commission."

I was silent. Perhaps even my mouth was open in amazement, but I was too taken with this unlooked-for eloquence that I just let him run with it. Then I realized how good Friedrich's English was. *That little shit!* I thought and considered the various ways I could beat out of him the source of all these hidden talents.

We discussed the price of the wood, the tides, the weather and the prospects of the codfish commodity market. Eventually Farnsborough brought out some claret and we drank it while he answered several questions concerning a former acquaintance of mine in England.

"Retired to Stratford with all his money, eh? Well, I cannot say I blame him," I remarked.

"I think Bill just grew rather tired of the whole scene, you know and that partnership with Fletcher..."

"...you don't have to tell me."

"Aye, it's all masques and such now. No real depth to the words. I don't know how much longer Jonson will even last. He tends to make people angry."

"A master wordsmith, but sharp man."

"And an excellent calligrapher."

As pleasant a host as Farnsborough was, I knew we couldn't stay long.

"What do you plan to do with the man? The one Friedrich here shot."

"I planned to give him to the Guards if he makes it through the night. Well, I'll give him over if he doesn't."

"It would be most excellent if our involvement were…"

"…forgotten? I will do my best. Now about the wood."

We settled on the price, took the yew, thanked Captain Farnsborough and left his ship.

"Where did you learn such excellent English, Friedrich?"

"My mother was English. From Sussex. It was my cradle language."

"There is more to you than I would expect. You seem down. Worn out."

"I may have killed that man."

"Do I need to mention what he and his friends would have done to you?"

"No, I'm not a fool. But I'm not a killer. I may know how to carve a pretty thing and yes, I can speak English, but I haven't been trained to kill like you."

There was more he was going to say, but he thought better, or worse, perhaps of it. I let it slide and the enormity of what we had set in motion settled in on me as well.

"I told you, Friedrich. I wasn't born to this life. I was a librarian once in this City. I've told you that."

"No, forgive me. You're my only real friend, I think. Besides Kalbenski, maybe. I guess it means we can be honest with each other. Anyway, you're a woman and you probably had to learn all of that to survive in the world. It's an ugly place."

"And maybe your path is to make it a bit brighter for the rest of us. I am sorry it had to come to shooting."

"Maybe he won't die."

"Probably not." I looked at him. "He bled a good bit, but he'll be fine."

We walked back to the secret passageways unfollowed. I made sure of that this time. But it wasn't night-time marauders we had to fear. For now.

The morning had barely got underway. I had only drunk one cup of coffee and Friedrich was still asleep when the pounding at my door commenced.

It wasn't the threatening kind. I knew what an unpleasant cohort of visitors bent on taking my life in vengeance sounded like, so I assumed that the Black Cranes were still back at their nest licking their wounds. No, this was the insistent pounding of law enforcement fists. Besides, there were only a few of them who knew how to reach me. I was a bit sad for I thought Farnsborough had already sold us out before noon even. I learned that wasn't exactly the case.

"Tell me, Herr Dettin. Was the Vesalius helpful?"

"Yes, the human body is really a beautiful thing you know. This is excellent draftsmanship and printing..." and Friedrich opened the book on Gudrun's desk and pointed out several of the drawings, especially one of a rather pert skeleton, a man I assumed, strolling down a country lane in Italy as if it were the most natural thing in the world.

"You know, I don't think my colleague's presence is really all that necessary here," Gudrun said. "I'm fairly sure she was responsible for the wreckage down at the pier last night. While I often chide her for her methods, her capabilities are without question which makes her methods all the more irritable. Frau Ludenow, you're free to go, but I'd like a word or two more with Herr Dettin. Thank you."

And she smiled that big Swedish smile that let me know what I already knew. She'd won. I shrugged and walked out the door. Ferdinand was waiting to escort me from the Tower.

"Who ratted us out? Captain Farnsborough?"

"Him? Oh no. It was that bloke Dettin shot. Sang like a thrush in a hawthorn bush he did although he didn't know your name. But he just had to describe you and Frau Surgeon Sigurdsdottir and the rest of us knew exactly who it was. Nice work. I wish I could have seen it. I wouldn't have interfered, but just to 'watch the Mistress at work.' It's like watching a master painter or chef you know. Oh, we found that one chap's knee cap. That must be a sharp sword you have."

"I wish you had interfered. The outcomes would be the same and I wouldn't have had to do all of that. But now what?"

"You know Gudrun's method's Ada," Ferdinand said with a wink as we left the building and he was out of earshot. "But she's kind of odd. I figured she'd have that little scarper up on the rack before *you* to make you talk, but she's got something up her sleeve."

"Gudrun's no fool. She knows she just has to ask him."

Not having to watch out for Fritz, and being followed by two indescribably obvious inspectors from the Tower, I went to Minkler's in the great circle for some roast chicken and kölsch. The meal was excellent and exactly what I needed. I had a cup of coffee and a nice lemon tart, the sort they specialize in, and it struck me that I had left one very important part of the investigation unfinished.

I don't know why I hadn't considered them in all of my research other than my incurable and inexcusable bigotry towards those I misjudge as rural and stupid. But you have already guessed I am a snobbish, optimistic misanthrope, which one could even argue is actually a paradox, but no, there are several different kinds.

The martyrous misanthrope chiefly inhabits Abrahamic lands and is known for hating humanity through his excessive desire to see them all judged by a god who sounds like that incontinent old uncle you keep in the attic, the one with his arms tied to his sides lest he fling his own shit from a broken window at a neighbor and so your household would become an object of contumely. They so wish for the hideous world to go away that they attempt to speed its demise via long and dangerous swims in A Certain River in Egypt. (A pun which goes back to the Old Kingdom)

The cynical misanthrope is a deeply disappointed idealist. Perhaps someone with a torn perineum and a screaming child who smells of sour milk and urine, thinks that the lies about motherhood were bitterly aimed at her by the special hand of fate: not for singling out for undue punishment, but that she alone would know the truth about the world while the rest of its pox-ridden inhabitants danced away with death as if the white lilies would never grace their graves.

The pessimistic misanthrope convinces himself through inscrutable linguistic calisthenics that the difference between "realism" and "pessimism" is simply a matter of perspective. I prefer to consider myself an optimistic misanthrope because while I think that for the most part, people are stupid and hopeless, I am ever yet hopeful that I will be proved wrong. I seldom am, which is my despair and a rock that I push up my Sisyphean hill every day, but once in a while I am surprised.

So there I was at the Wünchi's farmhouse, listening to the men-mountains and drinking buttermilk.

"Well, this woman came by the farm early in the spring," Tolf started saying. "A very beautiful woman, but strange. She wasn't from here, or her parents weren't from here maybe."

"Yes, she came from the east, beyond the Rus." Rolf added. "She had those pretty almond eyes. And she was tall, but could speak the Hagentachte very well. She dressed in very nice clothes."

I naturally assumed this was Gretchen Wu, who had "taken over" for me as Kanute's favorite. The description fit her.

"What did she want?" I asked.

"She is the agent for our landlord: Kanute Eldredsohn. We feared her you know because she carried a bag," Rolf said.

"A bag?"

"What he means is that the foreclosure papers could have been in it," Tolf said. "Our father mortgaged the place to the hilt, ma'am. We thought Kanute was going to shut us down and this woman, this Frau Wu was his agent."

"Have you ever met Herr Eldredsohn?"

"No, they say he's very rich."

"Hmmm. He is. But go on."

"She came with a deal instead," Tolf said. "We were supposed to go and meet an old man in the forest. It was a bit out of our way, but the woman said the old man was a relative of Herr Eldredsohn, a crazy old cousin who needed taking care of and we should watch over him and do whatever it took to protect him."

"And so we did. For a week we followed him through the forest. We thought he was gone simple, you know," Rolf added.

"And then one day he seemed to notice us and gave us the slip through the forest."

"How long did it take him to figure out you were following him?" I asked.

"He knew all along," Golf said, breaking his silence.

"You're probably right, Golf, but we had orders. It seemed simple. We didn't have our debt forgiven, Frau Ludenow, we could just delay our fault for a while until we got on our feet. That was Frau Wu's deal."

"Default, but go on."

"Anyway, he gave us the slip so we followed him as best we could. Golf knows the forest well, but this oldster knew it better. We heard some tussling up ahead, some foul business and these men shouting obscenities and threats."

"They were going to bugger that little clerk, and he's a nice man. Then they would kill him, we were sure," Rolf said.

"Larcenous exaggeration perhaps, but who knows, you put a stop to it."

"Well, yes. They weren't much."

"One of them cut me."

"And you killed them."

"We didn't mean to."

"But you didn't know your own strength."

"Frau Ludenow," Golf said. "We're not professional bodyguards. We're smiths, farmers, slaughterhouse men." I nodded. He made sense, and it made sense in the bigger picture to have these charming, ham-fisted boys carry out the dirty work.

"You've done nothing wrong. Technically, except not coming forward, but I don't really care about that."

By this point I thought I knew enough. I knew that I did not know everything, for if it is one thing Philosophy teaches us is that *we can't know everything*, but that bit of knowledge is often hard won if it is won at all. Many of my peers build systems of thought when they reach this point as a sort of consolation activity: "something to keep the hands busy" as a barber would say.

When I reached home, I found Friedrich there already carving away at the skeleton.

"What are you doing that for?"' I asked.

"This? Frau Gudrun said I should complete the plan and see what happens. She said you'd take care of everything else."

"She did? Hmmm. She did."

Things were strange. And easy. Too easy, and that is what made them strange and of concern for me. Although I suspected the Cranes had perhaps triangulated a more precise guess of my residence, I didn't see anyone. Still, I had inflicted a lot of damage but without the coup de grace, which is more for those who survive after, in these cases. This meant I had dire enemies on my hands and while it seemed natural that they were off regrouping, it seemed more natural for them to bring damnation and fire on whomever dealt out the blows.

I went over to Friedrich's old residence to check in on it for him. Rather than risk the clothes of the beggarwoman, I wore another disguise, this time as the seller of trusses for ruptures and treatments for *prolapsis ani*. All I had to do was walk down the street in my brown robes (stolen from a mendicant), and the red tasseled hood along with my cart, ringing the traditional jingle bell (hollow sounding, like a cow-bell) with the guild flag (a rose growing between two hills, they were not subtle) and everyone seemed to shy away from me, save one desperate client who required an enema of particular power. But I wasn't allowed to sell enemas—the guild only allowed the sales of items, treatments and unguents that assisted with the retention of things, another guild facilitated the violent and shuddering expulsions of things *from* the body. It was all a matter of direction. She made several disparaging comments about unions and guilds and stalked off elsewhere to find relief for her fecal plug.

As I had feared, they had ransacked Friedrich's old residence. Nothing was taken as I originally said, but everything was broken, every window, the crib, every carving. I felt like a large rough stone had slid into my stomach. Without a mouth it could still speak. *You will have to tell him something. I bet you'll lie to him."*

So I knew they were still on the trail and judging from the age of the piles of shit in the middle of the floor (they were thorough in their insults) and given the season, I figured this happened the night after our affray at the *Jenny O'Neil.* But nothing had happened since then. They were probably lying in wait to see what we would do next. It would only be a matter of time before some English sailor or some Guardsman slipped up and the curiously deliberate trip of their prey to get English yew would be discovered.

I thought about this as I walked back through Hagen. Fritz had told Gudrun nearly everything it seemed, although I wasn't there for the conversation so I couldn't know for sure. People, even with the best intentions, can leave out important details. And when a person, especially a lonely man, starts talking about "how golden the Frau Surgeon's hair is..." I know I have to triple my watch on the foolishness of reported dialogue. Fortunately, he seemed to have related the idea that the old man was tied to Wodenists, perhaps was a priest even since he seemed to take up the guise of Wotan himself. (Kanute, in his vanity, was fond of that trick as he grew older). Then again, Gudrun might see through *my* trick which was to have an honest man tell her exactly what he thought the situation was. Gudrun had been married before. That much I knew, but she left her husband in Sweden and didn't have very many good things to say about him, so I knew that she wouldn't believe any oafish fool with a dick between his legs on principle. No, it was all move and countermove, my stone there, and Gudrun's there to block my maneuver. But was she slowly encircling me? Was I just playing this game to get out?

I finally arrived back at my lodgings. On my way, I did manage to sell one truss to a visiting merchant from Bavaria who had blown his out after losing an alimentary battle with Hagen's famous Skallbenner Soup—a potent mixture of dried beans, peas, cabbage, smoked mutton and onions which is fancifully described as being able to "give wind to the sails when the sea is becalmed." Such humor is an inevitable experience in a seaport like Hagen. The less said about the resettlement of his rupture, which was accompanied by a lot of schnapps and a barking dog nearby, the better. The lengths I will go to remain *incognito*.

"A note has come for us, from the Frau Surgeon."

"Well, what does it say?"

"I can't read it." He handed me the note and there was Gudrun's scratchy Greek, like she was writing out an invoice for Retsina.

"Ada Ludenopolopolis. Since yer Mann here seems to think the last toy will brung out them thiefs, I wood recommend you proceed tonight. I will send Ferdninand and some Argives armed in Bronze to guide you two the Tree. He would be there at 8:00 dark." I laughed.

"What does it say?"

"Oh, who cares what it says, the Greek is atrocious. She even seems to be borrowing a device from *The Iliad* without even knowing it. And she calls herself a doctor. She can't even read Galen in the original!"

"Are you finished? I don't know why you make fun of her so. She says she respects you but…"

"Oh Gods, you're taking her side. You've fallen in love."

"No, I just think she's here to help us, really."

"If I am translating this Greek according to what it hopes to say… a Guardsman will be here after 8:00 to escort us to the tree where you will hang the skeleton."

"And then what? Are we going with just one man? Won't there be more?"

"Oh, we'll be accompanied by the Army of Agamemnon."

"That sounds promising."

"Friedrich, it means a few guards at the most. I suspect this is a trap to lure out the Black Cranes."

"Ada, my house…"

I looked at him. He reminded me of a faithful dog—I could not question his loyalty and as much as a lie would be convenient at the time, I knew he would find out: there was no veal chop waiting back at home. But it was worse than that, his life had been destroyed and I chastised myself for drawing him in too deeply. *But they would have found out. They would have killed him.* I steeled myself with this last ratiocination, although as with all such ratiocinations, I knew its purpose lay not in providing the safety of a truth which could not be verified absolutely but rather provide comfort for my own heart.

"…Friedrich, I'm afraid…"

"Do not tell me any more. I can read it on your face. I am glad you are honest with me though. I still consider you my friend. Perhaps my best friend. I suppose it couldn't have been avoided. Life isn't a garden full of roses and milk for people like me."

"But perhaps it can be now," I said. And I wished to really mean it. Perhaps I even did, but the terrible means of Friedrich's freedom had a steep price that doused any condolence hope could offer.

Ferdinand and three Guardsmen arrived at our predetermined spot where they met us. Friedrich tightly held onto the skeleton. I hadn't even seen it and was curious as to what it would do in the boughs of The Oak, but for that I would have to wait.

Caution had long been "thrown to the wind which dropped it on a dung heap" as we say in Hagen. We rode forward through the dark streets in a Guards' carriage so that perhaps only a flying banner stating "here we are, come follow us" was the missing element.

We drove through the South Gate and quickly came to where the agricultural station was. The Oak Tree did indeed wait inside of a much-improved enclosure. We stopped before its gate. A pair of slimy lackeys stood there, attempting a pose of daunt, I suppose. Ferdinand spoke first.

"You will get out of here. Everything has been arranged. My men and I will scour around the perimeter and see if anything is up. It probably will be. Are you armed?" he said to me.

"Of course."

"I would almost rather you were with us, Frau Ludenow. I daresay you'd be an asset in either close or range fighting, but I think it's best if you accompany Herr Dettin here to the tree."

"Agreed."

We got out and Ferdinand waved off the lackeys and we entered through. The Oak Tree waited for us: an island of stillness. The wind had been blowing in chill from the North Sea as usual, but here it seemed to pause, as if the Tree had bidden it to wait for the final instrument to be placed. Ferdinand and his guardsmen then disappeared into the darkness and we hoped they knew their business. There was nothing left but help Friedrich up into the Tree and I performed my human ladder trick for hopefully the last time.

I waited at the bottom of the tree for what seemed a very long time. Time itself had seemed to slow down, and I was reminded of other dimensions one entered in this world. Some were the fantastic realms of beings we cannot understand: they are given various names by us: elves, kami, manitou, but those are simply words we apply to consider their marvelous worlds in the remote abstraction of language. Their true names, if they even have them, were a mystery.

But slowly, I heard the wind, or rather I heard the branches of the tree move and the leaves begin their divergent strains of conversation, like the hum of humans at a party. The limbs creaked and groaned like viol de gambas and I fancied they were tuning up like an orchestra. And then I heard the faint, random but distinctly unique melody of the nightingale trill down from above. It was such a sweetly seductive line that I missed when the aeolian harp began to offer its chromatic, unearthly drones. Friedrich still did not come down.

And then tones joined the other notes, pure wood percussions but so soft they sounded like the moan of the wind in nooks and caves by the sea. Each note sounded in counterpoint to the notes of the nightingale. I had expected some kedonking twonkle, like a simple windchime, but this was different. The sustain of each bony note was incredible—not as long as the seemingly infinite hum of the harp, the pitch of which would wind up into a helix of self-reference so that there was no end, they were simply again at the bottom of the octave starting again like an ouroboros—nor were the notes short, fleeting footsteps or wing beats within the immeasurable distance of space as were those of the nightingale. No, the triads of sounds came and came again weaving together like some endless braid.

My head had nodded. I had been leaning against the tree, but I hadn't thought better of it. A voice spoke in my ear: "Oh!

Sentinel Pastoral, Would ye stop Apollo from Flaying Marysas unless he had the right paperwork!" What did that mean?

It means mountain streams of hair and black scarves, the tinkling of silver chains, charms of little hammers, skulls, and the wings of ravens, in the wind of the smart horses. This is the Old Poetry walking the earth.

Was it evening, or early morning? I looked and could not tell for the horizon all around me was a banded girdle of purples, pinks, and oranges, as if the rosy fingers of dawn had interlaced with those of evening around the earth.

The Oak was gone, but a man stood there. He was stark naked and beautifully constructed. Not in some Hellenic conception of youthful perfection, but rather the knotty muscles and weathered skin of a man in the prime of middle age. His skin was dark like chocolate as were his eyes. His lips were full, sensual and given to smiling the seductive expression of a well-traveled man who had kept his heart enfolded in the golden armor of empathy, endurance and experience. His hair was long, in sumptuous kinky braids woven through with threads of gold and scarlet. His feet had long beautiful toes with shining perfect nails. His legs, like his arms were well muscled and his dark penis swung like some marvelous undiscovered fruit. *Ikembe* I wanted to say, but I knew it wasn't him.

"This is not your true form," I said.

"It isn't but this is your dream, so I am only visiting here. The form is one I am borrowing from your memory. I must say I rather like it."

"It suits you well. Do the muscles pinch?"

"Not at all. It feels quite homey, actually, although a bit limited since I only seem to have four branches."

"Five."

"Oh, well, yes, that one too. It seems a strange way you have with these things. How do the bees get the pollen into your flower?"

"They don't, let's not discuss mechanics at this point."

"That's right, I'd have to stick this thing in your flower, wouldn't I? Doesn't seem very romantic, and you all make such a fuss over it. I suspect this was someone you were close to?"

"No, actually you bear the likeness of one who got away."

"How?"

"His boat was tied to the back of a parmacetty. It's a long story."

"A couch from Italy?"

"No, a whale."

"I'm sorry."

"No, he didn't die, not that I know of. The boat he was on was tied to the whale by way of the harpoon stuck in his back and the whale was just swimming off to the horizon and we never saw them again because…"

"Never mind. The ocean is a strange place, I would be quite lost in it. Floating around. Washing up on Ireland eventually and being carved into quaint pieces of bric-a-brac."

"What are you doing here?"

"You would know the answer to that better than even I

would. You were the one who laid down under me. But I knew from the first time I felt you that you were different. Touched by the Waterpeople." he said.

"I told you that was a long time ago."

"Ah, yes, now you're too old to be of service to them."

"How would you know?"

"The age isn't difficult, even though the span of your years is miniscule compared to mine. No, I merely meant you can't make babies for them, so they are probably withdrawing their power. Did you give them any waterbabies?"

"No,"

"Really? Usually they get at least two or three out of a woman like you."

"I can't have children. Couldn't I suppose I should say."

"Oh, I see. Perhaps that's for the best. I don't get any sense that nursing children, wiping asses, getting them out to the fields to work or to school was really your root in life. And then with waterbabies there is always the problem of giving them up to the rivers, the streams."

"Well if this is a dream, then why don't we make something of it?" I asked.

"What do you mean?"

"I mean stick that thing in my flower."

"Oh, you mean fuck."

"It's a dream. No harm done to either of us. We won't say anything while were awake."

"Ada"

"That's my name. Come here, it might help if I get things going." He approached me and I reached out for him.

"With your hand? Actually, that feels really good. When do I turn you around?"

"Are you ready?

"Can't you see that, Ada?"

"Just stick it in there."

"I can't wait. What are you talking about? Ada."

"Put your hands on my shoulders." I said. "Gods, can you grow another arm and pull my hair? Oh you're feisty."

"Ada, wake up," but it was not the voice of Ikembe, or the Oak. But he did chime in:

"Ha ha ha haha ha… have to some other time you saucy bit of ass!" The laughter died away and I opened my eyes and Friedrich was furiously shaking my shoulder.

"The Guards are gone! There was some shouting out in the darkness. I drifted off to sleep in the tree, but it woke me up. I think the Cranes are coming. Dammit well this tree is tricky. We don't know what sort of things he can do."

"And we never will. Shit," I said.

We both stood up but there was nothing to do. There had to be twenty of them at least, and I had no idea how many more were in the darkness beyond my sight.

"Go ahead. Shoot, darling. There are no Englishmen here to save you and your Guards. Know they put up a good fight." I knew the voice was Pinky's. I was about to say something but there was a soft thud. Something had been thrown at us and it rolled over on the grass before us. It was Ferdinand's head.

"What do we do?" Friedrich whispered.

"Try and think of something." The first thing I remembered was to quickly take the thin strip of leather I had kept in my sleeve. I usually had it there in case of emergencies like this, but I'd never hoped to use it. I had only practiced with it a few times.

"What are you eating?" Friedrich asked.

"Numbmtrffing. Shut up."

Pinky came up, his arm in a sling, but he was smiling. I couldn't really blame him. He had us caught. I kept hoping to hear the shouts of the real contingent of Guards that Gudrun had dispatched but none came. More of the dark men, cloaked and hooded against our eyes and the night, came up. I didn't have to wait long for the cudgel. I just remember the feeling of intense pressure across the back of my head, like I had thrown myself off a cliff and landed headfirst into the receiving earth. Everything was a strange memoryless mixture of nothing which is the best I can describe, because what is narrative without memory but speculation and I was quite incapable of even that.

I came to my senses with a splitting headache and blood running down my face. They had bound me securely. I couldn't reach the pen knife I normally kept in my shoe, because I didn't have a shoe. I was naked. That was the problem. And so was Friedrich, although I noticed he was barely tied up.

The brooding guard, a thick lipped man sneered. "None of

that Chinko magic fighting this time."

I examined myself as best I could and was surprised that I hadn't been molested in the least. Neither my vagina nor asshole felt any sense of violation. They hadn't cut off my nipples and it looked like Friedrich was still in possession of his manhood. (Purely average, I have to say, neither too big nor too small). We were tied to steel bars put into holes and I would have been able to ascertain our situation faster if it weren't for the oppressive smell of rotting fish and alder smoke. Perhaps I should say *fermenting* fish for the sensitive, but the sensitive can stop reading right now if the thought of being just outside a high ceilinged, warehouse, surrounded and engulfed by the smell of putrefying, cured herrings, mackerels and… eels is disturbing. The air was cold and you could feel the wind and hear the river rolling by. Oh, and add standing in this place stark naked, tied to a post with a bloody head and the knowledge you are about to discover, once and for all what Rabelais has called "The Great Perhaps" and you may quail even further. Place a gag—a filthy oily thing that was soaked in a spittoon—in your mouth and the effect is complete. There was a smell of urine, for Friedrich pissed himself, mmmming something I assumed was "what do we do, dear Gods!"

At this point the more shrewd readers may think, "ah, but she's saying all of this in past tense, so she must have made it through," and yet I should add that this story may have veered into the parallel unknown world of Undiscovered Country. Perhaps I am reporting on this from the privileged position of the dead. Perhaps I am piteously wailing in the afterlife. Stuck with Friedrich. Regardless of the condition of my corporeality, I will continue. I heard something like a conversation coming toward us and then finally heard words I could clearly understand:

"These two? They both don't look like much. Still, this is the one that did in the boys in the forest and the chaps in the alley, eh?"

"We're not really sure about the forest, but it seems a safe bet."

"How?"

"Some kind of "Chinko Magic" is what Pinky here says. We tied her up good. Nobody's had her either. Probably has teeth in her pussy."

"You didn't check? She probably has a good old-fashioned knife up there. This is one of those special assistant secretaries they hire at the Coroners." At that point a man, of average height and build, obscured in the darkness approached me.

"Hadn't thought of that boss." Was all Pinky said.

"That's why I'm in charge here. Sorry about this." And he proceeded to give me a complete pelvic exam right there. Friedrich's rectum, I can't say was spared either. I can say the man was clean and efficient.

"Lot of trouble, don't you think?" 'Pinky asked him.

"I just don't want any escapes."

"What are we going to do with them?"

"What the fuck do you think? C'mon. They're waiting for them."

Who? I wondered. Friedrich was whimpering and crying by now and Pinky punched him several times. Alas, I had to wait for the right moment.

"Yes, here. It's the pen they keep 'em in. Nobody'll notice 'em here once they're finished.

"I can see them wriggling around down there."

That was the second to last thing I heard. Sadly, the person whom I assumed was the leader didn't stop, reveal himself in full elegance, and regale Friedrich and I with an origin story of how he had come to this place in life, for you must remember that the Villain is the Hero in his own Narrative. Nor was there any sort of explanation regarding his master plan and how much time Friedrich and I had before the City exploded. There was no saving moment of recognition, that he was my long-lost brother who shared the same tattoos as I had. No, I simply stood there, and wondered hard at how I was going to get the blade out of me and cut free in time. But I said second to last. The last thing was the sound of the Elbe as it rolled by and at least I knew where I was.

After that, I felt the steel bar removed from behind me and before I could do anything, a hard pole or axe handle struck deep into my stomach, knocking the breath out of me and pushing backwards into the void.

I didn't think I was going to die. I had trained myself against it all those hard years of travel, and though I had seen death many times, dished it out occasionally—reluctantly and only when I had to—I did not expect to feel The Old Boy tap on my shoulder with his polite "time's up" following. So, I hurtled through the darkness, stark naked as the day I was born and I did not experience any slowing down of time as my life rushed before my eyes. I merely heard Friedrich's high-pitched scream as he too was clubbed into the whatever we were falling into.

And what exactly were we falling into? I wondered that as well. It was outside, I knew that. It was cold, so I was fairly sure we weren't being thrown into a coking furnace. It didn't smell sweet, so I knew it wasn't roses, and then I hit the water and felt them: serpentine, slimy, wriggling in a great muscled dark mass. Several forced their wedge like heads in my ass cheeks, another was at my vagina, they squirmed around my mouth and they pushed at my eyes. The elvers wriggled into my ears and they wrapped around and around my arms: dark, slithering, far quicker than any snake, yet they were the epitome of serpentine movement. Eels, thousands of eels and I could feel them begin to feed just as Friedrich landed on top of me.

Have you ever been… of course not. Well, maybe you have, and I don't have to tell you how they wriggled all over me and Friedrich in that cold water. I fought to keep my breath and was lucky to keep my sense for I could feel Friedrich slipping below me. How was I going to bring the blade up and get out of this?

Actually, it was so nauseous being in that pen full of squirming eels all over and almost in my body that I could bring the sheathed blade up easily, but controlling it in my mouth, and angling the sheath so it slipped out between my teeth and cut the ragged gag was difficult. Master Chang never told me about the eels when I practiced this in his watchful tutoring in the Wudan Mountains. Blindly, I bent forward and cut the rope between my legs that held my hands, but that opened my rear up to the eels and I twisted back quickly hoping to break the neck of the one that had gained entry to the foyer with his head. I had to do it again and went for my feet to kick free.

I didn't have much breath left and I could feel Friedrich go slack in my hands. Things began to slow down and I knew I had a few moments left. I made two quick kicks and broke the surface for fortunately the mass of eels buoyed us up slightly. I think I heard laughter. Then a "shit, she got loose!"

Then I looked up at Pinky and the top of his head magically lifted in the darkness so that his beautiful blonde hair fluttered in the moonlight streaming behind him. It was beautiful in a way but then heard the crack of the rifle follow. Pinky began falling toward me. Someone had blown the top of his head off and now he joined me, the ultimate in white meat feast for the eels and they fell on him immediately and seemed to leave me and Friedrich alone.

I could finally get my bearing in the pool. I realized we were in one of the eel storage tanks in Fosthorpe. I did not see the leader anywhere up above us, but heard several shots fired and then a great deal of shouting. Most of the eels left us alone at that point or burrowed into Pinky's opened skull (they love brains), and I could finally slip my hands around and under my feet to cut them free. I reached out behind me and felt Fritz's scalp still near me, so I pulled hard and brought him close. I could reach out and feel the sides, there were handholds for the tank was designed to allow water through.

"Is she down there? What about the man?"

"I think so."

"Well shine a light down there, damn you. Give me that." I knew two of the voices quite well. I looked up, an eel still wriggling in my hair, and saw those unmistakably white robes. And next to Gudrun was Kanute's white hair blowing in the wind. He shone the lantern down on my faced and then laughed, the bastard.

"Hold onto him, here is a rope ladder" and it was thrown down. I know I must have grabbed onto it, held onto it with that desperate, unconscious strength we possess just before we die. But I did not remember anything more.

It was still dark when I opened my eyes. I was under a dry blanket but still stark naked. I could see the stars and heard the sound of retching. "Seems your friend here hasn't had enough of the eels and he's giving them some a chum. You're safe, Ada." It was Kanute. I looked up at him and he had a strange bundle in his arms. "I would go back to sleep."

"Herr Eldredsohn. I think we had better take care of that now."

"Just a moment. Ada here, breathe deeply." I did as I was told and was it some kind of smoke? Opium perhaps. I felt it drift over my face and into my nostrils. Some powerful soporific moved into me, whether it was exhaustion or shock or narcotics or a pleasant mixture of the three, I don't know. I remember seeing Kanute rise and throw the bundle over my head into the eel pen but then I closed my eyes again and the faint memories are gone at that point.

"Oh, I don't know if it's a bad thing or not, Klaus. After all, the tree's an attraction now. Lots of people will be taking shortcuts through the South Forest to get here. With money for offerings, and shouldn't Hermes get his due on this road as does the Lady and Donner? Think about it, man. You might even have some *legitimate* businesses around here that can rip people off. Apples on a stick, souvenirs, a means to launder your other income," Kanute said. "Von Dietzen shouldn't be making all the money here."

"You mean go straight?"

"I didn't mean anything quite that drastic. Perhaps diversify a bit is all, we can all do without the hidden razor blades, the poignards, the black jacks and the killing."

The man was quiet for a while and finally spoke: "Kanute, I think these newer arrangements you speak of will work much better. A legitimate businessman. I like that."

I was in a carriage, an expensive one because I could barely feel the swaying of it back and forth on the road. I was dressed in a simple black dress, but it was of rich silk. Next to me was Friedrich, peeping out at the other two occupants of the carriage with a look of fright and wonder. He was also richly dressed: in a bright blue surcoat with a new linen shirt and black silk trousers.

"Good morning, Ada." Kanute said.

"Ah, the legendary Frau Ludenow. We finally meet." I was sitting across from *the* Klaus Hunser, the leader of the Black Cranes.

"Where are we going?"

"To a concert, Ada. One you and the esteemed Herr Dettin here have made possible. Are you hungry? There is some excellent ham and hard-boiled eggs in the hamper. And nice bottle of Rhine to ease that headache you must have."

When we arrived at the Oak, for where else could we be going, the day had reached mid-morning. We entered through a side entrance, by which the fat and resentful Graf von Dietzen eyed us with something between bald resentment and jealousy.

"Never mind that fool," Kanute said. I held his arm, still feeling somewhat shaky from the previous night. "He wouldn't have any of this without you and he knows it. I've enjoyed reminding him every chance I get."

The Oak was festooned in ribbons of every color and a group of men and women slowly circled it in a dance. They were all naked and seemed enraptured. If they were fundamentalists, at least they seemed like the kindly sort.

I recognized the blue coats of the agricultural inspectors clustered around a bright impromptu table proudly burdened with beer steins. They even wore their peacock feather hats, looking self-pleased and silly rather than abashedly asinine. The Kashubian doffed his cap and raised his glass at me and wished us all *Prosit*.

"We're not even going to bother with the pretense of appearing to work today," Kalbenski said as we walked by.

We walked to a small pavilion. The music drifted out of the tree, just as I had heard it the night before but of course it was completely different since each note depended not on the mind and will of some man or woman enslaved to tempo and tone, but rather the wind which did as it pleased. Gudrun Sigurdsdottir was there and at first, I could not recognize her because the faintest traces of a grin spread across her rosy face. But more importantly, she wore a bright green dress. She was quite pretty after all.

"Friedrich, I believe the Frau Surgeon has some questions for you," Kanute said.

Hunser bid us goodbye, said he wanted to stand by himself for a moment to listen. "It's as though it's speaking to just me,' he said. "There's some regrets, some anger of course. Yet I know it must be speaking to everyone in such a way, but differently." And he walked off across the rich barley field.

I don't know how long we actually sat there. Perhaps an hour judging from the shadow of the tree.

"Well, seems you have Wodenists all over the place. This must increase the value of that Loire wine." I said.

"Ada, you know I always have a contingency set. It's why rich people always come out ahead. If a market crashes I can buy up a commanding interest in various businesses. If it booms, then I make a profit. In this particular case... the good Frau Surgeon and I have come to the conclusion of your investigation."

"Ja," Gudrun said turning around. She had been speaking

to Friedrich, but I had not caught any of their conversation. "It seems the bones of those three thieves were found in the bottom of an eel pond on the Elbe. The City is of the opinion they died at the hands of their peers, for reasons unknown and perhaps best left that way. The City does not feel there is a threat of bloody Wodenists."

"Ah, that's what you threw in there last night. What is the state of that trade treaty with the Kingdom of France?"

"No, Ada, my dear if you hadn't been so wrapped up in this affair and those ridiculous costumes you take such pride in, you would have heard: Mazarin has died and the new King of France wishes for our friendship and our continued enmity towards his neighbor to the South, His Most Catholic Majesty of Spain. Some special business arrangements have been made that will keep everything in order, and we're not turning Protestant here either any time soon, although (and his voice hushed) *I have some doubts about that new king in Sweden.*

"Tell me, Kanute. I know it was you who engineered all of this. I spoke with the Wünchis. It still seemed a bit dangerous, goading those three thieves."

"Well, you know very well it wasn't all my idea, Ada." He glanced towards the Tree. "I liked to help out an old soul you know. I had been out here to conduct some business with that lout von Dietzen last year and stopped for a while beneath it. It seemed so lonely, and I knew it for a very great tree just as you did. On a whim, I asked "what can I do for you? And now you know the rest."

"Hold my hand for a while. The music is beautiful," I said.

"Of course. You've earned it my dear."

If you find yourself in the Free and Hanseatic City of Hagen, you will doubtless wonder at the Rathaus Clock set above the white stone façade, with its moving statues: the goblins and elf-women, the prancing carven bears, snickering apes and the moon's changing face. Any local will tell you that the clock is magical, paid for by one of the richest men in the city and built by their own horological wizard whose fine crow-stepped house and emporium is "right over there."

The sign above the richly graven doors proudly says: *Friedrich & Gudrun Dettin, Purveyors of Instruments of Wonder."* Inside their atelier you will find luthiers, carpenters and machinists crafting tools, ornaments and of course toys. The nightingales are always in high demand, for they most loudly sing of old love, but once-childless women swear by the cuckoo clocks. Friedrich is working on a breadbox that suggests new types of flax loaves. Frau Gudrun is known throughout much of Europe for her matchless prosthetic limbs (still sadly needed in this violent and unsafe world.) Their daughter, her golden hair tied up neatly, crafts a duck that always suggests the right thing to say to an angry teacher. And there are viols full of Winternight songs, and cunning metal globes that spin and show any dream of travel that you wish, complete with itinerary, exchange rates and recommendations for clean inns. Many people come and simply gaze at the wonders in his workshop, and if they cannot purchase anything, there is always the Oak in the Dietzenpark that sings to them the songs kept in the treasuries of their hearts.